A Cursed Cleaning

Ellen Taylor

Contents

To my Uncle Marc

Thanks for letting me borrow the house

Chapter One

Isolation

Springs squeaked as I shot up, letting out a cry. Another second passed before I touched the tears racing down my cheeks, wondering why I was sobbing. My gaze traveled around the room to see torn wallpaper and a haphazard painting job to cover it up. The scent of mildew hit my nostrils as early dawn filled this space with a red glow. I was in a bedroom. Perhaps the mattress on a bedframe within four walls should've been my first clue. Though this place was so crowded with junk that I had thought the bed was only being stored here. My bare feet landed on the crusty shag carpet. I shrugged it off and walked to the window. Stiff lace curtains bent as I lifted the broken blinds. Nothing but trees outside. How odd. Is it odd? I didn't remember this house, or this view.

An additional detail came to me I should have considered first. What was my name?

The crusty carpet prickled underfoot. I hopped back onto the bed, dust shooting into the air. Should I panic? What about? I'd woken up sobbing for some reason, not knowing where I was, or my name. Perhaps that's what I needed to panic about.

First things first. Slippers. My tolerance for grossness had reached its limit. I'd rather jump onto a dusty comforter than walk across the carpet again.

My eyes traveled to the sagging high ceiling above. That couldn't be good. Trash, empty packages, beer cans, old shoes, and bottles littered the ground. A sliding closet door hung off the track and clothes spilled out. On the clustered nightstand was an ashtray filled with cigarette butts. Across from the bed was a desk that doubled as a dresser, cluttered with mountains of papers, letters, and drawings.

I almost missed the cracked, dusty mirror behind the chaos. The pale pink nightgown I wore wasn't familiar. With lacy sleeves and neckline, it gave off a more girlish look. Big blue eyes and brown hair stared back at me. Did I always have these features? How did I not know this about myself? My hands rested on my hips as I tried to guess my age. That, too, fled my mind. I seemed past my teenage years. Perhaps early twenties? Old enough to feel a creeping panic about greater responsibilities.

A mouse scampered over the brown shag carpet to its hole. The king-size mattress groaned as I stood on it, then paused. Mice didn't frighten me; I'd lived with them before. Was this my house? The answer came to me as quickly as the question. This was not my place, but I had a similar experience with these creatures and never felt scared.

As my gaze traveled over the room, they stuttered to a stop on some slippers by the bed. The pale-pink bows on each matched my nightgown. With relief, I shoved them on my feet.

Two doors stood on either side of the room, both with intricate frames of carved lines. The one on my left had a comically large padlock hanging from the knob. The other had no such mechanism.

I jiggled the handle of the locked door first, but it held firm. There was no logical reason for it to remain closed. I should turn the knob, padlock and all, and this door should open. Something kept me from entering that next room.

Decision made, I tried the other door. It squeaked open into a new room, and I walked onto the brown shag carpet with protected feet. I flipped the light switch, but nothing happened. It didn't matter; this section boasted two windows that filtered in the dawn glow through more broken blinds and yellowed lace curtains with dead flowers on the windowsill.

A huge TV sagged on an old stand, thick with dust. A bookshelf full of VHS tapes stood next to it. I leaned down, scanning the movie titles.

Alien, The Haunting, Sixth Sense, A Nightmare on Elm Street, The Blair Witch Project, The Exorcist, The Birds

I scurried away from the movies. Despite waking up with no memories, the sick feeling in my gut did not lie. Mice didn't terrify me, but these tapes did.

Miscellaneous takeout bags littered the ground. No identifiable logos anywhere, just different colored sacks with wadded wrappers. I rubbed goosebumps from my arms.

The ceiling in this room wasn't as high as in the bedroom, and brown paneling covered the walls. I'd gotten a turn of the century vibe in the bedroom. These two rooms came straight from the 70s or 80s.

Odd. How did I know all this and not my name?

A floral recliner sat in front of the TV, with two other couches behind it. A small table stood in the corner that held an ashtray and a dusty candy bowl filled with bright pink circular candies on a stained doily. I opened the lid, then hesitated. Was I actually reaching for sweets from a dirty glass container next to an ashtray? I shrugged and plopped a candy in my mouth. A second later, mint burned my sinuses.

This place was a literal grandma's house. 80s paneling, VHS tapes, doilies, bright pink candy, and ashtrays everywhere.

Across from the couches I saw a built-in cherry wood bookshelf. It was beautiful, but someone had stuffed paperbacks in every corner they could find. I brushed some of the dust from the titles.

It, Dracula, I am Legend, The Call of Cthulhu, The Shining.

Mint-flavored air filled my lungs. I'd seen enough. Looks like I wouldn't get my entertainment from this house.

The TV room connected to the next room, creating one long rectangular space. This new room, too, shared the brown paneling, the cluttered and crispy brown shag carpet, and the artificially lowered ceiling. A massive corner desk had shelves stuffed with papers and old mail, with a large computer in the center. I jiggled the mouse, but it didn't wake the screen. Right. No electricity. Underneath the desk were haphazard stacks of newspapers and magazines. I grabbed one to find a date. Each paper displayed blurry pictures and articles, like the printer had created a poor copy. The magazines were no different. I couldn't tell if I flipped through an entertainment or a travel magazine.

A rectangular card table stood in the other corner of the room near the windows, sagging under the weight of torn packages, more blurry newspapers, and dirty dishes. The only sounds were flies zooming around the table. I searched through the packages to find names but saw empty spaces for sender and receiver.

Hinges squeaked as I opened the front door to reveal a forested area beyond the shredded screen door. The cement chill crept through my slippers as I stepped onto the porch. Four skinny poles with wood rot barely held up a metal awning overhead. Dead plants hung between the posts, and a dirt path stopped right before a cluster of pine trees.

Shading my eyes, I glanced at the hazy yellow sky. I remembered skies like this. When forest fires happened, wind blew in smog and ash, creating a haze.

Was there a fire? The thought alarmed me, surrounded by trees as I was. I didn't smell smoke. I pushed the concern away as something to be aware of, but not worry about. Figuring out my name was top priority. No, never mind. Why I turned up in this strange house with no memories took top priority.

The house offered more comfort inside than out, though I'd have to address the mildew soon.

Crossing the living room, I walked into a tiny kitchen. At the entrance stood a partially hooked-up stove. The exposed wiring and dangling outlets lying on the countertop made me pause. If a child lived here, CPS would've been called.

Next to the sink full of dishes was a drying rack on a musty towel. A sturdy block of cherry wood cut the already small kitchen in half. Bags of groceries covered the surface, spilling onto the two chairs tucked underneath.

On the wall adjacent to the refrigerator was a gorgeous cherry wood cabinet. The amber glass bubble doors caught my breath. Old, yet beautiful. Inside, I saw stacked plates, cups, and bowls. One of the bottom panels was hanging off its hinges. Canned goods tumbled out, and more grocery bags, coats, and purses littered the ground.

In this tiny kitchen were three doors. A pale green one next to the refrigerator, then two more doors side by side. The green door had that same comically huge padlock over the knob. From my guess of the house's layout, this must lead back to the bedroom.

I opened the door closest to the sink. A windowless bathroom proved difficult to explore with little light. The toilet worked, though. A broken and warped linen closet stood beside a dirty bathtub. I played with the tub knobs and heard a trickle. At least the water worked, even if I had no desire to take a bath. I wiped my fingers on my nightgown, since no towel in this house had my trust.

Next to the bathroom, the final door led to a covered back porch layered in dried-up leaves. I kept this in mind, but I wanted to explore more of the old kitchen.

A cold stench hit me when I opened the fridge. A light flickered on, and I couldn't help but stare despite the smell. The electricity didn't work, yet this appliance started humming and light showed me in crisp detail the moldy food inside. This defied logic and made my stomach quiver.

Not wishing to see that rotten food anymore, I shut the door and straightened, studying the cluttered kitchen island again. Among the chaos was a simple black landline phone. No twirly cord like I expected. It rested on a base plugged into the wall. A memory unearthed itself, and I vaguely remembered a phone like this from my childhood. Whenever someone left a message, the base made a red blinking light right...

There.

Even the buzzing flies quieted as I stared at the blinking light. Not a single house in the vicinity, trees for miles, no rows of electrical poles connecting me to anything or anyone. Yet the phone worked. The fridge I could explain away, but this?

Here, in complete isolation, someone had left me a message.

Chapter Two

Game Logic

Perhaps it was a clue. I picked up the base, turning it over to figure out how to replay a message. Or to remember what button to push. Receiving messages was my mother's job.

Huh. I have a mother.

I lifted the phone, placing it against my ear.

"One new message," a robotic voice said. *"Press one to hear it."*

Easy enough. I hit the number.

"Hello." Nothing about this female voice triggered any memories. I needed to listen to her, though. My gut told me that much. *"In seven days, they will come. In seven days, they will destroy. If you wish to survive, follow your to-do list.*

"The list is being created now."

My gaze darted around before resting on a notepad and a calendar mounted on the wall at eye level. A mug stuffed with pencils, pens, crayons, and paint brushes sat next to the phone. I reached for one as the female started speaking again, but finding a writing utensil wasn't necessary. Words materialized on the paper as she spoke. The cursive handwriting was eerily perfect.

"Declutter one room of your choice,

"Inspect food in the kitchen. Dispose of expired food outside in the dumpster,

"Clean out the refrigerator appliance,

"Store what is fresh in the refrigerator appliance,

"Further instructions will follow..."

On the notepad, it showed up as five bullet points. I stared, brows furrowed. The phone next to my ear beeped, and I screamed. It dropped to the table, and I clutched my heart.

"Jumpy, are we?" I asked myself. Of course I was. I'd woken up in isolation, in a house full of junk with no memories. Anyone would be on edge.

I snatched the phone from the clutter and placed it on the base before tearing off the paper. The second I ripped it from the notepad, two bars appeared at the top left-hand corner of my vision. My eyes bounced around, but those bars remained in the corner. I was familiar with this setup. I'd somehow stumbled into... no. That was impossible.

A game. This was like a video game. I glanced down at my hands. I was real. Absolutely real. Except... I'd woken up in a bed I didn't recognize, in a house I had no recollection of, and no memories.

The top bar was yellow with a lightning bolt symbol on the left. Stamina. The one underneath was blue with an outline of a person's head with white lines scribbled through the brain.

Sanity.

I tapped the table, my fingers jittery. Parts of this were familiar. A dirty house, miles of land. Without seeing it, somehow I knew the yard would contain a garden to grow vegetables. This was a farming game. I *adored* these games. I'd spent hours making my virtual homestead pretty, growing my food, and decorating my space. But this?

They will come. They will destroy.

The VHS tapes on that bookshelf and the dusty paperbacks stuffed into the shelves returned to my memory. Whatever *they* were couldn't be good. Someone had merged my favorite game with my least favorite genre.

I wasn't interested in meeting whatever *they* were. The paper crumpled in my hand, and I glanced at the instructions. I didn't want to face evil. There was enough of it in the world. Why did anyone have to make up more? How was I here? Could I trust this woman? Could I trust anything?

All I knew was *they* would come in seven days, and the way to protect myself was to follow the list in my hand. I had to trust somewhere, and this was where I'd begin.

It was time to clean the house.

None of the clothes stuffed in the closets or scattered around the bedroom tempted me; therefore, I remained in this strange nightgown to clean. Since part of my instructions were about sorting food in the kitchen and cleaning the fridge, I decided to tidy that room up, too.

I sorted through the grocery bags to find fresh food. Some bags gave the impression of being from this week's shopping. Some had forgotten produce from months ago. Those I placed by the back porch. I opened the fridge again, bracing for the stench. CPS definitely would've been called if a child lived here.

The stench never came. I frowned, opening my eyes as I stared at the appliance stuffed with rotten food. There was a stench before, but not now. In fact, I remembered sorting through the bags of spoiled items on the counter and didn't recall a smell then, either. How did a stench disappear?

I picked up one of the less rotten containers of food with my fingertips and attempted to place it in a bag of rotten groceries by the door. For whatever reason, an invisible barrier kept me from cramming it in. I would have had better luck shoving it through a brick wall. I needed a new bag to put this in.

Were there sacks under the sink? My fist instinctively curled around an empty bag, and I glanced down, eyes wide. How did this get in my hand?

It was worth testing. I dropped the rotten food inside the new bag, then another. And another. When it was full, I tied it off and tossed it near the door. I grabbed a package of moldy hot dogs from the fridge when a sack materialized into my fist. I stared ahead as goosebumps traveled up my arms. It was as weird as bars showing up in my vision. Or the fridge humming despite electricity not working. A fridge that didn't have a freezer, come to think of it. It didn't follow normal logic, but none of this did. At least I have bags to help.

Should I wear gloves? Why did this thought come to me after spending all this time already sorting through food? I examined my hand. Not even a particle of dirt after all that organizing. My mind suggested this wasn't real life, but I refused to go there. If anything, this was a sprinkling of game logic. But then why did I feel the carpet before?

With an uneasy breath, I took off a slipper, then placed it against the dirty floor. That prickly sensation didn't return. My brow twitched as I rubbed my foot on the kitchen floor. I would have to try this in the bedroom to see if the carpet felt the same. Something happened after getting these bars in my vision. In a final act of curious desperation, I set my palm against the fuzzier foods in the back, wondering how I had the courage to do this sort of thing. All that, and I sensed nothing. Despite the absence of gross textures, I still found it repulsive and quickly brought my hand back, giving my impossibly clean hand another look.

It took a couple of hours to empty everything from the fridge and the cupboards. If I ignored the logic defying bags, it was rather fun to organize, since I didn't have to worry about dirtying my hands.

When the rotten food was all placed into sacks by the door, I opened the fridge to admire my work. I almost set my hands against each other when a spray bottle and a rag popped into my palms instead. I brought them forward to stare at them, then at the inside of the fridge. Fine. If they wanted me to play a cleaning game, then I would play. I sprayed, then wiped down the appliance, watching as a few scrubs in one section returned the shelves to pristine condition.

The bottle and rag blipped out of existence once the entire fridge was sparkling clean. To keep myself from thinking about it too hard, I placed the orange juice, milk, and a container of mixed berries inside. I closed the door, and something happened to the front of the appliance. Since I only caught it out of the corner of my eye, I didn't understand what I had noticed. As I stared, information filled my head like it was being downloaded into my understanding. This storage unit was now decluttered and cleaned, equipped for storing unspoiled food for however long I wanted. This knowledge left me with more questions. Would meals in here remain fresh for months? Game logic told me yes. I forced myself to turn away and remember my to-do list.

Turning from the fridge brought me face to face with the many bags waiting to be tossed. It was painful to see so much waste, but I couldn't salvage frozen pizzas the previous owners had forgotten.

Besides, I needed to dump this stuff and then check what I had left in the kitchen.

I opened the door onto the covered back porch and saw two more doors. One to the outside, and the other leading to another room with a padlock on the knob. The windows on the back porch helped me see that the locked door led to a small storage area. It was partially buried in the ground to help keep food cool.

Someone had stuffed a vacuum, broom, dustpan, mop, and bucket in the corner. They were draped in cobwebs, as was everything else in this room, including the torn screen door leading to the backyard. The years' worth of dead leaves gave more protection than the screen. The brick walls were painted a salmon color, decorated with dirty cobwebs. A tattered maroon and gold diamond rug was the only thing between my slippered feet and the cold slab of cement. A bare lightbulb clung to exposed wires dangling from the ceiling.

I yanked open the screen door and walked into the backyard. My fingers brushed over the stucco exterior of the storage building without sensing the bumps or cracks. Outside, between the storage building and the edge of the house, was a slab of cement that I assumed was a small patio area. A fire pit had been dug not that far from it.

Four darkened buildings caught my eye. Upon further inspection, they turned out to be greenhouses. Not a garden, then, as most farming games had. I suppose that made sense, considering whatever was arriving in seven days wanted to destroy. Though a glass greenhouse wouldn't protect me that much from a monster.

I walked around the backyard, searching for the dumpster mentioned in the to-do list. A river roared somewhere in the distance. A short walk from the house was a rundown single-car carport. The sky was still hazy, with no smell of smoke or fire. Even though the storage building's exterior was done in stucco, the house itself was in a fading white brick with gray shingles.

With a gasp, I realized this home had a second story. Someone had painted the top floor a pale salmon color, and the window shutters in coral. It was a beautiful old place, if neglected. But how could I reach the next floor?

Right. The locked doors from the bedroom and the kitchen. There must be a staircase leading to the second story. No doubt I would have to complete my chores to earn rewards, and one might be the key to the comically large padlocks.

After admiring the old house, I refocused on why I had come outside in the first place. When I'd heard the word dumpster, I expected something big. What I found was only a rectangular metal box outside between the living room and kitchen windows. It seemed small considering the junk I needed to stuff in there.

I reentered the back porch and gathered armfuls of sacks. I took one step, and a huge chunk of stamina vanished. Bags tumbled from my arms, and I sighed. This wouldn't work. Not with how much stamina it would waste. I did some tests until I realized I could take two bags without it affecting my yellow bar. Two. Bags.

Despite knowing I could've done more in real life, perhaps this was part of the game mechanic. It frustrated me because I could have taken ten in one trip, but I started with two to save my stamina.

I dropped the expired food in the dumpster. Somewhere deep inside it hummed quietly, then numbers appeared in my vision.

+0.06

The number remained in the center of my vision before it zoomed to the bottom left-hand corner. Was that supposed to be money? Or points? It was something.

Shadows stretched toward the house's foundation when I finally dropped the last bags in the dumpster. Dopamine tickled my brain as more of the kitchen carpet revealed itself. It was the same maroon and gold carpet on the back porch.

With everything tossed, I had a grand total of 1.36... somethings. Either dollars, euros, pesos, or even regular points. Four out of five things were crossed off my to-do list.

Nice.

Now I had to declutter a room. The kitchen was almost done, so it made sense to finish it. I gathered dirty dishes from the cherry wood table and dropped them in the sink. I turned on the water and waited for a sponge to jump into my hand, but nothing happened. After a few moments, I ran the plate under the tap, scrubbing with my magical hands that couldn't feel anything. It wasn't long before the drying rack filled up. None of these towels looked sanitary enough, so I grabbed a paper towel. I started toweling off dishes when an overwhelming nausea came over me. I leaned over the counter, my head pounding and my vision blurring.

The stamina bar had a thin yellow outline, but it was empty. I hadn't been watching that. I had only noticed it when it made an obvious drop while carrying ten bags outside. Did stamina refill after a time? Or did I have to eat food to restore it? How could I finish my list if I didn't have any stamina left?

My feet shuffled from the sink. I couldn't pick up another dish, even if I wanted to. The thought made me ill. No timer appeared beneath the bar, and the stamina hadn't reset itself in the few hours since I cleaned. I might have to eat something. I had little food, despite the organized kitchen. A lot had needed to be tossed, and until I had a steady replacement, I had to use what was left sparingly.

Though...

I gathered some dishes from the sink, taking a few steps. No dip in stamina, no overwhelming nausea. I walked outside to the dumpster and dropped them in.

+0.03

Sweet. Whatever these points were, I wouldn't mind having more.

Chapter Three
Dopamine

The sun had dipped below the trees when I collected the last of the cups and tossed them in the dumpster. I had 2.75 total numbers that made my dopamine soar. Dopamine points. That was a good identifier.

The kitchen already looked better. I stuffed old coats and purses with no identifiable brand name into another magically appearing bag. When I tried dragging it outside, the same overwhelming nausea hit.

Okay then. Too heavy. None of my stamina had returned, so it should reset every morning. All I wanted was to get these last bags out to receive that sweet, sweet dopamine from a completed to-do list. Sure, the kitchen wasn't clean, but the clutter was gone. I assumed cleaning would show up on the list another day. Come to think of it, I was probably meant to wash dishes a different day, too. Oh, well. I had gotten points out of it.

On the back porch, I noticed something I hadn't before. A clipboard was hanging by a flimsy string by the door of the storage unit. I would have seen it during my first inspection. How was this here?

The oddity of it all made me forget my current job and walk over to examine it. In the dying light, I saw the reason for earning dopamine points. One page had multiple sets of clothes to buy. The picture of sturdy overalls and boots reminded me I had stayed in my nightgown all day. The pictures promised a reward, but perhaps I wouldn't know what it was until I purchased it. Each was in a different category. The cleaning outfit had a blue dress, shoes, a white apron, gloves, and a ribbon to tie my hair back. All separate purchases, all giving a bonus.

"This would have been nice to know, lady leaving messages on my phone." I said it out loud as I searched through the other pages.

The system grayed many things out, though it kept labels on the side. Like farming, housing, and traps. What traps were they thinking of? Did they expect me to trap *them*, whatever creature it was that wanted to hunt me?

The last page made me pause.

Progress for the woman who does not know her name

That was a mouthful. I cleared my throat, trying to focus. Five sections of the progress bar were grayed out. One bar, cleaning, was unlocked and approaching level three. I hadn't noticed I was gaining levels in this skill. Perhaps while I was cleaning, I got experience points, and it was reflected on this clipboard now. On that note, did I get any bonuses for reaching level two? Thinking back, I had sensed an increased ability, where I could've taken three bags without hurting my stamina, but I had ignored the thought at the time.

Well... that was on me. Game logic and reality kept messing with my head.

With that in mind, I returned to the stuffed bag of coats and took out a few. When it was a quarter full, I walked out the back door with no overwhelming nausea.

Level three was close, so I stayed aware of my instincts. As I'd hoped, after two more trips, I sensed the ability to carry more stuff. I dropped the last sack in the dumpster as the first stars shone in the sky. I brushed the nightgown I had worn all day. Despite working hard, I didn't smell of sweat, and I wasn't bothered about sleeping without a shower. No way was I stepping foot in that bathtub.

"Still would've been nice to know about buying clothes."

I pulled out my to-do list, seeing it all crossed off. A proud sigh escaped me. +2.00 more dopamine points were added to my total, no doubt my prize for completing my jobs.

Something outside started buzzing. I glanced from the list, frowning. The noise got louder until a lamppost flickered to life a few yards from the front porch. Once again, electricity decided when to work. My brain was divided into two halves. One side still insisted reality was a thing, and the other slowly accepted game logic. This instance with the lamppost chipped away a portion of my reality side, and it caused a chill to go down my spine.

The lamppost gave a soft orange glow, revealing deeper, darker shadows. It was the only source of light within miles. A wolf howled in the distance, and my knees weakened. This morning, with the sun shining in an admittedly hazy sky, isolating from civilization had seemed fun. Now, in the weak flicker of light that barely held back the darkness, anything might be in these woods. Like *them*, whoever *they* were.

My brain didn't register crickets chirping until they stopped. My breathing shuddered, too afraid to tear my gaze from the lamppost. Something made a deep, guttural, *close* growl, and my sanity dropped.

I sprinted toward the broken screen door. After two steps, I collapsed onto the patchy dirt, moaning with nausea. I couldn't sprint without stamina. Clambering to my feet, I walked to the front porch despite the scream clawing at my throat to escape. Hinges groaned as I threw open the doors to get inside. Tears raced down my cheeks as a shriek exploded out of me. I stumbled into the house and searched for a bolt lock. Once I heard it thunk into place, I shuffled through the dark into the kitchen to fasten the back door, too.

My lungs tried to suck in all the air in the vicinity. *They* weren't supposed to be here yet. Not for another seven days. It's what the message said. Unless this wasn't *them* at all.

Nausea crept up in me, and not the kind tied to my lack of stamina. My imagination went wild. Anything could be out there. My gaze shot toward the blue bar in my vision. That growl had knocked out a chunk of my sanity.

"Absolutely not." In the dark, I shuffled through the house until I reached the bedroom door. Once it was open, I leapt into bed, covering my ears with the pillow. I was safe. I *had* to be. I hadn't lost any more sanity since that first growl.

Would you like to sleep?

Y/N

The words hung in my vision.

"Yes! Sleep!" I screamed it in case they couldn't read my mind. This is what I wanted. To forget what I heard. I did not want to know what would happen if my sanity dropped to zero like my stamina had done today.

Tiredness hit me. My fingers loosened around the pillow, and my body eased into sleep, my darkening vision alleviating my panicked soul.

Red dawn filled the room with light as my eyes snapped open. I sat up, and the pillow fell off my face. I breathed in the dirty bedroom, not thinking about what happened. Last night felt like a few seconds ago.

Both my bars were full. I sighed, bowing my head. It scared me how quickly the growl had made me lose some sanity, but on the other hand, I was a scaredy-cat. Being isolated during the nighttime freaked me out. Especially in the middle of a forest without memories. It was a miracle I hadn't been frightened sooner.

Was there another message on the phone? I climbed out of bed, touching the carpet. The crunchiness under my bare feet was gone. It was a revelation I stuffed in the back of my head for later examination. I still placed my slippers on my feet again. The red dawn gave the house an eerie light as I walked through the rooms. The kitchen, though far from clean, was at least decluttered. I was quite proud of my accomplishments yesterday. It was important to focus on what I had done instead of that ungodly growl.

My overactive imagination thought about it, so I closed my eyes to force myself to imagine something else. That didn't help, since my only memories comprised the first day of this strange game. No thinking. Only do. I picked up the phone and pressed one, full of questions.

"What is this house? Why am I here? Who am I?"

"—*days, they will come. In six days, they will destroy. Anything you didn't complete on your to-do list will be added. Please do the following to protect yourself:*

"*Purchase one article of farming clothes from the clipboard by the storage unit,*

"*Find the first greenhouse key in the carport,*

"*Prepare one soil bed,*

"*Further instructions will follow...*"

The phone beeped, and I closed my eyes, sighing. The to-do list finished writing on the notepaper, and I tore it off. Why couldn't someone tell me what was happening? Mysterious things in the darkness shouldn't growl.

People didn't wake up with their minds wiped in a house they don't recall while being asked to clean it. This wasn't common. Do rats in mazes feel like this?

I moved to the clipboard and flipped to the back page. My cleaning level was at three. Another skill, farming, was unlocked. I turned to the section on clothes, studying the farming outfit more. The overalls looked simple, sturdy, and worn, as did the boots, the straw hat, the checkered shirt, and the gloves. Each separate item cost five dopamine points. I had 4.75 in total. It shouldn't be hard to get .25 more. After all, clearing clutter gave me points, and this house had plenty of junk.

The window in the living room was sealed shut. Maybe that was for my protection. Tossing bags through the window to the dumpster would've been convenient, though. I stuffed old letters into another magic bag and walked outside to dump them.

+0.01

My shoulders sagged. This would take a while.

Letters gave next to nothing. When I dropped a sack of old magazines, I received a whopping +0.03 dopamine points. I focused on newspapers and magazines after that until impatience itched at me. This took too much time for too little reward.

After three more bags in the dumpster, I paused to think. My gaze lingered on the lamppost. It hadn't turned on yet since it was midmorning. The sky was still hazy, and I sensed it would remain that way for the foreseeable future. My eyes darted to the carport, more specifically at the junk stacked around the side door. I needed to find the key. I should kill two birds with one stone.

After further study, I realized it had no large front door at all. Perhaps this is what made it a carport. On the side, a battered wooden door hung on its hinges. I swung it out and saw mountains of garbage inside. At least the dumpster was close. Since I couldn't carry many bags, it was nice that the trip would be short.

Hazy midmorning light filtered in through the open wall, shining on all the junk. I stared at the piles of clutter, realizing I had wasted an hour on something not on my to-do list.

My fingers flexed as I checked them again. Letters, magazines, newspapers, and my hands were sparkling clean. Would the same apply to rusty nails and oil spills? I needed to be more careful with stuff in here. Not just rust, but useful resources might hide among the junk. I loathed starting a farming game and selling the important things before realizing their necessity. I wouldn't be able to quit and start a new file in this strange place. The woman on the phone didn't inform me of the clipboard until it was necessary, which I took as a warning. I shouldn't toss anything unless I was certain it was trash.

Still with slippered feet, I moved into the carport full of rusty nails, mysterious stains, and broken beer bottles. I lifted a hand, a bag already there, and started cleaning.

I dropped the first sack of oil-soaked rags into the dumpster. +0.04 was more of a dopamine rush than +0.01. At this rate, I only needed a couple more trips. Lucky for me, plenty of crumpled towels littered the floor. I'd buy some clothes by lunchtime.

The thought made me pause. I hadn't eaten breakfast. In fact, I never ate yesterday. No hunger pains hit me after almost two days of decluttering. Perhaps food only affected stamina. Did the same work with sanity? If I enjoyed a slice of chocolate cake, would I gain sanity? Because that would be nice. It'd be a plus to have cake, too.

Every crumpled paper and rusty nail became blueprints and re-sources to my nervous imagination, and I didn't want to toss them. This made it slower than shoving letters in a bag, but I refused to speed up.

Once I reached 5.02 total, I headed toward the back door. It wasn't until I entered the porch that it dawned on me. I had locked this the night before. Did locking it even matter? Being unprotected from whatever created that growl caused my sanity to tremble.

Focus. Don't get scared. I stared at that blue bar, willing it to stay full as I pushed other thoughts aside. I picked up the clipboard and focused on that. Different farmer and cleaning outfit options lit up on the page. Despite how tempting it was to pick cleaning gloves, I chose the farming overalls instead.

In an instant, my pale pink nightgown vanished. I was left wearing a simple pair of cream-colored shorts and a tank top. It startled me so much I dropped the clipboard and touched these new clothes, but my fingers didn't register the material. Where'd my nightgown go?

Wear overalls now?

"Uh...." Cleaning the carport in these flimsy shorts seemed more unprotected than a nightgown. "Sure. Sure. It'll be nice to be in pants."

I waited for the overalls to show up to put them on. They instead jumped onto my body. I touched them, holding in a gasp. Without a farmer's shirt, I still wore the basic tank top. This begged to be tested. I closed my eyes, imagining myself wearing the nightgown. I cracked an eye open, seeing it on me in real life now. Shouldn't I have sensed the sleeves? I raised my arms, wanting the overalls back. The change was fast, the pale pink melting into denim. Game logic. It was the only answer.

My slippers, though, were gone forever. I stared at my bare feet, imagining them covered, but they didn't come. My toes wiggled, sensing the cold, but not the carpet. As I walked outside, the bumps on the ground, the patchy grass, and the occasional prickly weed did nothing on the soles of my feet. I hesitated at the edge of the carport before stepping inside, not feeling the oil stain. I muscled through the unease and worked to find the key.

Two piles formed. "Definitely trash" and "possibly not trash". "Possibly not trash" became a mountain. Inspecting every item proved time-consuming.

The shadows stretched past the carport. Once the lamppost turned on, I'd run to bed.

My "definitely trash" pile was big enough to dump and make more room. I sensed an added ability to take four bags without it hurting my stamina. Perhaps I would unlock more abilities with cleaning clothes.

Once the shadow of the carport touched the house, I stopped saving stamina. An entire day dedicated to finding one key got me nothing. Where was that stupid thing? How big was it? Did I need to study the lock to guess the size?

Didn't this place apply game logic? Like a light guiding me as I neared the hiding spot? A hot/cold feature to help me out? Some games had the object materialize after searching for a certain number of minutes. Perhaps reality played a bigger part.

I filled another magic bag full of trash. Despite the enormous pile of things to save, the carport was getting cleaner. That much I could proudly say. Soon I'd need to turn on the bare bulb light to keep investigating. No, wait. Spotty electricity.

The key remained elusive as I approached 3.00 total dopamine points. How did this place seem so massive, yet small, at the same time? With the "definitely trash" pile gone, I noticed a tool table toward the back. Out of desperation, I climbed over the junk and opened some drawers. Even finding a flashlight would be a relief. Had I thrown away the key by accident?

The buzz made every muscle inside me freeze. I glanced out the carport opening as the lamp flickered on. I was near where I'd heard the growl from last night. Was it already nighttime? My heart did a double flip as wolves howled. I would not stay to hear that snarl.

I drained the rest of my stamina by sprinting into the house, holding my breath the entire way until I was inside. I locked the front and back doors. It might not help, but I'd rather be safe. In the dark, I stumbled through rooms before entering the bedroom, collapsing into bed.

"Sleep! Sleep! Sleep!"

Darkness filled my vision, and I was out before anything could scare me.

Chapter Four

The Process of Finding a Key

My eyes opened, the red light hitting the green walls. Three days, and I'd woken up the same time every morning. No alarm clock, no nothing, just a creepy crimson gleam filling this room.

I had slept in my overalls, but like everything else, I felt no itchy sensation, and no marks pressed my skin from the rough material. The game forced me to sleep, so it made no difference whether I was in this or a nightgown. I climbed out of bed, rubbing my face. If I kept going, I might accept this as my life, and I refused. Too many questions plagued my mind for me to embrace this lifestyle. Who am I? Who was my mom that I briefly remembered? Does she miss me? Is she alive? Worried about me? How did I get here? Would this be the rest of my existence?

Why did I wake up that first morning sobbing?

The red light blinked on the phone as I stumbled into the kitchen. I picked it up, listening.

"In five days, they will come. In five days, they will destroy. Anything you didn't complete on your to-do list will be added. An added rule: if you don't finish your list, you cannot go to bed until midnight, or until your sanity drops to 20 percent."

"No!"

How did this woman know I had dropped everything and ran the instant the lamp turned on? Was she watching me? She had to be. Watched, then changed the rules.

"Please do the following so you may protect your—"

"Who are you!" The fear was too much, and I started screaming. "Why am I here?"

"—chop down two trees—"

"Who are '*they*' you keep talking about? Why are you making me do this?"

"—ten firewood onto—"

"I can't do this! Not without answers!"

The beep on the other end stopped the one-sided conversation. I was hyperventilating as I slammed the phone on the base. Farming, home décor. I adored these games and played them for hours. I hated being a rat in a laboratory experiment.

The to-do list finished writing itself, waiting for me to rip it off. Yesterday's jobs were incorporated into it. If I failed to finish it,

I'd have to be awake until midnight. How would I know with no clocks in here?

The other stipulation was my sanity dropping to below twenty percent. I would have to stay awake for a while. Long enough to hear that guttural growl multiple times and perhaps see the creature who created the noise. Yeah. I wouldn't last until midnight. Everything was fine in the morning light, even in a hazy sky and red dawn. Once night came, all my sensibilities leapt out the window. The unanswered questions were bad enough. Any horrors the woman and her group of observers threw at me would make matters worse.

A panic attack almost took me, and I sucked in a few grounding breaths. My fingers ran over the cherry wood table without sensing the stickiness I expected, causing another spike of alarm. The smell of mildew hadn't come back. I opened my eyes to see the to-do list ready to tear off. None of this helped calm me down.

In a rebellious gesture, I focused on the calendar next to the notepad. The nice weather made me assume it was April or May, but I needed to stop assuming anything now. Instead of the month's name, it said SPRING/SUMMER. This calendar depicted the season lasting five perfect weeks of seven full days. An illustration at the top was of the house. It was a beautiful, sturdy home with no fading or chipped paint. Roses grew in the flower beds, and it boasted a well-manicured lawn. I turned the page to FALL/WINTER and saw another thirty-five days. This picture was of a snowstorm, camouflaging the white brick. A tiny red light shone in the second-story room. I furrowed my brows, studying it closer when the red light flickered. I gasped, dropping the page. It might have been my imagination. I wasn't about to check.

Why were the seasons stuck together? I wouldn't stay here until fall/winter, right? Surely I'd get back home by then. They couldn't keep me here forever. Despite farming games having no end, this one should.

The calendar glowed. My eyes widened as I braced myself.

Upgrade Calendar for -0.25

Y/N

The words hung over the house's picture. My work in the carport got me 2.75 dopamine points. 0.25 was low enough to catch my interest. I mentally chose yes, then waited.

My points dropped to 2.50. X's crossed the first two days out. A red circle displayed itself around the seventh. In the same perfect cursive as my to-do list, *They Arrive* showed up in the circle. Five days later, another circle materialized, with the same words in it. My stomach churned as the days shortened from five to four to three, before *They Arrive* was consistently three days apart until the end of spring/summer. The calendar glowed again.

Upgrade Calendar for -0.30

Y/N

They would keep attacking, and I had stumbled upon their attack list. I backed away from the many red circles on this calendar as things I had stuffed in the back of my mind forced themselves forward.

Some mysterious group sent me into this weird land to make me play a game. A movie franchise had that plot, I was pretty sure. I didn't know much about the horror genre, just that I hated it. No sane person should ever consider it entertainment. Even as I thought it, I knew those were controversial thoughts. *Someone* locked in my memory loved horror.

The calendar was the only thing giving answers, so I chose yes again and watched as I was left with 2.15 dopamine points. A moment later, a scattering of images sprinkled over some of the days. I leaned closer, seeing a few cartoon pictures of a bright sun. One of them was the day after *they* first arrived. Did it mean it would get hotter?

Upgrade Calendar for -0.35

Y/N

This was draining my points, and I hadn't even checked my to-do list. Did I need to buy anything else? I finally tore off the paper and studied it.

Find the first greenhouse key in the carport

Prepare one soil bed

Find an axe in the greenhouse

Purchase one article of building clothes

Chop down two trees

Load 0/10 firewood onto the fence

The beautiful cursive didn't stop my panic. This list was long. My evil overlords insisted I finish it or suffer the consequences.

Fear threatened to take hold again as I blinked back tears. I refused to lose control. For whatever reason, I was here. I needed answers, but for now, I'd focus on not hearing that growl. In the middle of the night. With no one around to help me.

I closed my eyes and forced those thoughts away and instead focused on my biggest questions: figure out who I was, how I got here, and how to get home.

On the clipboard, a new section of outfits for building had opened up. I eyed some boots for 5.00. Those 0.55 points I spent on the calendar felt like a stupid move now, but I also didn't regret the advanced information. For all the questions jumbled in my head, I craved any knowledge anyone or anything could give me. If the creature who growled gave me answers, I'd walk up and demand them.

It was time to clean. I walked to the carport and faced my pile of trash. My "definitely trash" mound was gone, but I had more sorting to do.

A warmth entered my right hand. I glanced down; relaxation fled from my body as I studied my spotless palm. Did I catch an infection? That would bring about too many problems I didn't want to acknowledge. At first I ignored the warmth, but as I started organizing, it got impossible to push aside. I took a few steps, and a tingle spread up my arm. Worry nagged at me, but I also couldn't deny the comfort this sensation was. Once my entire form was comfortable, one of the desk drawers glowed. I grabbed the drawer, pulled it open, and sifted through the junk. At the bottom was a key. Once my fingers brushed against it, the warmth faded.

My jaw dropped as I lifted the key to examine it. This was for the greenhouse. Whoever placed me here must have heard my idea from yesterday about a system of hot and cold to help me find it. Except I had never said that out loud. They could read thoughts. This was a clue. They saw me run into the house last night to escape the scary things. That first day, searching for slippers, not wanting to step on the crusty ground, I found them beside the bed. Then they left now that I was buying clothes. The repulsive scents that disappeared. The gross floor I could no longer feel. Was this all their doing, too?

How powerful were these people? They seemed helpful with my slippers, but wanted to punish me if I didn't finish my jobs for the day. Perhaps they were both, deciding when to help and when to enforce rules. They could also somehow read my mind. Which gave me a different, chilling thought altogether.

"I... absolutely do not want answers from whatever growled last night." It was easier to say out loud, partially so I knew they heard. "I'd rather go weeks with nothing than face that thing." Once that escaped my mouth, I let out a tiny sigh. "And... thank you. For helping me find the key."

It fit into the comically large lock of the first greenhouse, and I twisted it. It clanked to the ground before fading away. I pulled the door open and stepped inside. It reminded me of the carport, except this only had one junk pile at the back instead of being stuffed with it. Two rectangular boxes stood on either side, full of dead plants.

Find an axe and prepare a soil bed. That was on my list. I searched through the torn magazines, moldy newspapers, and old shoes to discover a small shovel and hand rake. My senses told me I would need these, so I kept them close. I heaved a bag of fertilizer into the start of my "definitely not trash" pile.

With my newly acquired tools, I approached a box and started digging up dead plants. As I wore my purchased overalls, information was downloaded into my brain about proper treatment of soil beds. Experiment time! My nightgown emerged on my body, and all farming strategies were gone, leaving me wondering what to do.

Back in my gardening outfit, I uprooted old vegetation, then set the hand shovel down before reaching for the other instrument. My fingers brushed against wood and air. Didn't I put that tool here? I shrugged, then reached for the spade instead, but that, too, went missing. A frown tugged at my lips, then an idea crossed my mind. I thought about breaking up dirt, and the small rake materialized in my grip. My eyebrows shot to my hairline, but I went to work loosening the soil.

Once I was done, a weird light flashed over the rectangle box, like a sheen racing over objects, indicating it was complete. Common in video games, but not real life. I was living in a mixture of the two.

I reached into my pocket and pulled out the list. The jobs I finished were crossed out. It was almost noon. I'd have the rest of the day to finish these jobs before the evil overlords tortured me with things that hurt my sanity bar.

It didn't take long searching through old shoes and newspapers to unearth a rusty axe. I stood up, brushing myself off, even though my knees were clean. My feet traveled over the uneven rocky ground and patchy dead grass outside.

According to my list, two trees needed to be chopped, so I chose one uncomfortably close to the house and whacked it. A chunk of my stamina evaporated. Had I lost some while working in the greenhouse? Would I have noticed a slow yet steady drip? I picked up the axe again and thwacked it against the trunk, and another burst of energy vanished. I'd have to watch that bar next time I worked on a soil bed.

Nine thwacks later, the tree groaned, then fell. Even with a shard of stamina left, I stood near, feeling no need to clutch my knees or take deep breaths. No doubt I wouldn't be exhausted until all the yellow disappeared.

Speaking of game logic, once the trunk hit the ground, branches vanished and three logs rolled to a stop. I didn't need those. I needed firewood.

An idea came to me that I wanted to try. I scooped up the rusty axe and smacked a log. It turned into a couple of perfectly cut boards. My curiosity was too much, so I struck one of them. Two bundles of a handful of chopped wood sprung into existence on the ground, bound with rope I never produced. This was the firewood I needed.

I whacked until the second plank changed into a picturesque grouping of firewood. I was about to lift my arm again when it became a thousand pounds heavier.

"Alright." I straightened, dropped the axe and studied my empty stamina bar. "Guess I better eat."

Chapter Five

Fast Decluttering

Almost three days in this strange place, and this was my first meal. No hunger pangs whirled in my stomach.

"If this is some experiment, I don't like it," I said, walking into the covered back porch. "Your virtual reality sucks because it's not realistic. Look at me." I lifted my hands. "I've cleaned out oily junk from the carport, prepared a soil bed in a greenhouse, *and* chopped down a tree, yet they're squeaky clean. Not even a blister. To prove my point, I won't wash before I eat...." I hesitated, mulling over what I had just said before shrugging and opening the fridge door. Why, when all other electricity failed, did this still work? I almost asked those evil overlords when I realized I should keep them unaware of this. They might stop it, and then where would I store my orange juice in this strange spring/summer season?

If I was right, though, these beings read my thoughts, and it wouldn't matter if I said it out loud. Perhaps they were studying human nature through video games. An interesting theory.

"Are you guys aliens or something?" I pulled out a gallon of milk. "Is this what it all is? Have you abducted me and is this how you're probing me? Because if you are, I still expect you to treat me with dignity. I've heard stories, and I'm not interested in that level of investigation."

In the cupboard, I grabbed a clean bowl and a bag of off-brand Lucky Charms. I sat at the clutter-free cherry table and ate in a game logic way. After taking two bites, the cereal and milk disappeared. My stamina bar filled a quarter. I crinkled my nose. "That isn't enough."

So I poured more. The odd thing about never being hungry is I never got full, either. I finished my second helping, my energy at halfway. "How can I cook when the electricity doesn't work?" I eyed the stove as I kept chatting. "And milk? How will I replenish my supply? These games often have a barn with cows and chickens. I didn't see one out there. Also, there's usually a village within walking distance with a bunch of NPCs to buy from and talk to. Isolation is no joke. You end up talking to yourself a lot."

A long sigh escaped me as I poured a third bowl. "I wouldn't mind taking care of animals. I could gather eggs." My gaze fell on the stove again. "I'm assuming there's cooking, too. Because... every farming game has that."

Two bites, cereal gone. My stamina reached three-quarters full. One more serving should do it.

"Orange juice and a container of mixed berries can only get me so far." I froze. Did I slip up and say something that could be misinterpreted? "I appreciate the fridge keeping things cool, by the way. Please let it keep working. And maybe the stove, too?"

After finishing my fourth bowl, my stamina filled up. I hopped off the chair and returned the milk. It was halfway gone, with one more gallon left. My brain churned out ideas, preparing to ration food. Eating half a slice of bread was easier than eating nothing all day.

I stared again at the empty fridge, cocking my head. That was strange. I knew how to make plans to stretch simple meals out for weeks.

"I've been starving before, haven't I?"

I spoke to whoever was forcing me to play this game. Though perhaps I said it to myself. It was a clue about who I am. A primal instinct, not a memory to be wiped. Much like my distaste of horror.

Speaking of which, it was time to finish my to-do list. I walked outside with renewed stamina and picked another tree. With many thwacks, I brought it down, and with a few more, the logs and boards changed into beautiful firewood. After all that, I still had a bit of yellow left, which was nice.

The shadows stretched, and so did I. I had a few more hours until nighttime. I pulled out the to-do list and studied it again. Everything was crossed out except purchasing building clothes and placing ten firewood in the fence. How would I build one on this patchy lawn? Buying clothes might help me understand. If I remembered right, all the articles of clothing cost 5.00 dopamine points, and with my current 2.15, I needed to dump clutter.

Exactly ten bundles of firewood rested on the ground, which was a pity, because I wanted to see how much the dumpster gave me after dropping a bundle into it. I couldn't give one up, because I didn't have enough stamina to chop more trees. Instead, I needed to clean. There wasn't enough "definitely trash" in the carport to get me to 5.00, and organizing took forever. Maybe I could clean somewhere else? I didn't enjoy waking up to the mess in the bedroom. Waking up to it organized, with no mice scampering over the piles of junk, would do wonders. I could begin decluttering there, then move to the carport later.

My levels must have been higher, since I carried an entire garbage bag stuffed with shirts from the closet to the dumpster. Once I cleared out the previous owner's wardrobe, I noticed my night-gown hanging inside. The sliding door still hung off the track, but I just left it there. This now had the only other clothing I owned. Perhaps this is where the clothes were stored when they weren't leaping onto my body. My other apparel would have bonuses, but did this nightgown have any? Like any magical properties to help me while I slept?

"That'd be nice!" I shouted to the scientists controlling my lab experiment.

I gathered the ashtrays from the bedroom and the entertainment room before dropping them into the dumpster. They each gave me a measly +0.01 dopamine point. Oh well, they were gone.

2.26 total. I tried not to imagine what it would be like if I had never upgraded the calendar, because that wouldn't do any good. Instead, as the shadows of the trees stretched toward the house, I buckled in and gathered up junk.

The bedroom was coming together. I'd appreciate it better in the dawn light and not the setting sun. Right now, I was stressing more about reaching 5.00.

When I dropped another large bag of beer cans into the dumpster and received +0.04 for all that effort, my legs got restless and my insides quivered. Weak sunlight filtered through the thick forest trees, and it already felt dark. I didn't want to feel terrified until my sanity left. My points crept ever closer to 4.00, and it was time to move into the carport.

My pile of "definitely trash" wasn't big enough, but it was something. Crickets chirped in the distance as I finished filling a bag. I monitored the slivers that left my stamina as I ran to the dumpster. I dropped a bag in, finally reaching 4.02 total dopamine points, but I didn't celebrate. The shadow of the trees inched up to the roof, and I focused more on them than on what I was tossing, until a phrase entered my vision.

Are you sure you want to throw that away?
Y/N

The climb to 5.00 was slow, and I needed to get this finished, but the question stopped me for a solid five seconds. I had stumbled upon a built-in system to ensure I wouldn't toss anything useful. That changed everything.

I mentally chose no, and the sack reappeared in my hand. I shook the contents of the bag onto the ground and began plopping things into the dumpster one by one until I received the phrase again.

Are you sure you want to throw that away?

Y/N

What I thought was a rusted bullet was actually an old battery. Did I need batteries? Not one in this state, but since I got the prompt, I was too afraid to toss it now.

After mentally choosing no, it reappeared in my palm, and I ran into the carport. I stuffed my bag with as much of the "possibly not trash" pile as my stamina would allow and booked it to the dumpster. I dropped it in, holding my breath.

+0.08

No message about whether I wanted to throw something away. I forced myself to think of other things besides how quickly the orange and red sky turned to purple and blue as stars twinkled above me.

The carport would look so organized now that I was throwing out garbage. Someone might even fit a car in here.

I sprinted toward the dumpster again with three new bags of junk, dropping them in one at a time.

"I bet whoever owned this house had a gorgeous car." What was I saying?

+0.05

"So lovely." I stared at my total.

4.46

"I guarantee it was a charming green car. They aren't often pretty, but the previous owners must have had one. Probably a Model T. That's the first vehicle invented, right?" Who was I asking this question to?

I sprinted into the carport, stuffing things into the sack. "I have a feeling it had some glitter on it, too. Like a green, glittery Model T. I bet the lady of the house was beautiful. Back in the late eighteen hundreds."

Halfway to the dump, the bag slipped out of my fingers and I collapsed, my stamina gone. I couldn't move, even if my survival was at stake. Which it was.

"Come on, whatever your name is. You can do it," I said to myself as I gathered a few of the spilled items on the ground and dropped them in the dumpster. I crossed 4.52 total points and walked to gather more trash in the bag before returning.

"I believe in you. You've got this. You—"

A guttural noise cut me off.

Chapter Six

Not So Isolated

I was talking to myself. Out loud. Why was I doing that? Only idiots in horror movies did that.

My eyes shot toward my blue sanity bar. The growl from the first night had caused it to drop; this time it held firm.

You can do this. You'll be okay. Your sanity is fine, so you are too.

I dropped the items in the dumpster and strolled into the carport, gathering more. I stifled my breath as I walked as fast as my empty yellow bar would let me before unloading the bags.

My ears tingled. The crickets weren't chirping, and the river roared behind the greenhouses. The growl was deeper in the woods, yet too close.

Tears fell down my cheeks, and a splinter of blue evaporated. I dumped the trash; my mind scattered. If I didn't get this done, I'd be awake until midnight.

The creature growled again, closer to the carport but still hidden by the trees. Light from the lamppost created dark shadows as the stars above twinkled in a black sky.

The dumpster vibrated with my last bag. 4.65 total. I wouldn't make it. If I hadn't upgraded that stupid calendar, I'd have been in bed already.

Don't get scared. You can't change the past. Use the energy to work on what you have now.

My knees knocked together as the growl rumbled at the forest's edge. Every hair on my arm stood, blue fading from my bar. I needed something more valuable to sell. But what if I sold it, and couldn't recover it, leaving me incapable of completing another task? I'd be stuck with a continually piling list of to-dos that would keep me awake until midnight and drive me insane and I—

Milk. I had an extra gallon.

I let out a breath and sauntered through the back, even though my anxious muscles demanded I sprint. I snatched two cans of beans from the cupboard, opened them, and drained them in one swallow. A small flake of stamina returned, making me open and drain two more as I reached the fridge. Food always sold in these kinds of games. Since this place had no village of NPCs, the dumpster must be where I got points for it. I grabbed the full gallon and tried not to think about how much this might hurt to lose. The beans might have given me something, but the small amount of stamina I had received in return made me believe they weren't as valuable.

The front door squeaked open as I emerged with the milk and a bag of empty cans. I tiptoed around the house. I wanted to save my extra energy for emergencies. The river flowed behind the greenhouses. My breathing might have been louder than the creature as I let the sack fall into the dumpster. It hummed, making me wince at the noise as it gave me +0.02 points. The creature must not have noticed the humming, so I dropped the gallon inside.

Are you sure you want to throw that away?

Y/N

Yes, yes, yes.

+1.50

I sucked in a ragged breath. 6.17 total. I briskly walked through the back door and purchased the first item on the building list, an orange hard hat. It popped onto my head. I must have been a sight in this and my worn-out farming overalls, but I didn't care. When I moved into the backyard, a ghostly impression of a wood fence circled around the carport and house. Words hovered above it.

0/50 firewood

With a sinking heart, I realized I had stacked the wood by the dumpster. The last place I heard the growling. At least I only had to do ten, but even the thought made me want to scream.

Every instinct told me to hide in my bedroom, but I pushed through, stepping onto the concrete front porch before easing around the side of the house. Silence pressed into me, which gave me a slew of emotions I couldn't identify that ended up like a rock in my stomach. Ten bundles of firewood were against the white brick, and I started gathering. When I picked up a third bundle, the other two tumbled to the ground. A wave of nausea hit me as my precious stamina left.

Fine. Two it is.

The information given to me from my hard hat told me to stack the bundles inside the phantom fence. My ears ached as I listened for the creature. Knowing it was out there and not hearing it felt almost worse than hearing the growl itself.

Unsure, I placed two bundles into the glowing outline, and the wood disappeared. The numbers ticked upward before stopping.

2/50

That was a good sign. I snuck back through the house, eating a handful of mixed berries to get more stamina. I got a nice chunk of yellow that helped ease my anxiety, then left to gather more bundles.

At least I can carry two.

I repeated this phrase to myself. Ten trips would be horrible. Five was doable. I dropped more firewood, checking that it worked.

4/50

Six more, then bedtime.

The lamppost cast a shadow of a four-legged creature coming out of the forest near the carport. It stepped onto the ground, sniffing. My feet froze in place, and my breathing turned shallow as my sanity took another dip.

No. No, don't freeze. Come on, dear girl. You can do this.

It required a mental force to get my legs moving again. I gathered two more bundles and tiptoed to the fence, blue dripping out of the bar as I shoved firewood into the image.

If the carport wasn't there, I'd see exactly what that beast was. The jagged silhouette it cast, though, was enough that my sanity continually dropped every second. The sniffs coming from behind the carport were wet and slobbery. I might be in bed in a few minutes, whether or not I finished the job.

The creature had four legs and—according to its shadow—thick, mangy fur. A wolf was the first thought I had, but I refused to accept it. I'd heard wolves howling in the forest. They didn't make the noises that this creature made. It sniffed around the cement foundation as I picked up two more bundles, tears streaming down my face. My sanity was officially halfway gone. The creature's sniffing became more intense, with snarls intermixed as it grew more fervent in its search, moving away from the carport.

It must not have a keen nose. Shouldn't four-legged monster creatures have a better sense of smell? They hunted, after all. This thing should have smelled me already. Best not to think about the logistics of it all. I should just be grateful this beast stayed distracted by something else.

I placed the bundles of firewood and turned to retrieve the last two. As I picked them up, the creature stopped sniffing, and I remained frozen on the spot. Tears dripped from my chin onto the patchy ground below. I waited, my breathing nonexistent as my heart roared in my ears. I could do these final two bundles. Please let me do this.

Sanity was dropping fast, but not low enough to run straight to bed. Maybe I could stay here, rooted, until it was at twenty percent. That could work, right?

The creature barked, one of recognition and anger. I gasped, hugging the bundles to my chest as I sprinted toward the fence.

What was I doing? Get in the house! Why wasn't I running for the front door?! I only have so much stamina, and I shouldn't waste it like this! Don't run for the fence, go for the DOOR.

Fear was a strong stimulant. I shoved the remaining firewood onto the image as four paws pounded the ground, headed for me.

"Done. I'm done." I pumped my legs, hoping I had enough stamina to make it to the house without collapsing in nausea.

Out of the corner of my eye, I saw the shadowed beast. It snarled, saliva dripping from its jaw before a deafening crack filled the air. At first I thought a gun had gone off, but then the creature squealed in pain before it stood up on its hind legs and sprinted for me. The speed was inhuman, and I screamed, throwing myself against the front door as the last of my stamina was gone.

It could run. On its hind legs. What *was* that thing? What was it doing here at this house?

I slammed the door and locked it, tears dropping off my chin as I scrambled to the back door in the dark, making sure it was secure. I tried to bolt to my room, but I collapsed in nausea. Moaning, I got to my feet and stumbled into bed.

"Sleep! Please! It's done! My to-do list is done!"

The last two nights didn't produce any dreams. I begged the overlords that the same applied tonight because I couldn't have a nightmare. I was already living in one.

Chapter Seven

The Greenhouse

The dawn light woke me up once again, and I slowly lifted my head. I spent a solid minute staring at nothing. No dreams or nightmares, but it felt like it had happened seconds ago. That cracking noise I heard, was that the creature's spine? Did bones shift and break to cause it to do that? If so, how could that beast stand, let alone run? I remembered the squeal of pain, and maybe I should feel pity, but I didn't. It wanted me dead. This was a game, though, and I had no hit points. That might mean something, right? I stared at my two bars, wondering if—

My sanity. Unlike stamina, the blue bar only filled up halfway. Did only a certain amount refill every day?

When my chest stopped rising and falling so much, I stumbled out of the partially decluttered bedroom and into the entertainment room. I refused to look at the VHS tapes on the bookshelf. I couldn't have another night like yesterday. Not with half my sanity gone. My body certainly felt the effects of it, leaving me a trembling mess.

With a shaking hand, I grabbed the phone, pressing one.

"In four days, they will come. In four days, they will destroy. Anything you didn't complete on your to-do list will be added. If you do not finish your list, you may not go to bed until midnight, or until your sanity drops to 20 percent."

"I know." Why did I bother talking? It wasn't like the woman leaving a message ever replied.

"Purchase and plant ten tomato seeds,

"Water those ten tomato seeds,

"Finish building the rest of the fence,

"Further instructions will follow..."

The phone beeped, and I studied the jobs. It was short, but it would take me all day again.

My eyes closed, which made my mind replay the image of the creature's inhuman sprint. I gasped, opening my eyes, and tore the to-do list off the notepad. This fence was important. Four more days until *they* attacked, and this was the first time my instructions were anything toward my safety.

After flipping through the clipboard pages, I reached the farming section and saw how much the seeds were. A packet of five cost 0.50 dopamine points. I needed two, which would completely drain me, which is when I glanced at my total. I had 3.17. How did I have more?

The first day came back to memory. When I finished my to-do list, I got +2.00. Last night I was so focused on running that I didn't register the bonus. I have it now, which means I don't have to worry about it being a huge drain to buy what I needed.

With my new purchase, I walked to the greenhouse, a glare on my face. This structure of metal and glass had put me through grief because I couldn't find the key fast enough.

My farming overalls told me to plant the seeds in the soil bed. Once I did, I glanced around for a watering can and a place to fill it up. When I found neither, I shrugged and reentered the house to get a cup of water. I was almost out the door when an invisible wall blocked me from leaving the kitchen.

"Come *on*, evil overlord alien people! I'm being creative! Finding a different way to do a job! Doesn't this help you understand human nature better? Let me do this!"

The barrier remained, and I glared before draining the cup, filling my cheeks full of water before setting the glass on the counter. I then moved out the back door, toward the first greenhouse. When I got to the soil bed, I spat everything out on the tomato seed, except... nothing came out. The water in my mouth just evaporated.

The overlords must have been glitching out, because a text showed up in my vision.

Insufficient for growth. You will be incapable of doing that again. Find a watering can.

"Ugh, come on! Let me have this one! You guys took half my sanity. It's only fair."

No reply. With a grumble, I turned toward the mound of garbage still in the greenhouse. I gathered the junk into a bag, slowly unearthing the watering can. I tossed the fourth sack of trash to the side as I picked up the rusted can and returned to the kitchen. As I waited for it to fill with tap water, I wondered if I should be worried about whether this was safe to drink. I quickly pushed the thought away. After cleaning out a carport with no gloves and not getting blisters after chopping down trees, I wasn't about to get a parasite now.

Once the seeds were watered, I checked my to-do list. I heard a squelching noise, which made me pause. I glanced around to see ten little mounds of squirming dirt. My eyes widened as baby plants inched out of the soil and unfurled their leaves. This was one magical place if they could grow tomatoes this quickly. I scurried out of the greenhouse. It was time to cut down those trees. I was not staying here after sunset, or when the lamppost light flickered on.

To get forty more bundles of firewood, I'd need to start chopping. I started with the ones closest to the house. In order to make the yard look nice, I wanted to remove the trees close to the foundation. I approached a tree, and the axe materialized in my hand, like with the shovel and garden fork. My mind recoiled at how unusual game logic was. Did I have an inventory? I set the watering can on the ground. Would that magically appear, too? Something told me yes. I found it and therefore gained it. Tending those plants was most likely part of my daily jobs.

Also, I realized I had slept with the hard hat and overalls on. This required so much game logic.

The first tree fell, and I broke the logs down into firewood, placing them into the fence.

15/50

This would take a while.

For every tree that I dropped, I took a break to regain my stamina by eating. I monitored my sanity, but it remained half full the entire time. I had hoped that in the sunlight it would have trickled back to full, but no.

When the fence read 50/50, I collected a scattering of empty beans and soup cans on the cleared-off table. I gathered them and dropped them into the dumpster, giving me +0.04 dopamine points. The temptation was there to drop more food to reach 5.00 again. I was eyeing some of those logging clothes. If I had some, would it take less stamina to fell a tree? Or get more logs out of it?

"Are you guys taking notes? Because I have some suggestions," I said to the sky as I walked outside. My fingers twitched as I rubbed them against my overalls. "Also... please don't blast me with unfair rules if I talk too much. You sent me here, after all."

I examined the lawn with my hard hat on. When I reached 50/50, a partially made fence erupted into existence. Firewood turned into crisscrossing spikes. The ghostly imprint was gone as the wood circled around the entire house and the carport. The greenhouses remained unprotected. Would they be fine from *them*? I couldn't be sure. Then I noticed more red numbers and words above the spikes.

0/10 boards

Right. I pulled out my to-do list to see everything crossed out except for *build the rest of the fence.* How much more was there to do? This was a lot of trees to chop down, and I was running low on food.

The hazy yellow sky turned more orange as it approached early evening. As long as ten boards were the last request, I could finish it well before bedtime. If the fence needed another resource after this, I should buy a logging shirt. Or boots. Or gloves. So far, I had the farming overalls and a hard hat. Was this a challenge to make my outfit weird?

I walked over to a tree near the living room window; the axe sprung in my fist. "Alright, let's get this finished."

After many hits, the tree fell and broke off into logs. I moved to chop them again when a glittering white orb rose from the remaining stump. I backed away, my eyes widening as I gripped the axe for protection. What I mistook for glitter was really ethereal, pulsating luminescence, spreading fractal light against the ground. It floated until it was chest high, hovering in the air. I stared at it, refusing to trust it. What even was this thing? How did it get here? What was it supposed to do?

The white orb continued to bob, trailing an afterglow. It was daytime, so I wasn't nearly as afraid, but I still wasn't sure what it did.

A solid minute passed with me staring at that ball, figuring out what it could do without me needing to examine it any closer. My mind was both racing and stuttering.

The orb vibrated, and then it shot toward my chest. I screamed before everything went black.

Chapter Eight

The Orb's Message

" ⸻ then I went into my room and played with dolls. I was pretending we were off on a desert island, but it had machines."

The little girl, perhaps five, finished setting the table for dinner and was leaning against the countertop away from the stove, arms folded. She had brown hair to her shoulders, watching a woman in her late forties making dinner. The woman stirred a pot full of corn on the stovetop. She stopped to catch some bread popping out of the toaster. The kitchen was large, with dinner preparation cluttering the countertops.

"What machines were they?" the woman asked.

"Like food or books or an arcade, or a zoo!"

The woman chuckled at the lack of machines in the girl's list.

"I didn't have to buy anything, because I own the entire island. And we just played and pretended we were the world's richest people. The food machine was great because it made those delicious burgers from that fancy restaurant you took me to the first time I met you."

The smallest of smiles crossed the woman's face; one the child didn't notice. "McDonalds?"

"Yes! It was so good! The island gave those burgers away, and everyone was happy. Then Felicity came and said—"

"Ah, wait a moment. Did Felicity give you permission to tell me what she said?"

The little girl crinkled her brow, studying the woman's face. "Why would I have to ask permission from Felicity to say you wanted help setting the table for dinner?"

The woman went back to stirring the corn. "There are things people want to keep private. It makes them feel uncomfortable when others know too much about their lives."

The little girl blinked again at the older woman. "I don't understand."

"It's okay not to understand yet. Just remember we still have to respect other people's privacy."

"But we always need to tell people what's going on. Mama is getting better because I told everyone what my life was like at home. That's what Ms. Nichole said."

"I know that too." The woman turned off the stovetop, moving the pot of corn to a different burner to cool down. "There are things that are dangerous to keep secret, but there are also details

Felicity may not want others to know, and it makes her feel embarrassed."

"But if no one ever reported that Felicity's mommy was getting beaten by her boyfriend, she would've been in danger. Right? So people know she's safe now. Right? If I didn't tell anyone I hadn't eaten in three days, no one would've brought me here so I can eat. Right?" The little girl sighed, then crinkled her nose again. "It's more important to tell everyone everything all the time."

"Ah, Quinn." The older woman ruffled the little girl's hair. "You may not mind what other people think, but Felicity might feel embarrassed."

The little girl, Quinn, almost asked another question, but the oven beeped. Quinn beamed. "DINNER!" She shouted it with all the energy in her soul as the woman opened the oven door and pulled out the casserole. Quinn leapt off the stool and ran to the dining room table near the kitchen. Her shouts were better than a ringing bell. Though the phone did start ringing. The older woman wiped her hands on the apron before picking up the handset. "Hello?"

Quinn sat happily at the table, holding her fork and spoon. The woman moved as far as the cord would let her.

"This is Brenda..." The woman's face changed from a slight smile to a frown tugging at her lips. "Yes, hello Shauna."

Quinn waved as another little girl with braids entered the dining room. The other girl returned the wave. An older man walked in.

"Hello Doug!" Quinn shouted.

The older man beamed at the little girl. "Hello, dear."

The woman, Brenda, craned her neck, motioning toward the man. "Doug, dear. Can you come here for a moment? Shauna's on the phone."

"Ah, what does she need?"

The two of them moved into the kitchen. A teenager slumped into a chair. "Oh, no! Shauna's calling? I'm starving! I don't want to wait for them to be done talking!"

"You're always starving, Derrin," Quinn said.

"Because I'm always growing. What about it, girls? Should I get the casserole?"

"Yes! Yes! Yes!" Quinn beat on the table with her utensils. "I LOVE tater tot casserole!" She said it with the same vigor she'd used to scream that dinner was ready, her spoon and fork shaking in her fists.

Derrin smiled as he entered the kitchen. When he returned, the smile disappeared as he placed the casserole in the middle of the table and left to get the corn.

"Mom says we can eat. They're not sure when they'll finish talking to Shauna," he said as he entered with the side of corn.

"Does that mean another kid is coming to our house?" Quinn asked.

"Possibly."

Felicity turned toward Quinn. "How long do you think this kid will stay?"

"No idea." Derrin grabbed the two girls' plates.

"Does it ever bother you to share your house with other kids?" Quinn asked.

"No." Slowly, Derrin started smiling again, dishing up dinner.

"What about me sharing my private life? Does that annoy you? Brenda says some people get embarrassed and don't want to talk about it. Like how Felicity hates how I tell everyone her momma's boyfriend beat her up—"

Felicity's braids hit her shoulders as she whipped her head around to glare at Quinn. "Hey!"

"But does it bother you when I talk about my life?" Quinn asked him, ignoring Felicity.

Derrin finished putting the plates on the table in front of the girls. "No, I don't mind. You are talking to Ms. Nichole about it a lot, though, right?"

"Yeah. I am. She wants to hear all about it."

The older couple walked in, and Derrin glanced up at his parents. "So?"

"A boy is arriving in about an hour. Emergency placement. There's nowhere else for him to go." Doug sat down and dished himself up. "We'll give him a tour of the place. Derrin, make sure you clean your room."

Derrin looked up from his mountain of tater tot casserole. "Your tours never include my room."

"True. It's a reminder to clean your room." The older man ruffled the boy's hair. Derrin grumbled, but allowed it.

"What's the boy like? Is he staying long? Why's he coming here?"

Quinn asked more questions before Brenda held up a hand. "Calls with Shauna are never so informative. We just know a five-year-old boy is arriving."

It didn't appease Quinn's avalanche of inquiries. Throughout dinner she filled the room with questions, supposes, and dark wonderings of what his life might have been like to come to Doug and Brenda's house.

Quinn was in the playroom with Felicity, still asking questions, when a car pulled in. Both girls dropped their toys and pressed their noses to the window. A woman helped a boy out the back of a car. Brenda and Doug waited on the front porch.

"I don't see any bruises on him." Quinn's palms were flat against the glass.

"Some adults are tricky and sometimes hit kids where they have clothes to hide the bruises," Felicity said.

"Oh, yeah. You're probably right."

Quinn and Felicity passed stories as they stared at the boy who stood on the lawn steps, his eyes focused on Brenda and pointedly ignoring Doug.

"He looks like he saw his dog get run over," Felicity said.

"Yeah." Quinn's already wide blue eyes grew wider. "Do you think he's actually five? Remember when Shauna told Brenda that Trevor was six, but he was ten? That was funny."

"That boy looks five, but then again, you don't look five either."

"That's cause Mama drank while I was in her belly," Quinn said.

Doug chatted with a worker as Brenda knelt to get eye level with the boy and talk to him. The boy's face remained the same. Wide-eyed, haunted, and with his mouth glued shut.

They were outside for an eternity. Doug entered the house and left again with a booster seat under his arm, which Brenda took and placed in her own car.

"Brenda's taking him shopping! It's time for our instructions!" Quinn said as the car left the driveway.

Doug smiled as he entered the house and heard the tail end of that. For anyone but Quinn, they would have noticed how small the smile was on his face, how the boy's haunted look leaked into Doug's eyes.

"Does he prefer girl company or boy company?" Quinn stood as if she were receiving instructions from an army sergeant. Her hands were behind her back, shoulders straight.

"Girl company," Doug said.

"So that means you need to be more careful around him, right?" Felicity asked.

"Yes, that does," Doug said.

"Felicity only liked girl company, but she eventually started liking you." Quinn patted Doug's shoulder. The man didn't smile as he patted Quinn's hand back.

"We're not to force my company on him if he doesn't want it. It's all up to him."

Derrin had his arms folded, leaning against the wall. "What about teenage boy company?"

"Still unsure. But we'll play it super safe. His name is Theo, and he'll stay with us for a while."

Chapter Nine

A Few More Answers

Doug and Derrin went to a different room when Brenda brought Theo home with two bags of clothes. The haunted look had not left the boy's eyes. Quinn was the perfect model of welcoming the new boy, asking questions deemed 'harmless enough' by Doug beforehand. Theo never answered, and Brenda smiled before taking him on a tour of the house as Doug motioned Quinn and Felicity over to him.

"Come on, girls. School's tomorrow. Let's get ready for bed," Doug said.

Felicity's smile dropped, and she gripped her braids. "I only want Brenda to comb my hair."

"And she will." He nodded in Felicity's direction. "Don't you worry. Once you're in your pajamas, I'll fetch her."

It was a while before the night settled. Felicity stopped tossing and turning, sleep taking her. Brenda and Doug stayed up talking in the living room, their voices solemn. Brenda started crying, and

Quinn checked on her. The little girl wanted to help, but Brenda told her that this was an adult problem. It meant Brenda would turn to another adult for assistance, however, she'd always accept hugs. So, the little girl gave her the best hug she could before returning to her room as Doug comforted his wife. Quinn wasn't too worried. Those two solved a lot of problems together.

An idea struck Quinn. She reached under her bed, grabbing an empty ice cream tub before leaving her bedroom, tiptoeing through the hallway. She had been the model example of behavior when Doug and Brenda introduced Theo, but now she had this opportunity to not pretend.

"...why? Why is the world so cruel to the ones that are the most innocent?" Brenda's voice came through the hall.

Quinn kept moving, sneaking into Theo's bedroom, still holding the bucket.

"Hi," she whispered.

Theo jolted up, turning toward her. His haunted eyes grew wide with fear. She knew he wasn't asleep, because no one slept well their first night. He grabbed his blanket, scooting back from her.

"My name is Quinn. I already introduced myself before, but I wanted to give you this." She handed him the bucket. "It was mine when I first got here six months ago. Brenda said I could have it to keep food under my bed if I felt scared. It helped me sleep better because I could wake up and eat a snack. I haven't needed it in a while."

Quinn's smile turned into a frown as she lifted the tub. "Oh, but there's nothing in here. If you want, I could sneak into the kitchen and get you some snacks. Brenda and Doug never lock the fridge or the cupboards, and they showed me where they put all the food when I first got here. They keep them stocked, too. I tried, just to make sure. I once emptied the entire basket of Ritz crackers into my bucket, and the next day they restocked them!" Quinn said, a huge grin on her face. "Not off-brand things! Actual ritz crackers! They're so good, and crispy, and buttery. Would you like me to bring you something?"

Theo shook his head fervently. Quinn frowned, tapping a finger against her chin. "It's okay. They don't beat me if they find me out of bed at night. Trevor was worried about that, but I told him Brenda and Doug don't do things like that. I even ran down to the kitchen and dropped a box of food to prove it. Trevor was shaking in his boots, but nothing happened. He's with his family now. Oh, not his momma, though. Just his daddy and all his siblings. His dad never punched him, only his mom. Doug said Trevor would come back here if he isn't okay, but he hasn't been here for months. So Trevor's good."

Theo kept staring at her. Quinn returned his gaze. "You don't want to talk, do you?"

His eyes retained their haunted expression, his mouth glued shut.

"It's fine. Really. No one expects you to talk if you don't wanna. My mommy never spoke either. Sometimes during the day she did, but she'd mostly moan. Or she'd scream. She hated it when I made noises in the morning or while she was taking drugs. I usually just played with my doll and talked to her so my mommy wouldn't get angry with me. That was before, though. Before I came to live with Brenda and Doug. I visit Momma with Brenda now. She never screams when there's other adults in the room. People say she's getting better. Mama doesn't take drugs much anymore. She even got a job. It'd be nice to be in a bed and not sleep in the park when I go live with her."

Quinn lifted her arms and shook them. "See that! Oh, wait, maybe you can't. I have the sleeves on." She tugged at the night-gown until her arms were showing, then moved them again. "I have some jiggle in them! The doctor was happy." She brought her sleeves down before kneeling and sliding the bucket under his bed. "It's there if you need it. Don't worry about me. If I get hungry, I go to the kitchen and eat! They never run out of food here."

Quinn placed her head on the mattress as Theo kept looking at her. "Did Brenda take you to McDonald's? They have the best hamburgers! I love them so much."

Moonlight shone through the window. Theo hugged his legs, listening.

"I don't have a dad. My mommy said he's out of the picture, whatever that means. Doug told me not to ask you about your parents. So, I'm not gunna." Quinn brushed hair from her forehead. "But you're okay now. Brenda and Doug are fun! They never get super mad. They also have a lot of food. Someone's mom said I talk as much as five kids. So, if you never want to speak again, I'll say enough for you."

Theo remained silent, and though the haunted look lingered, he wasn't gripping his blankets as tightly as before. Quinn brushed her nightgown out. "I love nightgowns. With Momma, I just slept in old clothes, but this is better. Brenda bought this for me my first night, and I love it! It's so comfortable. Way more comfy than wearing hole clothes. That's what I call them."

She beamed at him. "Brenda will take you to your appointments, since you don't want Doug's company. Some kids get nervous about how many meetings you have, but everyone just wants to help. I bet you won't even have to talk if you don't wanna. Ms. Nichole actually makes me draw. Do you like drawing?"

Despite looking less scared, Theo didn't react to her question. Quinn shrugged and kept going. "Also, don't feel bad if you're nervous about Doug. I asked him if he felt sad that sometimes kids don't want his company, and he said it doesn't make him sad. He's way more concerned about what the kid wants. Oh, but he told me not to force you to be near him. It's your choice when you want to accept his company." At this, Theo winced, unnoticed by Quinn. "Offended. That's the word he used once. He's not offended kids don't want to be around him. I don't know what that means. Brenda steps away too, if you decide you don't like girls anymore.

"Don't feel scared if you wet the bed in the middle of the night, either. Trevor used to hide his pee because he was afraid he'd get beaten, but Brenda and Doug don't hit kids. In fact, they prefer if you wake them up right when it happens. Apparently, you can get a rash if you stay in your own pee so much, and they want us to be healthy. Do you pee the bed?"

Theo said nothing, staring at her.

"Oh, this might be one of those things where it's personal and you don't want to tell. It's okay. You don't even have to nod or shake your head. Just know that Brenda and Doug are happy to help at night. Also, if you have nightmares—"

"Quinn."

Brenda's voice was soft, but it still stopped Quinn's words. Brenda was leaning against the doorway as the little girl looked up.

"Oh, sorry. Was I talking too much?"

Brenda gestured for her. "No, honey. Remember what we talked about with personal space? Don't walk into someone's room, because this is their place that they make their own and they want to control who comes and who goes. Knock on the door and ask if you can come in."

"But he doesn't talk," Quinn said.

"Quinn," Brenda said again, remaining at the doorway.

The little girl glanced at Theo. "I'm sorry. Am I talking too much?" Theo hesitated, then shook his head. "See? He's not bothered."

"It's getting late, and you both need your sleep," Brenda said.

Quinn sighed, then stood up. "Okay. I'll see you tomorrow, Theo. Remember, the bucket is under the bed. I don't need it anymore. If you have nightmares, let Brenda or Doug know." At this, Quinn frowned. "Oh, you don't like Doug's company, that's right. Brenda gives wonderful hugs. But you just wait until you get a hug from Doug." She wrapped her arms around herself tight and twirled. "He gives the best teddy bear hugs. I love Doug hugs."

Brenda chuckled. "I'll tell him you said that."

"I already did."

"I have no doubt."

"Good night, Theo." Quinn pointed down the hall. "My room's over there. Just enter my room. You don't even have to knock."

Quinn walked out, taking Brenda's hand.

Later, when the blue night sky turned black, Theo experienced his first nightmare. He covered his mouth to stop his screams as he ran to Quinn's room. She woke, rubbing her eyes to see him trembling, tears running down his cheeks, his palm over his lips to smother the noise, begging to escape. She didn't hesitate as she grabbed his hand and led him to Brenda and Doug's bedroom.

Nausea hit me, and I gasped, moving away from the stump. The orb was gone. No time had passed, even though I had spent hours inside those scenes.

I stared unblinking before I dropped the axe and ran. I was chasing after a theory. Something about all that was familiar. Too familiar.

My feet stumbled onto the covered back porch, heading straight for the clipboard. I flipped through the pages until I came to the last page.

Progress of the woman who does not know her name yet

I held my breath. An invisible eraser removed that sentence, the stroke marks clearing it away. Once it was gone, someone wrote two short words.

Quinn's Progress

Chapter Ten
More Chores

The last board tumbled out of my hand, fading from existence right before it almost crashed into the spikes. Boards popped up to keep the wood in place. A sheen raced across the fence. I didn't speak, hands to my mouth. I'd used up most of the remaining food to chop logs into boards. It helped with getting more stamina for decluttering, but I hoped I would already have something to replenish my empty cupboards by now.

I pulled out the to-do list from my overall pocket, relieved to see it was complete. +2.00 was added to my total for finishing the list as a few stars emerged in the sky.

My feet shuffled into the house as I hugged myself. Once I had both doors locked, the lamppost flickered to life. Then I entered the partially cleaned bedroom and collapsed on the bed.

Would you like to go to sleep?

Y/N

The words floated in my vision, but I didn't reply. Instead, I stared at the ceiling. That white orb was unsettling. Was it a memory? Clearly it must have been, because the paper had changed to Quinn's progress. I had studied the page before leaving to finish the fence. My cleaning and logging had reached level three. My building level was two. Farming was at one. I had two more areas on my chart to unlock.

A part of me still wrestled with the idea that my name was Quinn. The scenes didn't feel like memories, because I hadn't seen through the little girl's eyes. I had watched the entire thing being played before me, feeling someone else's detached emotional commentary. Yet it felt familiar. Once I'd seen them, a portion of my own memories was unlocked. I remembered the rough metal edges of the bedframe pressing against my shoulders as I talked Theo's ear off. I was such a talkative child with no filter. However, that's the extent of my memory; those few glimpses. I didn't recall Brenda and Doug talking in hushed whispers the night Theo came, and I still didn't know what happened to Theo and Felicity afterwards. Thinking about my foster parents, the only emotion I remember was security. They had my complete and total trust. Did they keep being safe? Were they only in my life at that moment in time?

What about now, in this strange game? Had I been teleported to my childhood home? This house was not for a child, and I'd thought on more than one occasion that CPS should have been called. But nothing about this place triggered any memories.

Would I get more of those white orbs? Or was that the only one? I craved more of the information the orb gave me. It was my first real clue, even if it just resulted in me figuring out my name and a hint of my childhood.

"Quinn," I told the ceiling, hearing the word roll off my tongue. Why couldn't I remember everything all at once?

The list of things I knew was short, but I mulled them over in my mind, anyway. I had gotten teleported into this farming game, a genre that I love, with a prowling supernatural wolf creature that now knew what I looked like. Some overlord alien people watched me and my progress. I had not stumbled here by accident.

Tears filled my eyes as I turned on my side. I remembered nothing else from my childhood. Little Quinn talked about it so easily, but I had no further memories. I simply listened as that girl explained her life. Her extremely short five years, full of trials and hardships, and yet she took it. That's what surprised me. Was I really that little girl?

On the second floor, the floorboards creaked. My eyes widened as my sanity dipped. What was that?

Would you like to go to sleep?

Y/N

Was someone else in this house? I had finished a to-do list well before nightfall, and I didn't want to be conscious while the wolf creature searched the woods. Were there other things in this house, too? I had all of tomorrow to think about this and find more clues to who I was and why I was here, preferably in the morning light. I mentally chose yes, and my eyes closed.

Then they opened with red dawn filling the bedroom. I sat up, not rested, yet not tired, either. Whatever strange limbo this was, I'd never get used to it.

With the new day, my sanity was almost full. If I had to guess, it was seventy-five percent. Maybe my blue bar only filled up twenty-five percent each day. If I had another horrible night where I stayed awake until it hit twenty percent, it would take four days to recover.

I headed for the kitchen, passing the grimy mirror. I promised myself that I'd sleep in my nightgown tonight to see if the alien overlords would let it boost my sanity recovery. My stamina refilled every day no matter how low it got, so that was nice.

After dodging trash, I entered the kitchen doorway and picked up the phone. I pressed the button and leaned against the countertop, waiting for my instructions.

"In three days, they will come. In three days, they will destroy. Anything you didn't complete on your to-do list will be added. If you do not finish your list, you may not go to bed until midnight, or until your sanity drops to 20 percent. Please do the following to protect yourself:

"Purchase an article of clothing for cooking,

"Pick ten tomatoes,

"Water the tomato plants,

"Build a fire in the fire pit,

"Make tomato soup,

"Build the base of a chicken coop,

"Further instructions will follow..."

I studied the list, double-checking on the calendar to see another X. Three more days. My spike wall was set. Perhaps that would be enough to protect me from *them*. I simply had to hope that doing what the woman asked would keep me safe.

"The boost to my sanity while sleeping in my nightgown would be nice."

My eyes lingered on my dopamine total. 4.21. At least I had finished my to-do list yesterday to receive that bonus. I headed for the clipboard and found another page added to it titled *Buildings*. It had the option to purchase one chicken coop, with an asterisk next to it saying, *some assembly required*. Perfect. The coop, though, cost 10.00 dopamine points. That was more than I had ever gotten. I might have to chop down this entire forest to get enough wood.

If it required 10.00, then that's what I needed. No time to waste. I entered the carport and went through my sorting process again. The stuff in here gave me the most points, and my food was almost gone. It sounded like they were teaching me how to cook, which made me optimistic.

I gathered items in a bag. This place was close to being decluttered. It was still a grimy, tetanus nightmare, but with the kitchen clutter-free, I was eager to declutter the rest of the house, too. I assumed that this first week was a tutorial period, and I wouldn't have as many things to do later. Once I survived *them,* I could do what I wanted. Hopefully. If *they* weren't a constantly hanging threat over my head, I would've ignored everything on the list and cleaned.

Once my dopamine points reached 5.03, I purchased cooking clothing. I now had my hard hat, my farmer's overalls, and a chef's button-up jacket. The oddity of this combination struck me, but I didn't mind.

This was the first time since building the fence that I needed to get past it to check on my tomatoes. I walked toward the spikes, hesitating as I didn't see a door or gate. Perhaps... game logic? I stepped through the fence, and it turned translucent as I crossed it. I glanced over my shoulder to see it solidify. Yep. That worked.

The plants in the greenhouse were fully grown, each with a tomato on it. My fingers reached out, a basket emerging into my hand as I plucked the first tomato. The change was instantaneous. My mind whirled, and I sensed more information on the clipboard had unlocked. I was too curious not to check, so I gently set the basket down and raced back inside.

Another tab was added to the clipboard; this one called *recipes*. It had multiple grayed-out sections, but I focused on the two I could see.

Basic tomato soup
0/5 tomatoes

Creamy tomato soup
0/5 tomatoes
0/1 bottle of milk

Well, that was nice. At least I wouldn't have to guess about cooking. I ran back to the greenhouse and finished picking the tomatoes. I placed the basket down, and a watering can formed in my grasp. After sprinkling the plants with water, I checked my list. It wasn't even mid-morning yet, and half my chores were done.

The fire pit was still within the fence, surrounded by a few trees. It was a circular, crumbling brick pit. If I stumbled upon this in real life, I wouldn't use it. But in the game world, this looked like something with upgrade potential. I walked closer and noticed a list of resources.

0/1 firewood
0/1 sticks
0/1 match
Words materialized in my vision.

-0.01 for more information

Y/N

Sure. That was cheap enough. I accepted the cost, and details were downloaded into my brain.

If I put in what the firepit requested, then a fire would burn for one hour with a pot to cook things in. I also had a feeling that chopping down firewood would get me those sticks and matches.

Yep. Absolutely worth the -0.01 point. I did my best not to look relieved, because I didn't want the alien overlords to realize how much they had given me for so cheap. Then I remembered they could read my mind.

My shoulders sagged, but I kept the relief off my face. It was nice not to have spent half the day figuring all this out. It was time to get to work.

The tree landed on the ground, collapsing into logs. I chopped one log into two boards, then into firewood, then grabbed a bundle and cut that again. Five sticks rolled around. Chopping a stick produced two matches, and the last of my yellow stamina disappeared. I gathered what I needed before moving to the firepit. I dropped the items inside one by one, watching the numbers fill up. When the match fell in, a roaring fire burst into life, flames licking the bottom of a pot I never hung there. I placed my basket on my lap and thought about the basic recipe on the clipboard, wondering if I remembered it right. Over the fire, words materialized.

0/5 tomatoes

I tossed them in until it read 5/5. After a pause, a timer materialized. I couldn't see any numbers, just watched as an hourglass filled up with sand and the pot stirred all by itself. If I had to guess, it was probably fifteen seconds before I heard a faint *ding!* sound.

A bowl of soup dropped next to the fire. I raised an eyebrow and picked it up.

Unlocked! Storage!

The words blocked my vision again, and I glanced at the rectangular, crumbling storage area covered in a faint glow. Could I store this in there without it going bad? Stranger things had happened in this world. Was it only food? Or could I store some non-edible resources there, too?

For now, I needed the stamina. In three bites it was gone, and I had half my yellow bar back. That was nice, considering all the food in the house currently gave me either 1/4th or 1/8th stamina.

The empty bowl left my hand. I had five more tomatoes left, and still an hour on the firepit, so I cooked another soup. It appeared after fifteen seconds, and I blew on it as I walked into the back porch. The lock on the storage unit was gone, so I eased it open. Short stairs led down to the long, rectangular room. Despite the calendar saying it was spring/summer, a chill laced the air inside here. Cobwebs covered the corners and underneath the shelves that lined the entire area. Two bags rested inside, one with onions, the other with potatoes. I brushed my fingers against them, and more recipes unlocked on the clipboard. With my farming overalls on, I also realized that cutting up a potato and planting the pieces in the soil boxes would make more grow.

Once I placed the bowl of soup on the shelf, it shifted into a pre-designed place. I glanced around at all the cobwebs and wondered about its sanitation before walking back up the stairs and closing the door. Game logic. That was what I kept telling myself.

I checked the clipboard. Some recipes were partially unlocked, with a potato or an onion and ??? covering the rest of the mysterious ingredients. The only recipe I could use right now was another soup.

Basic potato soup
0/4 potato
0/1 onion

I still needed to buy that chicken coop. It was time to do some experimentation with dropping things into the dumpster. I had a whopping 0.02 total dopamine points, and I wanted to know how much the logs gave me.

Chapter Eleven

A Rat in a Maze

If I spent the entire day decluttering the house or the carport, I'd never reach 10.00 by the end of the night. My points needed to come from elsewhere, so I should experiment. My leftover wood was a perfect starting point. I had one match, four sticks, one bundle of firewood, and one board. I started dropping them in the dumpster, making mental notes of it all. The match gave +0.50, which felt insanely high after getting used to the +0.02 or even +0.04. I dropped a stick and received +1.00. One stick supplied the same as two matches. That was good to know. The firewood and board reflected the same idea. Each board gave +10.00, and firewood got me +5.00. Since two firewood emerged from a board, it was easier for my stamina to sell the board.

It came to my last experiment. I lifted the entire log onto my shoulder despite my tiny frame. I knew it was possible because game logic. It gave me +10.00 when I dropped it in the dumpster, the same amount the boards gave, but each log gave two of them. If I wanted to farm for points, I needed to whack logs into boards.

It left me with +29.52 total dopamine points. And dopamine I was given. My stamina was halfway, and I might regret selling all that wood, but I had enough to buy a chicken coop.

I walked inside and bought the coop. It grayed itself out, which likely meant my home could only have one. Something thumped on the other side of the house.

It was barely afternoon as I headed out the back door and around the rectangular storage area. I walked over to the house's side I hadn't explored yet, near the bedroom and entertainment room. Lilac bushes covered this area, and for some reason their delightful scent entered my nose.

Nestled in the trees was a concrete block that I noticed had red glowing words above it.

0/15 logs.

This must be the chicken coop base. It would take some time and all the food I had left. Because of my experiment, I was able to buy more clothes. At least three. I didn't have any logging clothes, which seemed odd, so I splurged. Sure, it felt nice to have a cushion of dopamine points, but I also needed to get this base done.

Fifteen points were taken from my total, and I received a plaid shirt, a pair of sturdy steel-toed boots, and a yellow hard hat instead of an orange one. I then headed straight for the trees covering the chicken coop. My axe slammed against a trunk, and in five whacks, the tree fell.

My eyes sparkled as six logs dropped to the ground.

"Yes! This is amazing! I—"

A sound like fuzzing electricity filled the sky. I frowned, glancing around. In one blink, I was back inside the covered porch, holding the clipboard.

"What?" The clothes were for sale on the page, two of them under a gray lock. "I... I just bought those. You can't..."

19.50 total dopamine points. The amount I had before buying all three clothes. This had to be a glitch. I frowned, then purchased the plaid shirt again. I went to buy the steel-toed boots, but it stopped me.

Cannot purchase until logging level 5 is reached.

I sucked in a breath as my fingers tightened over the clipboard. "Seriously!"

This was a jerk move that would've made me throw the game console across the room. I'd seen those beautiful logs drop to the ground, and now they took it from me.

"Come on! You can't do this! It isn't fair! You expect me to go from dropping six logs to... however many I can with one article of clothing? It's not my fault you didn't think about this before letting me buy three clothes at once! Give it back!"

My tone got sharper as I kept talking. I was tired. Exhausted. I wanted this one win where my to-do list finished well before the day was over so I could clean the house.

To answer my questions, words floated into my vision.

Would you like to forget that you saw those logs?

Y/N

A chill raced down my spine, and my anger evaporated. A lot of thoughts surged through my mind. I had been talking to these sky people, thinking they were aliens or overlords. I had projected a forgiving nature on them because I wanted to imagine kind captors.

The sensation of being a rat in a maze returned. Despite them taking my suggestions, it was a stark reminder that I was not on equal ground with whoever had shoved me here. Yes, sometimes they took my ideas. Other times they saw me do something they didn't want and rearranged time so it was like I had never done it. The most chilling thing was I couldn't tell if their question was malicious or not.

The words still hung in my vision, so I chose no out of principle. I refused to forget this. I needed to remember how much power they had.

Turns out, slamming an axe against a tree was an excellent way to work through frustration. Crying helped too. These alien overlords were not my friends. I had to remember that.

My logging shirt created four logs from a felled tree. Game logic dictated that I could carry an entire log on my shoulder to the chicken coop base without it hurting my stamina. Part of me wondered what it would be like with the hard hat and the steel-toed boots. Would I lift more? I already knew I'd get six logs out of it. I only needed to chop three trees if I had the other two clothes. Now I had to cut four. Not only that, but I had five cans of beans and a tomato soup left. I'd eaten so much food today.

It still hurt, the excitement of all those logs hitting the ground then getting it taken away like that.

Are you sure you don't want to forget?

Y/N

My eyes lingered on the phrase in my vision, a reminder of their ability to read my thoughts.

"Look, alien overlords, or whatever you are." I lifted the last of the four logs. "If you're really here for a lesson on human nature, let me explain. No doubt you've heard me say how uncomfortable I am about being a rat in a maze. It's true."

I dropped the log onto the chicken coop base. It disappeared before it touched the cement slab. I wasn't winded as I returned. "I don't like this. Any of it. I understand I'm being placed in some sort of game, and you are slowly giving me pieces of the puzzle. You also take some suggestions, which is lovely. Nice boost to the ego." I hoisted another log, placing it on my shoulders. "But you still have a level of control I've never experienced before with anyone else. It unsettles me deeply."

Are you sure you don't want to forget?

Y/N

"No. I never want to forget that you have the power to do this. It helps inspire me to get out of here. My family will welcome me home with open arms, whoever they are. I'll regain my memories, all of them, and I won't be part of your experiment anymore. You have abilities no one should have, so I need to remember you have it."

So I can stop you.

It surprised me to think that as I dropped the second log into the chicken coop. It shouldn't have, because it was true. I needed to make sure overly powerful beings were in check. If they hurt my family, my friends, they would pay. How, I wasn't certain since I had no memories of my relations, but the instinct of needing to protect was there. I didn't remember anyone's face, but if anyone caused my family pain—

Inability to focus while still remembering. Begin deleting memory.

"STOP!" I fell to my knees. "NO!"

The words in my vision faded. I panted; the log on my shoulder slipped off as I clutched my chest. "Please don't. Please let me keep it." Tears raced down my cheeks. "I need it. Don't take another thing from me."

Distress will go away. Seems logical.

This didn't feel like a rat in a maze. Instead, I was an ant in a farm, begging a human to not pick up the container and shake it.

"I can't forget." The words slipped out as a whisper, but I knew the overlords heard. "Please. Let me keep it."

I hated how much this hurt.

We are not your enemies, nor your friends. We are a neutral party and will remain so. Does this ease your distress?

How well could I trust them? They still held a power over me that caused beads of cold sweat to form at my hairline. But, as with everything since the day I woke up in this mysterious house, what choice did I have?

"Thank you for telling me a bit more about yourself." My throat ached from the crying and the panicked screaming, and it barely came out as a whisper.

If it distresses you again, we will take away the memory.

How was I to interpret that in any other way except as a threat? I swallowed before climbing to my feet, my legs trembling. I picked up the last log and hefted it onto my shoulders before walking toward the chicken coop. Once the final log dropped on the base, all the logs melded together on the cement slab. New words materialized.

0/100 boards

The moment of panic passed before I pulled out my to-do list. Everything was crossed out. I didn't have to finish it completely, which was a good thing. The number of boards alone made this impossible to complete in one day.

I closed my eyes, breathing away the unease. It would never leave. I remained in the game, with a wolf monster trying to attack me. I needed to pay attention to clues and find a way out of here.

Technically, I could sleep now, but I didn't want to. This was the first time I had half a day to do whatever I wanted. Part of me itched to get those boards started, but with little stamina and not enough food, I couldn't justify it.

After a check-in with the clipboard, I was finally the proud owner of yellow rubber gloves. My outfit was a sight to see. Orange hard hat, plaid logging shirt, farmer overalls, and now, cleaning gloves.

I gathered more junk from my bedroom, as I wanted that to look nice. Waking up to a clean space would do wonders for my happiness. I worked faster, my stamina not affected by a quicker speed. It must be a hidden gift from getting the gloves. I forced myself to forget about this morning and fell into the rhythm of cleaning.

No, I refused to forget. Only partially. Enough for the panic to not control me. I picked up a picture frame, seeing it blurred to unrecognizable lengths. I needed to figure out this puzzle, but I wouldn't get clues from the stuff here.

Who was watching over me? They called themselves a neutral party. It's what anyone would say, except sometimes I believed them. They took my suggestions, yet also changed things, so it wasn't too easy for me. I just didn't understand their motivations.

My mind eased off this thought process, as dwelling on this group made the unease return. I tried not to let it terrify me, but I remembered what they had said. Memories they deemed unimportant would be erased if it caused me too much panic.

The last bag of clutter hummed in the dumpster, and I stood there, surveying my work. The electricity wasn't on in the house, so it was harder to clean the later it got. There had to be some way for the electricity to turn on. Sure, it was spring/summer, but soon it would be fall/winter. Sooner than I was used to, since the alien overlords smashed two seasons together and made them last thirty-five days. Odd, but not malicious.

I walked back to the clipboard because my gloves told me to. Now that I had cleaned the bedroom and kitchen, a tab had opened to buy chemicals. I was pretty sure that buying the gloves not only helped me work faster, but created this section so I could start cleaning instead of decluttering.

A cleaning kit cost 3.00 points, so I bought that and started working. I sprayed and wiped off the sticky cherry wood table, then cleaned the outside of the fridge, then the cupboards. I then washed the windows, watching years of grime and smoke melt away with a few wipes.

In the bedroom, I did the same, making the windows, night-stand, and desktop sparkle before turning to that grimy mirror.

I sprayed it before wiping it off. It followed game logic since the crack healed with a simple wipe of the rag. I was done when a sheen went over the entire surface.

This bedroom looked incredible. Clutter was gone; the night-stand wiped off. What I wouldn't give for the electricity to turn on so I could vacuum the floor. I tried wiping the walls, but they remained smoke-stained. Perhaps another article of clothing would unlock that ability.

The last beams of the setting sun filtered through the newly cleaned window and the still-broken blinds. I had a lot to do tomorrow, even if I didn't get a list. I needed to pick more tomatoes and build a stockpile of food. Cutting down all those logs today had drained my food supply. Whatever tomorrow's chores entailed, I could at least start storing tomatoes in the storage unit. When I had a large pile, I could cook it in batches. I could also try storing firewood, sticks, and matches, too. It'd be wise to keep fire-starting supplies on hand for—

A humanoid materialized behind me in the mirror. I gasped, spun, and saw nothing. I turned again to see a translucent gray-haired female reform in the reflection. She had curlers in her hair, tied up with a scarf. She wore a floral housecoat, and...

...and it was soaked in blood from a deep wound on her neck. Her nostrils flared as her gaze, eyes blazing with hatred, aimed right at me.

I screamed, jerking away from the reflection as I searched every-where for this woman. No one was there. I shot the mirror a wide-eyed look, and the woman's jaw dropped open. A shriek echoed out, reverberating around the room and through the house. I tripped onto the bed, not even climbing under the covers as I covered my head with the pillow.

"Sleep." I pinched my eyes closed, willing it to already happen. "Sleep. Please!"

Darkness came, and I didn't have time to think about what it might mean to fall asleep in the same room as a shrieking ghost.

Chapter Twelve

The Gift of a Friend

The room was clean as the red dawn light filtered into it. Dust was gone from the nightstand, and clutter was no longer crowding the place, making it feel bigger. The bedding was dusty, the blinds broken, and the once white lace was still stiff and crusty, but progress had been made.

The mirror was the first thing I saw when I sat up. It wasn't difficult to remember last night, because it seemed like seconds ago. Not only was there a wolf creature prowling around the woods, but the house was haunted. Of course it was.

Determination drove me as I threw back the covers and sprang out of bed. I filled a bag with the horror VHS tapes and carried them outside before dropping them into the dumpster. It hummed before a +0.00 floated in my vision.

"I don't care." I returned to collect the rest of them.

Once the tapes were gone, I dumped all the books. Those, too, gave zero dopamine points. This place needed to be comfortable for me, and I wanted nothing from the horror genre in this haunted house.

My sanity was at seventy-five percent. No doubt the shrieking ghost had taken another dent. I didn't check last night, as I was too busy with the shrieking to notice anything else.

With the entertainment room bare, I walked into the kitchen. I'd lost half an hour from the day, but it was worth it. Even if it wasn't reflected on the bar, I had to do this for my sanity.

I picked up the phone and pressed one.

"In two days, they will come. In two days, they will destroy. Anything you didn't complete on your to-do list will be added. If you do not finish your list, you may not go to bed until midnight, or until your sanity drops to 20 percent. Please do the following to protect yourself:

"Build a fence around your greenhouses,

"Find the river,

"Discover clay and stone,

"Gather 0/10 clay to the storage unit,

"Gather 0/10 stone to the storage unit,

"More instructions will follow."

Clay was here? And stone? Probably for more building options. Or to make fences stronger. A lot of possibilities came with these resources. I also learned the storage unit didn't have to be just for food.

With a rip, I collected the to-do list and got to work. I made sure I had my orange hard hat as I walked to the greenhouse. Another phantom fence blinked into existence, asking for a smaller amount of firewood. That would be easy enough. While I was thinking about it, I picked more tomatoes and watered them. I put the basket in the food storage unit before chopping a few trees to give more space near the buildings. The firewood filled up fast, then I moved on to boards before a completed spiked fence circled the greenhouses. Whoever *they* are, hopefully they couldn't throw rocks, or it would break my greenhouse.

I followed the roaring sound of rushing water. When the trees started growing thicker, I gave the house one more glance. I wanted to avoid getting lost in a vast forest with a prowling wolf monster.

Thankfully, it wasn't long after losing sight of the white brick home that I found the river. It didn't move too fast, but it still made me nervous. I approached it cautiously.

My vision was freaking out. Words vibrated above stones and clay to indicate resources discovered. Only one piece of clay or stone could be lifted at a time. The monotony of it all was what I struggled with the most. Farming games were fun, as long as the developers made sure the repetition didn't get too much.

"Any help, neutral party above?" I asked the sky.

No words came, so I kept going. My lips pursed together as I spent most of the afternoon taking clay and stone into the storage unit.

By the time the sun dipped toward the line of trees, I was done. All the stone and clay were in the storage room, and I sat on the concrete patio. A wave of emotions hit before leaving me drained. I closed my eyes, focusing on what I knew to keep anxiety at bay.

This was not reality. That much I was certain of. I was transported here somehow, and asked to play this game. The more I played, the more pieces of information I would receive. A group of people above me claimed to be neutral. My name was Quinn. A wolf monster and a shrieking grandma ghost haunted the house once it got dark. *They* were coming soon.

Everything swirled around me as I continued to sit. My to-do list was complete, the sun was setting, and I should go to bed. I was on top of things, and yet I felt like I was drowning. It was a similar feeling to swimming hard then getting a breath of fresh air and realizing I was in the middle of the ocean with no way to rest.

I climbed to my feet and walked over to the clipboard, flipping to the end to check my progress. It had six total areas, though the last one was grayed out.

Farming level 2

Cleaning level 5

Logging level 6

Cooking level 1

Building level 4

According to the new rules, I could buy another article of clothing once something reached level five. With 6.52 total points, I bought those steel-toed boots to drop five logs. I didn't care what tomorrow's to-do list would be. More logs always seemed like a good idea. The clipboard clattered against the wall as I dropped it. I walked inside and locked the two doors before climbing into bed.

"Please." I tried to imagine the neutral party as kind right now, because I needed some kindness. "This isolation will kill me. I... I need someone to talk to. Even if it's an NPC. Anything." I closed my eyes, tears spilling over. "And whoever it is, please... don't let them get hurt. I can't become friends and have them taken away by... by *them*. I want one thing. A friend who won't die."

The power of game logic forced me to sleep, then woke me when the red dawn lit up the room. I rubbed my head as I walked out of the bedroom. Tonight, I should sleep in my nightgown. I never cared when night fell. I was worried about other things. At least I had full sanity.

My feet froze in place after taking two steps into the entertainment room. The VHS tapes and the books were back, dusty and disorganized. The unease in my gut returned with a sharp, dizzying sensation. I couldn't deal with this right now.

I stumbled into the kitchen and grabbed the phone, pressing the button to listen to the message.

"At midnight, they will come. At midnight, they will destroy. As this is the night they attack, you cannot go to bed until after. Please do the following to protect yourself:

"Purchase one article of clothing from animal care,

"Complete all previous items on your to-do list.
"More instructions will follow."

The phone beeped, and I glanced at the list. The neutral party had planned to give me an easy day in case I had chores to finish. It was considerate of them. Since I had worked so hard, I could now do anything I wanted. Well, almost anything. First, I needed to buy something from the newly unlocked section of animal care.

Of all the things to do, I was eager to start on the chicken coop. The more boards I could place, the less I would worry about later. Also, I could dump a few boards to get dopamine points. I only had 3.52 total points, and I needed 5.00 to buy clothes.

With the plaid shirt and the steel-toed boots, I was dropping five logs at a time, and it wasn't taking nine or ten thwacks with the axe, either.

After sacrificing one board into the dumpster, it gave me 13.52 total dopamine points. Once that was done, I carried four boards to the chicken coop and dropped them in. I kept going until I had nothing left to carry.

9/100 boards

It was coming along, and I would get there. Eventually. I moved to the greenhouse, picked the tomatoes, and doused them in water before dropping the produce off in the storage room. I placed the basket on the ground before studying the soup I had made a couple days ago. Despite this place being covered in cobwebs and a chill in the air, that soup looked ready to eat. Still smoking, too. Would game logic ever stop surprising me? I grumbled and went to the clipboard. The animal care clothes included scrubs, bite protective gloves, shoes, and a hair tie. My hair didn't bother me, since game logic was applied, but it would be nice to have it back all the same. The orange hard hat vanished, and my hair pulled itself into a ponytail. I touched my now-bare neck. It would be easier to—

A noise sounded from outside. I lowered my hands, my eyes darting out the screen door. With the afternoon sunlight, I didn't feel as nervous as if it were night, but my heart still fluttered, my ears desperate to decipher what that was.

I walked out the back, frowning. The noise became more distinguishable the closer I got to the front. I might have imagined it, but it sounded like meowing. I peeked my head around the edge of the house to see the front porch. A kitten had her paw stuck in a rope, and my heart collapsed with how fast it melted.

"Oh, hey. Hey, little one." I rushed toward the kitty.

She cried at me and kept pulling on the rope. She was so small, black all over. I quickly undid the knot and picked up the kitten.

"Hey, where'd you come from?" I petted her head, seeing a blue collar around her neck with something printed on a tag. "What's your name, girl?" I moved the tag to read it.

Unkillable

My heart molded back into place before pounding in my chest. I kept petting the kitten's head. The kitten, who I guess was named Unkillable, purred. I hugged her. A black cat in a haunted house?

I suppose that made sense, but I found nothing terrifying about this adorable ball of fluff.

"That name better be true." I lifted the kitty and held her close as she continued to purr. "Because if something happens to you, so help me, I will light a torch to this entire forest and burn it to the ground." I glared at the sky. "You can read my mind; therefore, you know I'm not joking."

Chapter Thirteen

Them

Buying the hair tie for animal care meant I created dry cat food from thin air to pour into a bowl on the front porch. That turned out to be a clever trick. I also filled up the water bowl and placed it next to the other one. The kitten started eating, and I remained beside her, sitting on the ground, running my fingers through her dark fur.

"I think the tag around your collar was more to comfort me." The kitty munched on her meal. "But I won't call you Unkillable, because... I don't know. It just doesn't fit."

The kitten glanced at me, working on the hard food. She must be old enough for the dry kind, since that was the only thing this magical hair tie had given me.

"Unkillable isn't a name someone gives a cat. Or any pet. Seems like you're tempting fate. No, I'm pretty sure this was a message to comfort me."

The little feline moved to the water bowl, lapping it up. I ran my hand down her back again.

"Killie?" I asked.

The kitten didn't react, keeping her focus on what was in front of her. It made me smile.

"I like Killie better. Who knows, maybe you'll be a good mouse chaser. You could catch the one in the house."

She finished her food and, with little fanfare, sauntered off the porch and around the house. I smiled to myself, wondering if I was a cat person. I got up, following the kitten. She walked over to the cement patio and stretched before curling up and drifting off to sleep. It was probably for the best. I was done with my to-do list and ready to throw away the entire day to make sure Killie was situated well in her new life. With Killie taking a nap, I wanted to tackle the chicken coop.

I used up the rest of my stamina by sticking more boards into the coop and stockpiling some firewood, sticks, and matches in the storage area. Once that was done, I walked inside the greenhouse and readied another soil bed to plant potatoes.

It had been long enough that Killie woke up from her nap and found me. She rubbed her body against my leg as I worked on readying the second box. It was nice. This was the aspect of the games that I enjoyed. An entire day free to do what I wanted to keep my farm running and my house clean. I cut up two potatoes from storage and planted them in the soil. The neutral party above me didn't stop me, so I did it. If I received ten potatoes for every two I cut up, that would be excellent. I watered them, then watched the plants grow at an impossible rate.

It was early evening by the time I moved around the front porch to replenish Killie's food and water bowls. Now that I was at level five in cleaning, I bought an apron. It gave me the ability to wash walls, and so I sacrificed the dopamine points to get the supplies for it.

Whoever lived here was a smoker. Yes, the multiple ashtrays full of cigarette butts should have clued me in to that, but wiping the walls solidified it for me. I cleaned the bedroom and kitchen, getting a nice sheen. It was now painful to look at the carpet and be incapable of vacuuming it. These rooms were so close to being done, and I couldn't finish them because of the lack of electricity.

Once those were complete, I dove into the living area. I ignored everything past the TV for now. It was such a mess, and it somehow looked worse now that the kitchen and the bedroom were cleaner. I needed to tame this beast.

Killie walked inside the house, wandering around, staring at the trash. A mouse scampered across the floor, and she watched it, almost curious.

"Catching those would be nice." I gestured toward the mouse. She gave me a look that I interpreted as: *I'll think about it.* "I mean, I love your company and everything. But cats have a great job that would help me keep this place clean."

This kitty had grown today. She was a small ball of fur this morning, and somehow an older kitten this evening. Plants grew impossibly fast here. The seasons were clumped together and thirty-five days long.

My thoughts drifted to where I'd come from. What my family was like. How did I get here? Had anyone noticed I was missing? Did time move just as quickly back home as it did here? If I stayed for the full spring/summer season, would that be two entire seasons gone when I returned?

Was I in a coma? Fighting for my life in a hospital room while I was living out this fantasy? Was the wolf monster some deadly tumor? What an odd theory, and yet something about it would not let go.

"Wild." I walked over to Killie, who sat on top of the couch, watching over her domain. I gave her a pet, which she accepted, closing her eyes as she leaned into my hand. I smiled, then sorted through the junk on the card table. It wasn't too difficult to put all the dirty dishes in the sink, since it was empty. I could clean them now without it taking my stamina, but I didn't focus on those. I went back to the living room and kept organizing.

After stuffing more letters in a bag, something else peeked out of the pile. My fingers brushed aside papers as I discovered a flashlight. I stared at it for a few seconds before clicking it on. A thin beam of light came out, and I glanced up at the ceiling. Instinct told me I had gained a new tool.

"Uh... yes, please." I turned it off and stuck it in my pocket, where it promptly merged into the mysterious collection of tools that would show up when I needed them. This must be how I could use those batteries in the carport. That would be nice, especially with no electricity.

I wouldn't finish my list today. That much was certain. The red light of sunset warmed the room as I dropped the final bag of letters into the dumpster before scurrying back. I scooped up Killie from her spot on the chair and moved into the bedroom. I placed her in the little kitty bed in the corner. No way would I let her sleep outside. Not with a prowling wolf creature. Sure, maybe she was Unkillable, but I would not test it. I headed for my bed when new words came.

This is the night they are coming. Cannot sleep until they are gone.

Oh, right. I had forgotten about that. A sick feeling entered my gut. I stared at the dusty covers, wishing I could rest. The last of the sunlight faded as I tried not to panic. I didn't want to experience this. I wanted to go unconscious and have it over with. To wake up tomorrow and deal with the aftermath.

Killie jumped up, her back arched, and her fur rising. She hissed, staring at something in the corner. My stomach dropped as the flashlight materialized into my palm, and I clicked it on. Nothing was there, but my kitty still hissed at the emptiness. Her teeth showed, her paw up and ready to attack.

Transparent woman. Floral house coat. Blood. Shrieking. Perhaps Killie's job here wasn't to catch mice. She might have a different one entirely.

My kitten made a warning noise, and I backed away toward the door, throwing it open.

"Killie," I whispered. "Come on, girl. Come on."

Once I created an escape, she retreated out of the bedroom. When Killie was out, I slammed the door. I used my flashlight to triple-check both doors were locked before checking on my kitty again. She was in the middle of the floor in the entertainment room, her back still arched, her eyes fixed on the closed door.

"Hey, girl." I slipped into her line of vision. Killie was in attack mode, and I didn't want to startle her. "Hey, it's me. Is this place safe? Are there any...ghosts here?"

Were they ghosts? It certainly seemed so, but I knew little, since I had never watched horror movies. Killie kept her gaze on the door. I sat on the recliner, content to stay there until I could sleep. I fought the urge to check the doors again to be certain they were locked. Killie crawled into my lap, her body trembling, and I did my best to comfort her. I didn't know how well I had succeeded, considering I couldn't calm myself down.

"We'll be okay." I ran my hand down her back. "They're scary, but... they can't hurt us. At least... I'm pretty sure. They won't hurt you. The alien overlords promised me."

I had also threatened to burn everything to the ground if they broke that promise, so the ball was in their court.

Killie hissed again before leaping out of my lap. She scrambled to the living room, pacing the length of the floor as she stared at the ceiling, hissing and spitting. I approached cautiously. I saw nothing, but I doubted I would ever see it. My kitty kept her back arched as she remained focused. A floorboard creaked upstairs, making my sanity shiver. I stared, waiting. Shuffling feet was all I heard. My breathing turned shallow. I'd stop my heart, too, if it would help me hear better. Whisperings started, and it sounded like two women talking. At first it was quiet, but the whispers became more heated.

I dropped to my knees next to Killie, petting her. The female voices continued to whisper to each other, and I stared at the dirty carpet, trying to pretend this was a regular house. I was visiting a friend, and their relatives were having a conversation upstairs. It didn't matter that I'd never seen another human being since arriving here with my memories wiped. I had been wrong. For my sanity, I needed to imagine this was nothing more than family members having a chat.

Speaking of sanity, it was holding at one hundred percent. It rippled every so often, but Killie kept me alert of where there were spirits who might make blue stuff leave my bar.

"You know what, girl?" I asked, continuing to pet her arched back. "You don't need to catch mice. I like this ability so much better."

She remained next to me, her eyes never leaving the ceiling. The women continued to whisper, and I tried to ignore them. I couldn't understand what they were saying, which was fine. I really didn't want to know.

How long I was on my knees, I wasn't sure, but I refused to move. It was a few seconds after the whispers halted that Killie relaxed. I kept the flashlight off in case I needed to save the batteries. The kitten returned to the recliner, stretching. I wouldn't dare return to the bedroom until she gave the okay. It was dark, and wolves howled in the forest. Was the wolf creature out there, too? Not like I would walk out there and find out. I was fine to stay in here and wonder.

I picked up Killie and sat down, leaving her on my lap. She nestled into me, not asleep, even though she pretended to be. No doubt she kept one eye open, like me.

The silence became absolute. Cricket noises shut off. The buzzing lamp held its breath. I shot up in the recliner, hearing nothing but my breathing as the hair on the back of my neck stood straight up.

Killie leapt out of my lap, her eyes wide, ears flat. A growl came from the woods, deep and low. I shouldn't have heard it, because it was so quiet, yet the sound reverberated in my soul. The noise stopped, and silence pressed around me. The axe was in my hand. My sweaty palms made the handle difficult to hold, but I wouldn't let go. Killie was back in a corner, her pupils dilated. I needed to protect her.

The growl returned, choppy and uneven as it shook my core, syncing with my heartbeat and making it sputter. My sanity dropped. Tears filled my eyes as I stood before the front door, axe in hand. A rumble broke the silence as *they* approached. Despite all my hard work, those spikes seemed flimsy to me now. A faint glow outside gave enough light that I could move the curtains and see who *they* were. The thought turned my stomach inside out.

I could barely breathe. The stillness between the noises made me realize how isolated I was, how no one was here to help. It crushed every part of me. The rumbling growl reminded me I wasn't alone. I was here with *them.*

It was the longest stretch of silence between growls. Tears raced down my cheeks as my sanity dropped to the halfway mark. *They* were close enough to be at the fence. My knees buckled, but I kept the axe high. I didn't dare get closer to the door, and I could only pray my barricade held. I remained in the darkened house, refusing to let *them* know I was here.

A crack sounded, making the ground tremble, followed by a bellowing that rattled the entire house. My weapon tumbled out of my hands as I fell to my knees, covering my ears. My breathing came in quick gasps as the air evaporated from the room. The growl that had seeped into my being was now fragmented by that bellow.

Another crack split the sky, and the bellow that followed ripped my soul apart. I dropped to the ground, curled in a ball, whimpering. The spikes must have hurt *them*. The growl returned, shaking my bones. My stomach churned as *they* slipped back into the woods. The rumble faded away, but left its dark imprint.

Attack is finished. Force sleep beginning.

With the little energy I had left, I closed my eyes and went to sleep on the ground.

Chapter Fourteen
A Very Hot Day

Tears streamed down my cheeks as I opened my eyes, finding myself in the bed as red light filled the room. For the first time, I realized what it meant to sleep. To take a moment to breathe, to dream. To wake up rejuvenated.

This was not sleep. It was all quantitative numbers of sanity filling back up to the quarter mark, my stamina returning to full, and a monotony not of my own choosing. I did not feel refreshed. I wasn't ready to tackle another day.

My body curled in a fetal position, the exhaustion of last night lingering. Killie was nestled next to me, purring softly. I touched her fur, comforted by her presence. She was fine. Safe.

I stared at my sanity meter. How low had it gotten yesterday if it only filled up to the quarter mark this morning? I closed my eyes again, listening to her purrs and willing myself to be calmer. I don't think I ever would. Even though I didn't have hit points, that bellow had almost killed me.

The too-recent memory of it made me shudder, so I dragged myself out of bed and stumbled into the kitchen. The phone light blinked at me, and I prepared to hear the message.

"They left, but will return stronger. When that is, only you can find out." My eyes flickered to the calendar. *"They evolve, they adapt. It is up to you to get your house protected for when they come back.*

"Your to-do list will now be after every time they attack. You may finish it at your own pace at a speed we suggest you do as quickly as possible."

"But what am I supposed to do? What is the endgame?"

"Purchase the second article of clothing from the building section,

"Purchase the tools for brickmaking,

"Make bricks,

"Repair the damage to the fence,

"Build a brick wall around the fence,

"Finish upgrading the fence,

"Upgrade your axe,

"Finish decluttering the first floor of your home,

"Now that you have longer to complete your to-do list, you may not go to sleep for one hour past sundown until it's finished."

"No!" It was an instinctive reaction. "Please! I have only a quarter bar of sanity!"

The phone beeped, and I felt nauseous. Killie walked in, still a kitten, but older. She purred and rubbed her body against my legs.

I remembered last night before *they* arrived. Killie saved me from losing my sanity completely, because if I had a quarter of it now...

What happened to me when I had an empty blue bar? Would I die? I honestly hoped never to find out.

Tonight I'd sleep in my nightgown to check if it gave me a bonus, and I would have to remember to put it on before the things at night made me too scared to do anything else. I tore the to-do list off and checked the calendar. I had five days until they arrived. My list seemed short, yet monotonous.

The shadows in the kitchen flickered, and a ghoulish smile materialized in the corner of my eye, the mouth open too wide, a swirling dark void. I jumped, scrambling back as I tried to find the grin. Nothing. Just darkness. I dug my palm into my forehead, groaning. This must be what it's like to have a quarter sanity. It would all be in my head. At least that's what I had to tell myself. My heart still raced, and my adrenaline was pumping. Might as well put those to good use.

I studied the clipboard and realized I hadn't reached level five yet in building. I was almost there. A few more boards on the chicken coop would help, no doubt. With a sigh, I walked out of the house and crept over to the carport. The shadows remained with no ghoulish smile. Perhaps that only happened inside.

The fence was broken. I stepped closer, feeling nauseous as I saw black tar with a reddish tint to it. Was this something I had to clean? The thought of it made me sick. I didn't want this. I backed away before running in the opposite direction. Technically, I had five more days to deal with this. I could worry about it later.

I did my morning routine now of picking and watering the tomatoes. The potatoes looked like they would need another day, which was fine. They still grew at an insane speed.

Once the picked tomatoes were in the storage room, I checked the clipboard again to see an 'upgrade' section. Everything but the flashlight was on there. The axe needed 0/10 stones and 50.00 dopamine points. It was my only weapon. Even though I was completely useless last night, if something bad were to happen, I wanted some way to protect myself.

Purchase upgraded axe?

Y/N

It was a lot of dopamine points, but I didn't have to rely on clutter, just stamina to chop down a tree. I had the ten stones in the storage room, but I would hold off for now.

The mid-morning was heating up as I walked outside. Despite it being spring/summer for seven days already, this was the first time I reacted to the heat. I pulled out my axe and gave the tree a whack, but I watched in horror as almost twenty-five percent of my stamina evaporated.

"Whoa, whoa, wait. What's..."

Sweat appeared on my forehead. The sun was in the hazy sky, beating down. Too much yellow vanished after a single thwack against the tree. I couldn't keep doing this. What was going on?

Today was hot. Unusually so. Once I stumbled back inside the cooler house, the sweat vanished from my face. This was a game where the weather affected how I performed my tasks.

Most of my to-do list dealt with stuff outside. For now, I could finish decluttering the first floor. As I headed toward the living room, I noticed the calendar with an image of a sun on today. An unusually hot day. There must be something to combat this. These games always had a way.

I considered it as I gathered more clutter into a bag. I finished the first sack and carried it outside. The moment I left the shade, overwhelming heat smacked me. Beads of sweat formed on my head, and stamina trickled away.

"Seriously?" I asked before tossing junk into the dumpster. If I held nothing, my stamina remained strong, but something would still have to be done about this.

The coolness of the house was far more inviting. I gathered all the clutter into bags, placing them outside in the shade. I decluttered the bathroom too, using the small beam of light from the flashlight. It didn't take nearly as long to declutter, but I heard way too many ghostly moans from behind the locked door that made my precious little sanity to take a dip.

What could help me in this weather? If food helped with stamina, some might protect from heat. I sighed, leaning against the wall. The rooms were technically all decluttered, with all those bags on the front porch waiting to be dumped.

Shadows morphed around me, causing me to rush outside. I was terrified they would change into ghost people. Killie didn't react to the strangeness, so I assumed it was all in my head, something that had to do with having a low bar of sanity. The noises and the shifting darkness in the house frightened me, and being in the sun burned me up. I already had fewer days to finish this list, and I couldn't waste a day waiting for the heat to go away.

In the shade, I rubbed my arms. Soup wouldn't help me in this heat, which was most of my food. If it were something to eat, it'd have to be cold, like...

Milk?

Through the grimy window, I could see from the living room into the kitchen. It was crazy enough to try. I held my breath and walked inside to the fridge. A cup materialized in my hand as I poured myself some milk. I downed it in one swallow, then saw a timer below my bars. Ten minutes. I rushed outside before the twisting shadows grabbed me. I gathered as many sacks as my stamina allowed before dropping them into the dumpster. My energy remained steady, and I had a dry forehead. It worked. A glass of cool milk gave me ten normal minutes in the scorching sun.

With such a short time, I took multiple trips to get rid of the bags. When the last bag rumbled away, I pulled out the axe, ready to chop down a tree with the minute and a half I had left. Words in my vision stopped me.

Decluttering first floor is complete

Upgrade loading now

I froze, confused. What did that mean? Light circled around me. I tried not to panic as my feet momentarily lifted off the ground before I dropped back down. Movement forced me to look at the corner of my vision. The bars increased in size. They remained empty, but I realized what this meant. The more I cleaned my house, the more stamina and sanity I could hold.

"Wow, thank you."

This recent development shocked me so much that the rest of my timer ran out. The return of the unbearable heat brought me to the present. I slipped back into the house, hearing quiet whispers that Killie didn't react to. My sanity twitched, so I drank more milk and rushed outside again. It wouldn't do me any good to lose everything because of daytime murmurs.

I put those ten minutes to work. Trees fell fast, and when my stamina ran out, I ate a bowl of soup. Before, it had brought the yellow to halfway. Now with the bigger bars, it only filled to a quarter. I was still pretty stoked about the added bar length, though. No doubt, harder recipes would give me more energy.

Milk was running out. It was the only thing I found that beat the heat. I checked the calendar on the way to drink some more. This was the only different weather day until *they* came again.

After draining my cup, I hurried out the door. I grabbed the axe, turning all the logs into boards before placing them into the chicken coop. It took two more cups, leaving a small inch of milk on the bottom of the container. The sun was setting when I placed the last board I had cut into the structure. I checked my list, trying to remember what I was even doing. I wasn't supposed to be building this, was I?

Right. Get to level five to purchase another article of clothing for building. Rookie mistake. I'd gotten caught up in the excitement of a different job.

The worn and chipped bricks didn't feel like anything as I rested my head against them. This was fine. I had four more days until *they* came again, and I already had a good leap on my to-do list. Tomorrow would be better, because I wouldn't have to use milk. 21/100 boards were placed in the chicken coop, which got me to level six in building, and I bought a reflective vest. I had to trust the process, even though nothing made sense.

Two things were crossed off my list. I wasn't sure how to finish the rest, but I'd worry about it tomorrow. My nightgown materialized on me, as I was curious to experiment. Once that was done, I watched the last of the red light fade, then glanced at Killie.

"Wanna keep me company for an hour?"

The kitten that looked older now walked up to me, rubbing her body against my legs. I leaned down and gave her a pet, then left the bedroom. I sat in the recliner and rocked, waiting for the pull to go to bed. Absentmindedly, I took another small bright pink candy from the bowl, and I tried not to feel like a twenty-year-old grandma rocking in my chair with my cat. I wouldn't wait outside in the dark. Not with that wolf creature.

The shadows moved and danced. I shut my eyes tight, hoping they were figments of my imagination, or of low sanity. Killie didn't react to them. Instead, she remained curled on my lap, purring. The hour stretched on, and I refused to peek. Killie stayed on my nightgown, which was the only indication that nothing I saw meant anything.

A giggling child on the second floor made my eyes snap open as my stomach clenched. Killie opened one eye to glance at the ceiling before closing it again. My sanity threatened to drop as I calmed my breathing. Was it just in my head? Killie glanced toward the sound. Did that mean she heard it but wasn't threatened? I didn't care. Children laughing in the dark was creepy, and I hated it.

The instant I sensed the need to go to sleep, I scooped my kitty up and bolted for the bedroom. Once my body hit the bed, I woke with fifty percent sanity. I stared at it, confused. I wore my nightgown. Did it give me any extra? A part of me thought it worked, because I dropped below the quarter mark. If I were at twenty-six percent, would I be at seventy-five? It begged for more experimentation. Hopefully, being halfway wouldn't make the shadows dance.

I climbed out of bed and headed toward the back door, checking the phone on my way out. No messages. As I walked outside, I mentally chose both articles of clothing for building. Once they were on my body, I also wore my farming overalls, too, because I still needed to do my morning routine.

Numbers shifted around the cracked bits of fence.

0/3 boards

With my reflector vest, I could repair broken things. Good.

Since the day was a lot nicer, I whacked a few more trees easily enough with my bigger stamina bar. The boards were in, then it changed to a request for firewood, before it asked for a new thing entirely.

0/20 stones

My list said a brick wall, so I doubted stones were the last resource. This would take the longest time. Carrying things from the riverbed was monotonous. I walked to the river again, gathering the resources in piles. Killie followed like she knew I was about to do something mind-numbingly dull and meowed to warn me.

"Hey, girl." I scratched the top of her head. "I'm glad you're here."

I moved another stone when it vibrated. I scrambled to my feet, backing away as a white orb floated up. My breathing stilled, and Killie ignored the sphere. I needed this. Orbs gave me answers. With a shaking hand, I reached out and touched it. The orb hit me, and everything darkened.

Chapter Fifteen
Another Hint

The door to Brenda and Doug's house burst open, and Quinn walked through, an enormous smile on her face. "Helloooooo!"

She was missing a few baby teeth, proof that time had passed. Doug smiled as he followed her in. "Looking for someone in particular, Quinn?"

"Did anything change since I was here last?" She entered the kitchen, glancing around.

"People come and go. Felicity left soon after you did. She's home and thriving."

"Yay! Will she come back?" Quinn's head turned, her eyes scanning everything. Not much had changed. The house had recently been cleaned.

"Oh, she'll stay there. I have a good feeling about it," Doug said.

"You said the same thing about my mom, but see! Back here too!"

A sad smile flickered across Doug's face. "That I did."

"What about the snacks? Are they where they're supposed to be?"

He motioned for her to follow him. "Let me show you. Brenda wanted to be home already, but she's at work." Doug patted the cart next to the fridge, smiling as he showed her the recently stocked food. "Brenda bought you a huge container of Cheez-Its as a welcome present."

"Yes, please!" She skipped to the cart and snatched a bag. She tore it open and popped some into her mouth. "Why is it so quiet here?"

"Well, everyone's at school," Doug said.

"Oh, right. I haven't been there in ages. Mama didn't tell me when the bus would pick me up. She kept mixing up the times." Quinn swallowed before stuffing more crackers in, pushing them in her cheek to keep talking. "I waited outside for forever. Apparently, she was supposed to call the people to explain I needed to start school in the fall. It was all very confusing."

"I bet it was. You did a brave thing trying to get to school," Doug said.

"What about for here?" Quinn asked as she kept chewing.

"We've taken care of everything."

"But how do you do it? Just in case Mama doesn't remember when I go home. That way I can do it myself."

"Oh, sorry, honey, but you need an adult to sign you up."

Quinn groaned. "At least you set it up here."

Doug held back a chuckle as he grabbed his own bag of Cheez-Its. "That's our job. Brenda will even wake you up on time to make the bus."

"Yes! I get to go to school again!"

With a proud smile, he ruffled her hair. "You keep remembering this for when it gets hard, okay?"

She snickered, then glanced at the fridge. Whatever was on it wasn't visible, just Quinn's reaction to it. "Oh, is Theo still here?"

"Yes." The little girl didn't notice the quieter change of tone in Doug's voice. "Yes, he will stay with us for a while."

"Does he talk yet?" Quinn asked.

"He's saying single words a few times a week."

"Goodie!" She reached out and touched something. "I see he draws for Ms. Nichole."

"He does." Doug placed a cracker in his mouth before pointing to the fridge. "That's not from therapy, though. That was a school drawing."

Quinn lifted the picture, her nose crinkling. "Kinda scary, don't you think?"

"He likes to draw scarier things. That creature is his favorite. He is rather talented for an almost seven-year-old. Look at the detail on that fur!"

She kept her nose crinkled. "You said I'm rather talented."

"And I'd love to see how your talents have developed since you were last here."

With fury, she spun around. "Alright, where's your paper and crayons?"

Doug laughed. "It's not a competition."

"I know. But you want to see how my skills are developing, right?"

He gestured for her to follow. "Come on. To the arts and crafts room."

The two of them left. The page fluttered on the fridge before righting itself again. Drawn on the white paper with gray crayon was a wolf. Its claws were extended, red blood dripping from its jaw crammed full of teeth, looking like it had finished a kill. But the odd thing about it was that the wolf stood on its hind legs.

I didn't know whether there was more to the memory. It seemed like a dream, and the shock of seeing the picture brought me back. I was sucking in too much air trying to ground myself in reality. Or at least the realness of this place. Water crashing through the rocks. Not feeling the cold on my feet. Unable to smell anything.

My knees weakened, and I stumbled before resting against the grass. It was the same wolf creature. Theo had imagined it. At first, I thought these memories were to help me remember who I was, but I was now eager to figure out the identity of that little boy. He knew something.

For the rest of the day, I did my monotonous job, my mind whirling with questions and theories. I needed another memory orb, but I doubted they came on demand. It drove me to keep working. Theo must be a quiet kid with a dark imagination. Someone I sensed I had grown up with. That wolf drawing all but assured me he had *something* to do with this.

My list asked me to make bricks, but I didn't know how. After searching the clipboard, I found a brick mold, as well as a fire tool, almost like a stone oven. Both cost 10.00 dopamine points, which was so much. While carrying more resources from the river to the house, it gave me time to mull over what to do. Did I want to strengthen the fence? Or upgrade my axe?

Honestly? I wanted both. As the deadline for *them* came closer, I knew I was no fighter. I built barriers against scary creatures. My sanity would evaporate three minutes into any fight against *them*, even with an upgraded weapon.

If my list hadn't forewarned me about needing bricks for the fence, I wouldn't have bothered purchasing the brickmaking tools now. It was a nice heads up since I had a good supply of clay.

I gained information on how to make bricks once the purchase was complete and got to work. I shaped mounds of clay into the rectangle molds, leaving them to dry on the cement patio. After forming twenty clay rectangles, I sensed this concrete could hold ten more. The shapes needed half a day in the sun to bake before they were ready for the final stage in the tool. I built the fire tool quickly, sacrificing some stones from my precious reserve. It stood outside against the bathroom wall near the sunbaked clay. The tool held five bricks at a time and would need to take another half day to finish. It made me anxious enough to check the clipboard to see if I could buy an additional tool, but they only allowed me to get one. It would be close, but doable. When the clay finished baking on the patio, I tried to place them inside the fire, but something stopped me.

Cannot run tool overnight.

I flinched. My already tight deadline became even tighter. The trees were swallowing up the sun now. I'd have to work it every six hours tomorrow if I was going to make a brick fence. I spent the rest of the evening filling the stone requirement. When that was done, a new expectation showed up.

0/20 bricks

Good. I was prepared for that and was relieved it didn't request thirty. After letting out a sigh, I studied the greenhouses. After *their* first attack, the two fences had combined into one large barrier.

When the lamppost turned on, I was already in my chair, closing my eyes as Killie kept watch. We stayed out of the bedroom, and I listened to the giggling and the whispers. This time it sounded like a man and a woman talking, but I didn't want to get much closer to figure it out.

The next morning, my sanity returned to full, indicating my experiment was a success. The nightgown had a bonus, and I made a mental note that as soon as the sun went down, I had to be in it. Even with a larger bar, it still might not be enough for when *they* attacked in two days. Just remembering that growl caused ice to run up my spine.

The reddish dawn light found me stuffing five baked clay into the tool. I needed twenty of these and could only finish making ten each day. I couldn't fall behind, or I'd never get the fence finished.

As the bricks cooked, I worked on other things. *They* were coming tomorrow, and I wanted to be prepared. My to-do list was all crossed off except for upgrading the barrier. Since my farming had reached level 7, I bought a straw hat. Two tomatoes now hung on each plant instead of one. I also only had to use one potato to cut up and place in the soil bed. It still took two days of watering, but I got more produce with less cost. I had gathered so many tomatoes and potatoes that I figured it was finally time to cook more soups.

I spent the entire hour making food. It certainly helped, as I was pleasantly surprised when my cooking levels reached 4. It was nice to see that skill move past level 1. I used up the last of my onions; though. Replacing those would be a priority, since they were the other ingredient in potato soup. I only had six potato soups yet had stored almost fifteen of tomato.

After filling more shelves with my food, I studied the progress of all my categories.

Farming level 7

Cleaning level 7

Logging level 8

Cooking level 4

Building level 8

Animal Care level 4

I couldn't buy a third article of clothing until I reached level fifteen. Logging and building were moving along wonderfully. Also cleaning, as it was almost level 8. I had distracted myself in the evening by wiping off the surfaces of the living and entertainment rooms. The bathroom needed a different sort of chemical which was currently grayed out, so I would wait for that. It surprised me how disappointed I felt about waiting to clean someone else's toilet.

Chapter Sixteen

They Hunt

The next morning, I walked out of the greenhouse with my basket, giving a small sigh. My nerves were jittery, and a pit entered my stomach. Tonight, *they* were coming. The bricks were cooking on schedule. I had a strong supply of food. Almost too much, as the storage unit was getting full. Despite things going well, I remained distracted. I remembered how terrifying *they* were. Not having the fence done now made me linger by the tool, waiting to stick the final resource in its spot.

Halfway through the day, I switched out the bricks for the last supply, trying to talk myself out of my nerves. As I waited for them to finish, I chopped a few trees to get my fifty dopamine points and upgraded my axe. Tonight, the barrier around my property would be complete. The sun was setting when I carried the supplies and dropped them, one by one, into the fence.

18/20 bricks

19/20 bricks

20/20 bricks

I sat back, sighing as a brick wall braced the spikes. The words faded, then new ones showed up.

0/25 firewood

It took my heart a moment before my brain connected the dots. Panic seized me as I stood there, blinking.

"More?" My eyes trailed toward the sky. "There's... more?"

The lamplight flickered on. Darkness descended, and a wolf monster lived in the woods not that far. Yet I remained in the open, staring at the firewood requirement.

"No." My stamina was almost gone, and the only trees near me were outside the fence. Killie meowed at me, but I didn't turn toward her. Instead, I did math. Every tree produced five logs, a log gave two boards, and each board gave two firewood. I'm pretty sure I could chop a couple of trees and finish this requirement. I sprinted to my storage unit and downed some of my tomato soup. Killie kept mewing at me from inside the house. Against my better judgment, I ignored her.

My updated axe cut through the bark much quicker. The tree dropped in six thwacks that felt like cracks of thunder, alerting everything to my position.

A growl rumbled from the forest, and I froze, tears in my eyes. The wolf was here. Close. I hadn't even gotten to chopping logs into firewood. To save my sanity, I had to be in the house, but if I stayed inside until *they* came, my barrier wouldn't stop *them*.

My breathing shook as the axe slipped away. I could carry these logs into the fenced portion of the yard to protect me from the wolf. Then I could keep cutting until I got firewood.

I grabbed two logs, pushing my stamina. I had a lot from the soups, and the chunk was a small sacrifice to get them protected in the barrier.

Killie kept meowing at me, and I tried to shush her. I dropped the last log when the wolf came out of the woods. I dropped until I was flat on my stomach, covering my mouth with both palms.

Why did I risk this? I needed to go back inside now. I wouldn't have enough firewood with the logs I had. What was it about that beast that made me lose my head? It was better to have a full bar of sanity to prepare for *them*, but I hadn't considered that when I thought I could finish the fence.

The wolf started prowling. I hadn't seen it in a while, because before I was smart and slipped indoors when the sun set. Despite the tall brick wall, I still noticed puffs of matted fur. It remained on all fours, but I remembered that picture. What did Theo know about this creature?

The beast growled, and my sanity dropped. I pressed my hands over my mouth to trap the scream inside. The wolf's head popped over the fence. Soulless eyes darted around before falling on me. Tears spilled down my cheeks as the wolf snarled, low and guttural. The spikes would keep it away, right? It kept *them* out. No reason to be afraid.

With a spinal crack, the animal stood on its hind legs, howling. Killie meowed from within the house. The wolf's jaws snapped together, then it sprinted toward a tree. Once its eyes were off me, I scrambled to my feet and ran. Bark splintered underneath the beast's claws as it climbed. It leapt off the trunk, sailing over the fence and landing inside.

Fear strangled my throat as I pumped my legs, yellow draining from the bar. I couldn't look at that creature. Even still, my sanity plummeted.

I slammed the back door, giving it a firm lock. I didn't know if the monster could open the doors, but I also hadn't been sure if the spikes stopped it. It was better to be safe. I already resolved to chop down every tree near the fence tomorrow. If I lasted that long.

Once I locked the front door, I collapsed on the living room carpet. I tried to be calm, but my frame spasmed. Killie jumped from the recliner, purring as she rubbed her head under my chin. My sanity was down to less than seventy-five percent, and I still had to face *them* tonight.

I clutched Killie. My heart rate dropped to a more manageable beat, but my cheeks stayed wet. Time had passed without my being aware of it. The fence wasn't complete. My sanity was below seventy-five percent. Tonight, I would figure out what happened when my blue bar hit zero, and see what kind of destruction *they* caused.

The child giggled again, and I curled into a tight ball. Killie kept purring. She must have heard the laugh. Perhaps she only reacted to dangerous ghosts. Despite how much my kitten remained content in my lap, I lost another bit of blue. With a mental capacity I pretended to have, I analyzed why that happened. Sanity reflected my fear. This game scared me and did an excellent job. Could I train myself to be brave?

The terrified part of me wanted to laugh and never stop. Me? Never be afraid? The likelihood of that happening was as slim as the sliver of sanity I lost because a ghost child started giggling.

Footsteps ran from an upstairs room as the child hummed.

"Just a child. Killie's not afraid. If she's not, then I shouldn't."

My kitty turned at the sound of her name. She was calm, so I forced myself to feel at peace. Why did children being happy frighten me?

Because you've only heard this anomaly at night, meaning they're a ghost, and ghosts terrify you. That means the child is dead, and that is sad.

A deep, throaty growl echoed through the woods, and a yelp sounded close to the living room window. That yelp had to be the wolf scurrying away from the noise. My back arched as my sanity took a hit. *They* were here. The wolf ran, leaving no bait for *them*.

I struggled to my feet, pulling out my updated axe. The rust had vanished, and its handle was freshly polished. This would have to be enough. I felt tricked. Betrayed. The bricks had taken too long. I wasn't ready. Even though I knew *they* were coming, I had no more time. Now I was here, upgraded axe in the air, terrified. Farming games rarely had creatures to battle.

The growl echoed again. I closed my eyes, tears spilling down my cheeks. My sanity hit fifty percent. It was the second noise, and my blue was halfway gone.

Don't linger on that. You can do this. I believe in you.

I cracked an eye open to see Killie on the recliner, her back arched, fur sticking straight up. Her pupils were wide, experiencing the same primal terror as *they* rumbled again.

My sweaty palms slid down the handle. It didn't matter that the fence wasn't upgraded. My axe was. This would work. It *had* to.

A crack sounded, and *they* bellowed. I jumped, trying to keep my grip on my weapon. Another sound, like ice breaking, rocked the house. My spikes. *They* were beating against it, then everything went quiet.

Silence was torture. Cold sweat formed on my forehead as I ran through the different ways to use my axe. Whatever creature was there, it no doubt had a weakness. I could do this. I could be strong.

A squelching noise approached the front door, and I did my best to function without air in my lungs. The growling returned. Another chunk of sanity evaporated as I realized how close *they* were. Darkness pressed under the door. I strangled my gasp, backing away as the shadow grew. Thin reddish-black liquid pooled at the doorway before trickling in through the cracks, accumulating inside the living room.

I gripped my weapon, grateful no clutter threatened to trip me. It didn't stop me from stumbling over my own feet. I imagined a creature like the wolf or lion. A beast to hurt with my axe. Not liquid.

Killie was so terrified she remained on the recliner, mute. My heart pounded as I raised the axe. The reddish-black pool had formed at the base of the door, then shuddered. My sanity dipped below thirty percent.

The flashlight emerged into my other hand. I hoped it was sensitive to light. I clicked it on, pointing it at the slime. It dodged the beam, and for that instant I had hope. The liquid moved together, gurgling before splitting off into five mounds. Then all turned toward me. I thought seeing what it was would help dissolve the fear of ambiguity and leave me braver. Instead, I got a full view of the various-sized teeth and uneven lengths of hair stuck inside the matter that morphed into different densities of liquid. It was a small part of a bigger whole, a fragment of *them.* The sludge raced in my direction, and I scrambled onto the couch, dropping my flashlight. It was almost better to not see them. I swung my axe as soon as my feet left the ground.

"Get away. Get away. Get away." It came out as a murmur, even though I wanted to cry out.

The beam of light revealed a trail of liquid feeding the creatures. My sanity dropped to less than twenty. I had to try something. With an unheroic scream, I leapt over the five sludge monsters and slammed my axe against the connection to the main monster. At least, that's what I thought. Slime still dripped life into the entities who rushed at me again.

"No. No." I struck my weapon into the trail, but it reacted like water. It would have been easier to stop the river from running. "You've got to die!" What if it was unkillable? Every task I received was pointed toward defending myself against a more powerful foe.

The creatures lunged at me, the first one slamming into my leg. I no longer had the energy to gasp. It began sucking like a leech, and my stamina drained with it. Another creature slammed into me, then another. My body turned icy, my knees weak. They stuck onto my skin, pulsing with every heartbeat. My sanity and stamina dissolved, and the ground rushed up to meet me.

Chapter Seventeen
Alien Overlords

Two people talked, their words unclear. I tried to open my eyes, but all strength had vanished. The bed I was cushioned in was warm and soft as clouds. They might be actual clouds, considering the strange turn of events my life had taken.

"... too hard. She didn't have enough time."

It was a female voice, and I struggled again to lift my eyelids. Were these the people responsible for why I was here? That woman sounded familiar. Was she the one who left messages on the phone?

"Very well. We will not ask her the question."

That was a man. They didn't sound human. My mind was translating their words somehow, and it sounded like an alien language. The words seemed broken up for me to digest and left a strange echo after every word.

"She's waking up," the female said. "Don't open your eyes, Quinn. You will go insane."

I wanted to ask questions, but whatever slime creature *they* were, *they* had sapped every ounce of strength from my body.

"She can't see us. We made sure of that," the male said.

"There are some aspects of human nature I cannot predict." The female walked closer to me. "Specifically, what they do in a situation they deem dangerous."

The male chuckled. "That's my favorite trait of humans."

"We will send you back, Quinn. This was a miscalculation on everyone's part."

It took all my energy to part my lips and say one word. "Why?"

"You will get your answers. Just play the game," the male said.

Someone snapped their fingers before all strength returned to me.

My eyes shot open wide, and I sat up with a jolt. It was only after that I remembered the warning about going insane if I opened my eyes. What I saw was the red dawn light filling the bedroom. I glanced around, my sanity at halfway, my stamina full. With a defeated groan, I collapsed back onto the bed. I might already be insane.

Killie jumped onto the bed to check on me. I couldn't waste time, but everything inside me ached. I lifted my hand, running my fingers down Killie's fur.

"Hey, girl."

She purred in return. She was more cat than kitten now.

"Do you know what's happening?" I asked Killie.

She continued to purr. For her, I climbed out of bed. That, and curiosity. Curiosity and the cat kept me going. Hopefully, it wouldn't kill me.

Did those strange people actually talk to me, or was it a dream? Was 'people' a good qualifier for them? Alien overlords seemed far more descriptive of who they were. The longer I spent here, the more I questioned my mental stability.

My eyes remained half closed as I passed the entertainment room. I suppressed a shudder, moving past where I had been attacked by them. I entered the kitchen and picked up the phone, rubbing my head before pressing one.

"It seems we miscalculated your skill level."

Both my eyebrows shot up. Before they said it was everyone's fault, and now it seemed they placed the blame on me. I felt morally offended by that. "Excuse me?"

"As such, we will try this again. We will not give you the regular punishment because of this miscalculation. Therefore, your sanity has returned to fifty percent, and you will not need to repair too much of the damage they did. They will return in another seven days."

My gaze shot to the calendar. It already reflected the change. Seven more days.

"We have made the next list more manageable. If we find you did not complete it because of your own negligence, you will get the full brunt of the consequences, including an attack from them."

My shoulders tightened, the recent memory of their attack hanging over my head.

"Your to-do list is as follows:

"Repair the damages caused by them,

"Strengthen the wall around the house and the greenhouses,

"Finish the chicken coop,

"Purchase a third article of building clothing,

"Clean all the walls on the first floor.

"Your next list will be given to you after they come."

The invisible hand finished writing, and I stared at my chores. I thought of everything that had happened last night. Or whenever I was, as I seemed to be suspended in time. I recalled the conversation between those two beings. The female was definitely the same voice I heard over the phone, except without that weird echo when I listened to her just now.

"I... am not... your rat... in a maze."

They could read my mind. Whatever machine they hooked me up to no doubt helped them know my thoughts. Neither of them cared. They had watched as I got attacked and had the life sucked out of me. They calmly discussed my welfare while I was not that far from them. Then, they shoved me back into this game to watch me.

We are a neutral party

The words hung there in my vision, and it made my stomach churn.

"Why am I here?" I asked.

A memory from last night returned in the male voice.

"You will get your answers. Just play the game."

Despite how much I hated it, the guy was correct. Those memory orbs only came while I was working.

"Am I safe here?"

You are making it safe

I studied the words in my vision, then my head dipped as I sighed. I tore off the chore list, then glanced at the calendar. The last two days had a sun icon, which meant I needed to finish my outside stuff before then. I had wanted to see if cleaning all the walls on the first floor would lengthen my stamina and sanity bars like decluttering had. If it did, that would give me a strong boost throughout the week. Then again, I was running out of milk, and I refused to end up without a strengthened fence again.

After walking outside, I mentally dressed in my farming overalls and straw hat. I pulled to a stop. *They* had hit the first greenhouse. Three panes of glass were shattered, with four others cracked. I rushed inside to see the soil boxes destroyed, and my tomatoes and potatoes useless on the ground. I gave myself a moment to mourn the loss before glancing around. How could I repair this? Could I still fix the beds and grow crops? I needed to finish the chicken coop in a week. That would take so many boards, which meant stamina. If I didn't have enough food to replenish the yellow...

"Happy thoughts. Don't worry about what you can't control. We'll cross that bridge if we get there. Right now, focus on seeing if you can grow plants."

Those beings had said they wouldn't give the normal punishment for their attack. A bitter part of me wanted to shout at them that this was still a consequence.

In the end, it didn't take long to fix the boxes. A bundle of firewood for each and a few scoops of fertilizer. When those were done, I walked outside and put on my building hard hat. Three question marks hung above the shattered roof. The game hadn't revealed yet how to create glass. With farming gear on, I understood that a greenhouse in this state meant my crops would need an extra day to produce. It was better than nothing.

With that settled, I moved on to the fence. Despite the unease, I got to work. It would be monotonous, but I had Killie to comfort me and talk to. For the next two days, I gathered stone and clay and made bricks. The hole in the barrier required them, and those took the longest to gather. I waited for a memory orb, but it didn't show up in the riverbed. The first one had come after cutting down a log. It always arrived while I was working, so I kept at it.

When I woke up on the last morning before two days of unbearable heat, I realized this strange season was halfway over. I glanced out the window at the hazy sky and wondered if it would ever clear. It had been yellowish haze for so long I almost missed what it was like to look outside and see blue. My mind returned to my first conundrum. Who was my family? Was time going fast for them? Was I in a coma? If I was halfway through spring/summer, did that mean a full spring had gone by at home? Did anyone miss me?

So many questions bounced around my head as I finished putting the last of the firewood into the fence. I moved to one tree near the spikes and pulled out my axe to get more boards into the chicken coop. The wolf scampering away from *them* proved it didn't need a tree to jump the barrier, but I still felt driven to chop down all the trees. That coop required a lot, after all.

My building and logging levels had gotten higher together. Of all the groups, these two often surpassed the others since I had done so much of both in the past five days. I needed to get my building to level 15 before purchasing the third article of clothing. More clothes in logging would be nice, too. I already knew another log would drop with a third article. What would happen with building?

I took a break from making the chicken coop to eat soup for my stamina. The coop was close to being finished, with 68/100 boards in there and still half a day's worth of chopping to go. I tracked my progress on the clipboard.

Farming level 9

Cleaning level 7

Logging level 13

Cooking level 6

Building level 14

Animal Care level 7

I had been so focused on getting jobs done on my to-do list that I had forgotten about staying on top of clothes. I dropped dopamine points for animal care and cooking and chose a fancy little baker's cap and a scrub top.

More things unlocked on the clipboard. I flipped through the pages, unsurprised to see an option to buy chickens once the coop was done. The pages shuffled again until I found the next added item. It was a fishing rod. My eyes danced at the possibilities. Fish! Both clothes gave me another food source that didn't require a greenhouse.

I tried to put that all aside as I focused on making sure I had the chicken coop ready. It was the last outside chore. Repairing the damages from *them* was still uncrossed, which I assumed meant the broken greenhouse. Until I figured out how to make glass, I could do little about that.

With the sun finally setting, I placed the final board into the chicken coop and got 0/50 firewood for my trouble.

"Stupid firewood." I kicked the base. I needed to stop thinking the requirement I was working on would be the last.

I cut the leftover logs and boards down until my stamina was gone, then dropped them into the building. 14/50 firewood was nice, but the next two days would be too hot to do anything without drinking some milk.

Despite tackling these chores for five whole days now, the only thing crossed off was strengthening the fence. It worried me how big the list still was. If I didn't receive my dopamine point bonus, I was okay as long as they couldn't get through the walls.

When the lamplight flickered on, I knew I was tempting the wolf by not staying inside. My sanity was at full. I checked the clipboard to see building was finally at fifteen. However, the price of clothes was now at 10.00 dopamine points. I sighed, glancing at my total. I had only 7.42.

Tomorrow. I still had tomorrow. Then I might get more stamina and sanity added to my bar by cleaning the walls. That would be a godsend. Because I would make it out of this game alive.

Chapter Eighteen

More to Unlock

In the early morning, I tried to experiment if the weather wouldn't overwhelm me. I remembered the first time this happened. I hadn't felt hot until it was creeping toward the afternoon.

The second I stepped out of the shade, sweat formed on my face. This had to be the summer part of spring/summer.

"Alright, well, we've sufficiently tested that." I slipped back inside, unconcerned. I had things to do in the house, after all. The morning was spent wiping the entertainment room wall. I moved the VHS bookcase to get to the paneling there. Honestly, if today wasn't so hot, I would have thrown them all in the dumpster again. The books were no different. I glared the entire time I did it, but I cleaned, dusted, and organized the bookshelf.

As the sun got hotter, I entered the living room. With no bookshelves, it wasn't nearly as hard to clean. The gamer in me wouldn't enjoy going to bed with a full bar of stamina, as it felt like a waste. So, when I reached a stopping point, I walked to the greenhouse and sacrificed some energy to water and pick the vegetables. I wiped the sweat off my face. I had no desire to do any cooking today, so I returned to the house.

It was about evening when I finished cleaning the walls in the bathroom. I was glad that I did more at the beginning of this season. Scrubbing three rooms wasn't nearly as hard as all five.

Walls cleaned on first floor

Upgrade loading now

The excitement caused me to hold my breath as I watched the bars in my vision. Instead, something in the kitchen toppled to the ground.

Upper floor unlocked

"Oooh," I couldn't help but say. Sure, more sanity or stamina would have been nice, but the second floor? This was progress!

I entered the kitchen, pulling out my flashlight before hesitating. It was dark. All the ghosts so far had come from the second story. Did I actually want to do this? As if for an answer, Killie came up to me, giving my leg a rub.

"Keep me safe, okay?" She meowed in response, and my decision was made. "Just a quick peek. I'm curious what's up there."

I pushed open the unlocked door and entered the hallway. There was a window from the covered back porch, but considering the sinking sun filtering through the dirt and grime, it offered little light. It was a small walkway leading from the kitchen to the bedroom. Plastic totes stacked on top of each other blocked some cabinets at the end. The start of the stairs was near the bedroom door. Even after cleaning up the clutter, it would still be a tight squeeze to get to the first stair. The staircase was dark wood with a faded maroon and gold carpet on the ground. I got a good view of the closet under the stairs, which was also full of trash. At least the boy's bedroom wasn't under there, because he wouldn't fit. Though his being a ghost now might make it easier. I closed my eyes, the light from my flashlight trembling. I needed more sunlight before I thought about spirits like this.

After climbing over the clutter, I reached the stairs before making my slow way up them. They creaked with age. The staircase curled as it got to the top. Through my beam of light, I saw a small landing with four doors up here. One had a huge padlock on the knob. Not a bad house, really, except for the ghosts.

The landing had piles of trash, but I would have been surprised if it didn't. Someone had painted the walls mint green and all the doors an off-white. Not a fan of those two together, but I assumed I'd fix it. I entered the door on my right and found nothing but boxes. The space itself wasn't big, but there certainly was a lot of junk in here. It had wallpaper with images of grandfather clocks and spindles. Where the paper was torn, I saw a spotted green-colored wall beneath. The flashlight made the shadows deeper, and I didn't want to travel farther into this little area.

"I shall call you the green room."

The next door opened onto a much bigger room. I could barely move three steps inside. All the holiday decorations, like Halloween, Easter, Christmas, as well as some seasonal ones, were stuffed in this place. I was getting rid of the box of fake tombstones first. This room was a faded pink color. The thing that excited me though was the glimpse of the floor. Beautiful hardwood! I knelt, touching the wood. I bet this was under all the carpets in this house! Despite everything, this made my heart soar.

"You shall be the pink room."

The door next to the pink room had a huge lock over the knob, so I entered the one on the other side of the stairs. The hinges squeaked as I shone a light inside. It had a lot more clothes and baby things stored, like a high chair and a broken crib with a few mattresses leaning against it. Someone had painted this a bright blue color.

"And you shall be the blue room."

Out of curiosity, I jiggled the locked door across from the blue room, but it rattled. It was truly dark now. I wanted to check if the wolf was prowling, but too much clutter stopped me from reaching the windows.

With an hour left before bed, I used the time to organize. I stuffed junk from the landing into a bag, so I had a clean place to work. The plan was to rush them to the dumpster first thing in the morning. I would have done it now, but I wanted to save my sanity.

As I still had half a bar of stamina, I gathered all the boxes I could carry and walked down the stairs, setting them near the front door. I climbed upstairs for another load and grabbed a box when something below it vibrated. I backed away, not allowing myself to panic yet. A white orb floated up chest high. I hoped this gave more concrete answers. I touched it, and everything went black.

"...which is when Mrs. Beckers asked me to tell why four plus four equals eight, and I was so confused. Like, why do we even have to say why things are the way they are? I don't know, it just is."

Quinn sat cross-legged on the floor with her back against Theo's bed. It was nighttime, the stars twinkling. Theo was sitting up, staring at her. She was ignoring him, playing with a stuffed teddy bear, twirling it in her arms, making it do somersaults in the air.

"But Mrs. Beckers is proud of me. She says I'm catching up with all the other students, even though I missed the first three months. Did you ever miss school? When you were with your family?"

Theo remained silent, his legs curled up and pressed against his chest.

"You don't have to talk. Brenda and Doug said you are talking a little, and I guess you say yes or no. Do you ever speak long sentences with them?"

He shook his head, and Quinn shrugged. "I don't know if I could ever stop talking. I would burst. Don't you feel you'll burst? Sometimes I think you might explode, and it's going to be nothing but alphabet soup, because you keep all those words inside."

Theo raised an eyebrow. Him not speaking was still the same, but the haunted look had ebbed away. He had more expression on his face.

"I... don't understand," Theo said.

"Don't understand what?" Despite having talked about it before, Quinn wasn't surprised to hear him speak a full sentence to her.

"Why do you talk so much?" he asked. "Your mom, she... last week she..."

"Died?" She kept spinning her teddy bear.

"Yeah. And yet... yet you talk."

Quinn scrunched up her nose as she thought. "Is that why you don't speak? Did your mom die?"

Theo's silence answered her question. Both children came to an understanding. They knew deep down they weren't like other kids at school. Something about their families had been unique, and they were responding to it in two separate ways. One by never opening his mouth, the other by constantly keeping it open.

Quinn studied her teddy bear, giving it a spin. "Yeah, my mom died. It was weird. She was in that coffin, and she didn't seem different. She just looked like she was sleeping, I mean. I think it's what she always wanted to do, you know? Sleep all day and all night. Now she can."

Theo had hidden his haunted look away in a compartment, but tonight it burst in, flickering across his face as he bowed his head. He studied his toes under the blanket.

"So if you don't talk, what do you do to not explode?" Quinn asked.

He glanced up, then considered something. He then climbed out of bed and motioned for her to follow. She shrugged, then dropped the teddy bear and followed. Theo put a finger to his lips. Quinn nodded, then mimed zipping her mouth and throwing away the key. He opened the door, checking for Brenda and Doug, who were asleep in their rooms. Quinn rarely entered Theo's room until she knew everyone was sleeping.

They crept down the hall toward the TV. Theo worked quickly, opening drawers of DVDs. He pressed a few buttons to start the player. Quinn sat down, frowning.

"Is this what you do? Watch movies?"

He again placed his finger against his lips, and she pouted, staring at the movie. A few more clicks later, the eerie music of Sixth Sense came on. Quinn stared, curious, though it was clear she did not like it. The opening scene played on the screen. Theo watched, a smile on his face.

Quinn furrowed her brow when she saw the man in the bathroom. "Why is he in his underwear?"

He again quieted her. Quinn pursed her lips, but said nothing. She jumped in surprise when the character pulled out a gun and shot the other man. Theo tried to cover her mouth, but Quinn gasped. She watched, wide-eyed, as the camera panned away before it could show the guy shooting himself in the head.

She screamed. It rocked the silent house, and it wasn't long before Brenda and Doug stumbled out of the bedroom. Quinn sobbed, covering her face.

"What happened? What's going on?" Brenda asked, rushing to the little girl's side.

Doug spun to see the TV. "What are you two watching?"

Quinn couldn't answer. She kept screaming, backing away from the scene. Theo stared at her, a frown tugging at his lips as he attempted to understand why she had reacted this way. Doug stopped the movie as Brenda tried to comfort Quinn.

"No!" Theo shouted at Doug as he headed out of the room with the DVD. "Please don't take it!" The little boy was wide-eyed, his gaze never leaving the cover. "It's my favorite movie!"

Doug's jaw slackened. Quinn didn't understand his surprise, but Brenda stared too, just as shocked. It was the first full sentence Theo had spoken to them, and it was about keeping Sixth Sense.

Doug studied the case, twirling it in his hands. "This movie is… it's dark."

"I know. I love it." The little boy blinked away tears. "Please leave it in the drawer."

The two adults exchanged glances before Doug sighed. "Look, Theo, maybe... maybe don't watch these darker movies with Quinn. She gets scared easily."

Theo sniffed, wiping his eyes. "But we can still keep it, right? Please. I still want to see it again."

Doug stared, listening to the waterfall of words from the silent boy, before holding up the case. "I... would love to watch this movie with you sometime. Would that be okay?"

Theo dried his cheeks. "Okay."

Quinn kept sobbing, trying to scrub that image from her mind.

I gasped, returning to myself. I almost lost balance, stumbling over boxes of junk. With every memory orb, I felt more confident that Theo knew something. That kid was obsessed with the horror genre from a young age and had made a drawing of the wolf creature. Could he be behind all this?

No. The people responsible for this were that male and female. They were no doubt taking notes about how much I hated horror.

It had been an hour, as I sensed I could now go to bed. I turned toward the green room again when I heard a strange noise. I flipped on my flashlight and pointed it around the landing. A quiet dripping came from the locked room. My beam of light traveled over the off-white door. I crept forward, frowning. Killie hissed, then bolted for the stairs. My heart already skipped a beat when she did that, but it made me drop to my stomach when something wet touched my foot.

"No, no, no!" I wanted to scream as I stumbled away. It was blood pooled at the bottom of the door. I scrambled to my feet and followed Killie's flight down the stairs. I hadn't put two and two together until that moment, but that was the room directly over the living room, where I heard the most activity at night. The talking women, the talking male and female, most of it came from the place now dripping with blood.

I pushed open the door to my bedroom. Killie was on the bed, mewing at me as I shoved myself under the dusty covers.

"Sleep! Sleep!" I hadn't gotten into my nightgown, but at this point I didn't care. Beautiful darkness claimed me.

Chapter Nineteen
Experimentation

The red dawn came again, the last one before *they* attacked. My fence was strong. I could survive because the walls would protect me. I really, *really* needed to be protected. It was a blisteringly hot day, but I used some stamina to drop the bags of junk from the landing into the dumpster before checking the to-do list to see what I had left.

Repair the damages caused by them
~~Strengthen the fence~~
Finish the chicken coop
Purchase a third article of building clothing
~~Clean all walls on first floor of home~~

With *them* attacking tonight, my anxiety told me too many chores remained. My anxiety also painted a picture of getting attacked again by *them*. The list crumpled in my tight fist, and I forced my fingers to relax as I reminded myself that the fence was strengthened. *They* couldn't enter. If anything, the rest of the things on my to-do list were keeping me from a nice dopamine bonus. It wasn't necessary for me to complete it all. I hoped.

The day was way too hot to do much. I drained the last of my milk to chop more logs into firewood for the chicken coop. I worked fast, as I only had ten minutes to finish this. Each tree gave twenty firewood, and I didn't dare hope that this was the final resource. I had learned my lesson to not assume.

One more tree dropped to the ground before I sprinted inside. My timer ran out once I entered the kitchen. I stared outside, trying to decide what to do. I had things I *wanted* to do, and things I *needed* to do. My stamina was close to the quarter mark. If I walked out there right now in the heat and chopped those logs into firewood, I would have to eat through my soup supply. It was doable because I actually had a nice stash of soups saved up. A part of me still resisted, though. It was such a waste when I could declutter upstairs instead.

The fresh horror of seeing blood oozing out of the locked door returned. That sight alone made me promise never to go to the second floor when the sun set. My sanity was full, which meant I should stop dwelling on that image of blood trickling on the landing and other such haunted activity. I needed to save all my sanity for tonight.

What I *really* wanted to do was fishing. I checked the clipboard, and a rod cost 15.00 dopamine points. Eventually I'd buy it, but not now since I didn't even have the 10.00 points for that third article of clothing.

The river had a lot of trees around it. The heat wasn't as blistering when I was in the shade. I could be at the river, catching another food source. Relaxing with a cup of lemonade, not thinking about the horrors of why I was here.

Lemonade. That would definitely give me a timer to work in this heat. What did someone need for that? Lemons, sugar, and cold water?

I froze, then my head slowly turned toward the sink. I didn't have lemons or sugar, but would cold water be enough? It needed to be tested. It would be stupid not to. I grabbed a cup from the beautiful cherry wood cupboard and poured water into it, downing it. Nothing happened, but I wasn't done testing. I filled the cup again, then walked to the fridge and placed it inside. I closed the door and watched, eyes brightening, as a timer started counting like the fire had when I stuck food into it. The sand dropped way slower than the fire. My guess was at least twenty, maybe even thirty minutes until it was cold.

In a rush, I began shoving cups of water into the fridge. When I got to my sixth and seventh cups, something stopped me from placing them inside. I must have reached the limit. Didn't matter. I was riding this high. I had figured out how to make cold things.

As I waited for that timer to tick down, I entered the cluttered hallway and stuffed bags full of junk. This was not Doug and

Brenda's house, because the memories showed me their place and it was nothing like this one. Was this the home I had with my mother? My mother, who had overdosed and died when I was a child.

I waited, expecting tears, but they didn't come. For whatever reason, I felt the same amount of assurance that my younger self did. My mom had liked to sleep all the time. Now she could. Forever. I closed my eyes and shook my head. All of this was too weird. It was strange to remember who I was from an outsider's perspective.

When I reached the plastic tote containers, I gave them a good hard look. Everything else followed game logic, so it would only make sense to try this. I picked up the entire container, a bag in one hand already. Once the large container was heading toward the small sack, the container got sucked into the opening. It didn't look like a garbage sack covering a rectangular object, either, but a rounded, picturesque bag. I smiled to myself and did the same with the others, making sure they were all in bags.

With three sacks of junk in hand, I walked out the front door and set them at the edge of the shade. The ground seemed to steam, reflecting how hot the day was. I tried not to curse myself for dropping an entire jug of milk in the dumpster my first week here. I couldn't have known. Besides, I had needed the dopamine points.

The fridge timer faded, and I opened it and drank the water. Three minutes. That was fine. I'd use every second.

I sprinted outside and lifted my axe, chopping the logs into boards, then the boards into firewood. So far, I had 36/50 in the chicken coop. Once the timer was up, I downed a second glass and raced back out there. When it hit one minute and thirty seconds, nausea dropped me to my knees. I'd completely forgotten to watch my stamina!

Well, it didn't matter. I had three glasses of water. Instead of chopping, I walked around the house to the front porch and grabbed bags, dropping them into the dumpster. Stuff from the second floor gave a higher dopamine point. Not nearly at the level of boards, but between 0.05 and 0.08. I kept stuffing the dumpster until my timer had seconds left, then I made my way to the kitchen.

Alright, well, after drinking two glasses of water, I'd chopped a couple of logs into firewood. Three minutes was better than nothing, but I missed the ten minutes the milk gave. Plus, I was pretty sure running around drained my energy, too.

In the covered back porch, I opened the storage unit and stepped down. I grabbed the first bowl of tomato soup, promising myself to watch my stamina. I brought the spoon to my mouth when I froze. My gaze shot to the fridge. I wonder...

In the kitchen, I put the soup in the fridge. The same timer showed up. I pumped my fist in the air before rushing to the storage unit and grabbing one tomato and potato soup each to test. With the fridge door open, I eased the two foods inside.

An invisible wall stopped the potato soup, but the tomato soup entered. A smile crossed my face.

"I will take it."

The fridge stopped me after the fifth bowl of tomato soup. I was okay with that. I busied myself again with decluttering the hallway as I waited. With a few more bags in the dumpster, I'd have enough to buy that clothing.

After an agonizing wait, the timer disappeared. I took out the food and finished it in three bites. Fifteen minutes and a quarter of stamina! All the stress left me. I could get so much *done*.

With renewed energy, I walked back outside and chopped the rest of the logs into boards, then to firewood, my eyes lingering on the yellow bar as I did so. It was evening time, but I was still so excited about fifteen whole minutes that I didn't feel the nerves from before. This was a major discovery. I wouldn't be trapped inside on a hot day anymore. Chilled tomato soup would help me get things done.

The last firewood entered the chicken coop, and shingles emerged on top of the building. I took a moment to admire it, then watched as a sheen raced across the structure. I let out a breath of relief before using the remaining minutes to drop more stuff into the dumpster.

I rushed back inside before the timer ran out, then walked over to the clipboard. With 11.23 dopamine points, I finally purchased bright orange overalls. I put it on, also wearing my hard hat and reflective vest. As I waited for knowledge to download into my brain, I flipped through some pages. My fingers froze, my brows furrowed, then I glanced out the door. I looked at the brickmaking tool, and my mind started whirling.

Upgrade tool?

0/50 bricks

"Oh, cool!"

I had an excellent feeling that this was how I would make glass.

Fifty bricks was a lot, and I already knew I couldn't fix the greenhouse this week, let alone in one evening. But glass was possible, and soon. Repairing damages was the only thing uncrossed on my list. I ate another bowl of chilled tomato soup and did my gardening for the day, picking my tomatoes and watering my plants. Once I repaired the glass, they would grow faster again.

When I finished, I used the last minutes on the timer to study the property. With the extra building clothes, more words materialized on the smaller buildings, like the greenhouse.

Repair damages in the unit before upgrading

0/5 ???

I tried not to get excited about an upgraded greenhouse, because it was a reminder I was in a game. I needed to figure out why I was here, but my imagination still went wild with options. More room for produce would be nice. I wasn't sure when I would unlock the other greenhouses, but hopefully soon.

"Focus, Quinn. Don't forget why you're here."

Play the game. Get answers. Leave.

Chapter Twenty
Enough

Yes, I would leave eventually. But I also noticed the storage area had upgrade potential. Probably for more space, since it got crowded in there. I walked to the front porch covered with junk and had five minutes left to drop it in the dumpster. As I passed the carport, red words wobbled above it.

Must finish decluttering unit before upgrading.

Greenhouse, storage, *and* the carport? Curse this curiosity of mine. So many options!

I dumped a few more bags as the sun set before slipping inside. Killie stood in the middle of the living room, back arched, staring at an empty corner. She hissed, her claws out.

"Okay, okay, girl. Thank you. Come on, let's..." I hurried to the kitchen, but my cat remained. She kept spitting at the mysterious intruder. "Killie, you can't hurt whatever it is."

Despite most of the activity happening upstairs, the shrieking grandma ghost remained here on the first floor. I didn't want to see any other ghosts tonight.

With the hallway unlocked, it made a circular loop between all the rooms. Maybe I could travel between places to avoid all the phantoms Killie saw. In my mind, it worked. But Killie was a teenage cat that was fiercely protective of me because I fed her every morning. It's something I respected, but I needed her to not provoke the ghost. I didn't want to figure out if an apparition could strike back.

"Killie, please." I motioned for her to follow me.

She let out a snarl and leapt toward the computer. She sailed right through what I assumed was the grandma before slamming into the desk. I gasped, ready to help her, but she scrambled to her feet, hissing and spitting as she tried again. I ran out in my animal care clothes before she pounced.

"Girl, it's okay. It's me. Come on." I grabbed her, which in hindsight was probably stupid, as she kept her claws out. We rushed through the kitchen, then through the hallway into the bedroom. I dropped her and examined the scratch marks on my arms. Bite-resistant gloves were the next clothing to buy, apparently. To my surprise, the marks vanished.

"Hey, girl." I tried to pet Killie. Her body vibrated with rage and fear, and I did my best to calm her. "That was a ghost you saw. It'll be alright." That wouldn't have calmed me down, but I said it all the same.

Killie eventually stopped shaking, but it took a while of constantly running my hand down her spine. My cat had reacted badly to this haunt. I thought we only had that granny, but there might be more. I didn't know and also didn't *want* to.

We waited in the dark bedroom. I calmed Killie down as I wondered why I didn't have health points. The answer came to me quicker than I would have liked. My sanity would drop faster than my health. Not sure how I felt about that. Besides, *they* had drained my stamina and sanity out of me. It wasn't really anything that caused me pain.

Killie was on my bed when she leapt to her feet again, hissing, staring at the door leading to the hallway. I scooped her up and moved into the entertainment room. I would do this until bedtime. It saved my sanity, and tonight *they* were coming. I just didn't understand why Killie reacted like this. The only difference between now and before was that the second floor was finally unlocked. Did getting access upstairs create more activity in the house?

The child laughed again as we entered the kitchen. Killie ignored it because she was glaring at the archway leading into the living room. I shuddered at the sound. That child was not a threat. It didn't matter how many times I told myself that; it still sent a chill down my spine.

They were close to arriving because Killie had been calm for a while. The spirits must have left, and my arms healed of the cuts again. She dropped to the ground before sauntering into the living room like she hadn't spent the last three hours hissing and spitting at ghosts in the corner.

I was panting, staring at my sanity, which had lost about fifteen percent. Killie freaking out did not help my sanity, but at least it hadn't lost a huge chunk. I may not have finished my list, but the walls would hold. They had to.

Killie jumped onto the couch and started licking her paws as I moved toward the door, my stomach a forest of knots. I pulled out my axe, staring at nothing. Deep down, I knew *they* could not be hurt by my weapon, but I held it all the same.

The crickets, the wildlife, everything stopped making noise, and silence pressed around us. Killie glanced up from licking her paw. I stared at the door, axe raised, trying not to remember the slime that had attacked me before.

The rumbling started, reminding me of stronger ones that cracked my soul and shattered my bones. Tears leapt to my eyes as my palms grew sweaty.

"Please be enough. Please be enough. Please be enough."

I hadn't finished my list, but I'd finished strengthening the wall. The tremors deepened, and I gasped, tears streaming down my face as my knees weakened.

"Be enough. Be enough. Be enough."

The growls approached the fence, and I didn't know how I stayed on my feet. My sanity took a massive hit, diving toward the halfway mark as I kept staring at the door. The silence was such that it kept me from speaking.

A crack sounded, then a bellow; my entire being convulsed as I dropped the axe. My knees finally gave out, and I collapsed on the ground.

"Be enough. Be enough. Be enough."

Another roar rattled the windows before the growling returned. I was too terrified to sob as tears streamed down my face. The crickets in the forest came to life as *they* left.

"Enough." Relief slammed into me. "Enough. Enough."

My body didn't stop shaking as Killie ran up to me, rubbing her back against my arm. I held my cat with no energy to sob. My sanity was almost gone. If *they* had bellowed again, my remaining bit of blue would have disappeared. I wanted to scoop Killie up and run to the bedroom, but relief mixed with pure exhaustion made it difficult to climb to my feet. What was it about *them* that weakened me so badly? Last time they had forced me to sleep, but now I intended to go to bed on my own.

I kept a hand on Killie, my eyes growing heavy as I assured myself I was in my nightgown. She purred in my arms, and with every purr, I became more grounded. *They* were gone. The fence was strong enough. I didn't finish the list, but *they* couldn't attack me. My gamer mind told me that this was huge. As long as I strengthened the wall, all the other chores on my to-do list were more suggestions than anything. Yes, ones I should listen to, because now I could upgrade buildings, but my priorities shifted. I needed to repair damage to the fence and strengthen it every single time.

With trembling legs, I stumbled into the bedroom, holding my cat in my arms. In the house's silence, I held her close. "I'd never survive here without you." I didn't bother getting under the covers as Killie snuggled up. "Sleep," I said to the words hanging in my vision. My heavy eyelids already gave in as my body shuddered before it relaxed.

I held my new to-do list in my hand as I walked outside.

Repair all damages caused by them
Strengthen the fence
Buy a chicken
Upgrade brick tool
Make glass
Declutter pink room on the second floor

It was short, but I also had only five days. Upgrading the brick fire would take at least 0/50 bricks, and that was if that was the only resource it needed. I had to start now if I hoped to make glass before *they* came.

My feet skidded to a stop when I noticed the greenhouse. It had glass instead of ???, but that wasn't why I stopped. Before it had read 0/5 to be fixed, but now read 0/8. If I didn't finish repairing the greenhouse, then the damage got worse. I needed to upgrade the brick tool. I dove into work. Tomorrow it would rain, and I already had a hope that the soups would keep me warm.

The tree came down, and I cut logs into boards to get 20.00 dopamine points, enough to buy one chicken. As soon as I bought it from the clipboard, I heard it clucking in the coop. I entered and walked to the feeder. I dropped the feed that I magically had into the bucket and filled up her water. Killie watched the chicken, curious, but now she had an animal friend. At least... I hoped they would play together.

The first half of the day involved collecting twenty-five clumps of clay from the river and shaping them to cook in the sun. Would a blisteringly hot day cook the rectangles faster? It was enough of a question that I slipped it away for experimentation. The next sun icon on the calendar was after *they* came.

Once the mounds were baking, I repaired the damage to the fence. I bought the third article of clothing for logging—a yellow hard hat—and I finally made six logs drop with every tree I chopped down. My mind flittered to when the alien overlords had let me buy three clothes at once before taking them away. It brought other memories with it, too. Every experience with those overlords unsettled me. Could I believe they were who they said they were? A neutral party? How could they claim that when they stole me and placed me in the middle of this world?

Another memory returned. *Play the game, get answers.*

I placed my hands on my hips, giving myself a moment to rest even though the desire was never there. I noticed Killie in the grass, then watched as she pounced on a mouse.

"Huh. I guess she is learning to be a mouser."

At least that creature wasn't in a lab. I grumbled, but kept chopping wood for the fence. It didn't take long to repair the damage. *They* hadn't obliterated the fence, so it only needed 0/10 boards and 0/5 firewood. Doable. The fence was about waist high on me, and I watched as words and numbers shifted to read 0/50 boards. Was it about to get higher?

It would rain tomorrow, and I couldn't leave the finished sun-baked clay outside. Better safe than sorry, so I brought them into the storage room. The alien overlords must have realized it was the brick fire that was taking me so much time, because without upgrading the tool at all, I could now stick ten sunbaked clay and cook them for half a day. If I kept feeding it bricks, this tool would be upgraded in two and a half days.

Killie wasn't as jumpy tonight. Perhaps the nights *they* came had more malevolent spirits. I considered cleaning the pink room while I waited to go to bed, but quickly squashed the idea. My sanity was at fifty percent, and I refused to go upstairs at night. I instead spent the hour talking with Killie, having her chase my feet, and trying to make a good thing out of a bad situation.

Chapter Twenty-One

Sewing

The bedroom didn't fill with red light when I woke up in the morning. It was colder and much darker. I peeked out the broken blinds, hearing the thunderous sound of rain above me. It made me quiver, but at least I had my sanity back. I checked the clipboard to see if I had reached new levels so I could buy clothes, which... was a weird thought to have. What was this game doing to me?

Cleaning was the next closest skill at level 12. Cooking was still the lowest, and I planned on doing more tomorrow after this rain stopped. I ate some warm soup from the storage room, pleased to see a fifteen-minute timer. I ran outside and watered the tomatoes and potatoes. With the greenhouses so damaged, it was taking longer for the plants to grow. I did my gardening, then shoved ten sunbaked clay into the tool. Since it was so cold today, it would take all day for it to finish. I allowed myself a moment to be disappointed. I could make it. By tonight, I would have twenty total bricks.

The chicken clucked in the coop, and I entered to check on her, a few minutes remaining on my timer. She pecked at an empty feeder. I magically loaded more feed into it, which the chicken happily ate as I checked the box. There was an egg. I took it and ran inside as the seconds ticked down. I set the egg in the storage unit as the time finished.

Alright, I had all day now to declutter the pink room. This second floor felt like where these people hid their hoarding. That room didn't just have decorations, but old clothes that they no doubt had grown out of. I used some stamina to carry a huge load downstairs and onto the porch. The porch roof kept the cold weather from draining my yellow. I strategically placed bags of junk on the cement to be dumped. When it was full, I ate another warm bowl of potato soup and spent the next fifteen minutes dropping things in the dumpster. It was an excellent system, though it was discouraging when I walked back up the stairs to see the small dent I had made in the pink room after three hours of work. Oh well. I had more time.

As I chipped away at the junk, the hardwood floor revealed itself. I had a pretty good idea that this was what was under that brown shag carpet. I was fighting a powerful desire to rip all the carpets up to check. There would be a way to do that in the game, though, right? Take down the eighties paneling and whatnot? I forced myself to remember I was possibly in a coma in real life, and I needed to figure out why I was here.

The greyness of the day darkened, and I pulled out my flashlight and placed it against the ground to give me light. I didn't want to stay up here much longer, but I assumed it got darker faster in the rain. I wasn't able to depend on any hunger pangs to tell what time it was. It was odd that with no stamina; I was only ever nauseous, not starving.

I needed to move the table to reach the stuff underneath, but as I tugged the leg, it didn't budge. I stood up, brushed myself off, and ran my light over the surface. A few things remained on top, and I pushed the clothes and socks away. I then grabbed a strange cover and pulled it off to reveal a sewing machine. I raised an eyebrow, curious.

Cannot use sewing machine until room is decluttered.

A smile flickered across my face. This must be the reason the list had specifically asked me to declutter here. What did it do? I refused to get my hopes up. Instead, I spent longer than I wanted to upstairs. I could only see with the flashlight by the time I gathered the last of the clutter from the room and hurried down the stairs. I didn't want to chance it, so I'd wait until tomorrow to find out what the sewing machine did.

The rain continued to pound on the roof as I used my stamina to go outside and gather the ten cooking bricks. It took a chunk of my yellow energy, but I could spare it. To have this run all night would be a fantastic upgrade.

My eyes shot to the sky. "Hint, hint."

Inside, I brushed the rain from my face. Water evaporated off me, and I grew warm. Killie was on the couch, relaxing as she licked her paw. No weird ghosts, then. To kill time, I glanced through the clipboard and noticed the cleaning chemicals for the bathroom were unlocked. I tried to hold back my gasp of excitement. How long ago had this happened? I needed to flip through the pages more often. I spent the hour before bedtime scrubbing the sink, toilet, mirror, and tub. Once again, a few scrubs with this chemical and a healthy amount of game logic turned the disgusting tub into one I could see myself taking a soak in. When that was done, I sighed in relief as the bars of stamina and sanity extended again. All a win in my book.

I walked into the kitchen when I heard the stairs creaking. I froze, not sure what to expect. In the living room, Killie remained on the couch, licking her paw. A noise grabbed my attention, and I stared at the door next to the fridge. Blood covered footprints took shape, heading toward me. I screamed, scrambling away. Killie sat up, confused, but I scooped her up and ran into the bedroom. Was it time for bed? It didn't matter. I just wanted to get that image out of my head. I refused to let my mind linger on those footprints headed toward me.

I threw back the covers, determined, yet still shaking off residual fear from last night. I climbed out of bed and tiptoed toward the hallway door. Killie walked by my side like she didn't have a care in the world. It should have comforted me, but the terror of those footprints would not leave me alone. As the red dawn filled the room with its glow, I listened to Killie's calming purr and pushed open the door to the hallway.

The early light cast dark shadows. I clicked on the flashlight, shining it on the ground. No footprints. I took careful steps forward, the beam bouncing everywhere. I then entered the kitchen. The worn carpet was clear of blood. I turned off the light and leaned against the fridge, letting out a sigh. All other paranormal activity only happened at night, but for my sanity, I needed to make sure no footprints remained. I could *almost* chalk it all up as a figment of my imagination, but I'd seen too many things in this house to believe that. Then again, it all might be in my head, anyway. I still didn't know why I was here.

Play the game. Get answers.

Three days before *they* came, with no unusually hot or cold weather. I had plenty of jobs I wanted to do, but I should finish the chores on my list. For good measure, I glanced at my sanity bar and saw it was full. Perfect. It needed to stay that way.

I stuffed ten more sunbaked clay in the tool. I then dropped junk from the porch into the dumpster before rushing to the greenhouse to do all the farming. Once Killie and the chicken had food and water, I gathered an egg.

"Daisy?" I asked the chicken. "For whatever reason, you feel like a Daisy." The hen didn't reply as she kept pecking at her feeder. I shrugged. "That'll be your name unless you tell me otherwise." I chuckled until I thought about what might happen if the alien overlords granted this chicken the ability to speak. Game logic warned it was a possibility.

I started cooking. I tried a simple egg recipe, but until I ate it, I wouldn't know how much stamina it gave me. After I cooked the two eggs, I sorted through my collection of tomatoes and potatoes. My attention was torn between making more food and decluttering the pink room. I *needed* to know what the sewing machine did.

After a rainy day, it was nice to not have to worry about eating soup to keep warm. As I sat to finish cooking, I pulled out my list.

Repair all damages caused by them

~~Strengthen the wall around the house and greenhouses~~

~~Buy a chicken~~

Upgrade brick tool

Make glass

~~Declutter pink room on second floor~~

"Hey, alien overlords. Remember my first week here, when I stayed on top of my chores, so you gave me a free day to do whatever I wanted?" My eyes drifted over to the carport that I hadn't touched in a while. "That'd be nice. Just sayin'."

Again, I got nothing in response. I was probably pressing my luck with these people, if they even were people. If they were a neutral party, this wouldn't offend them.

"Some notes I had. From a lover of these games."

Words glowed in my vision, and I held my breath.

Get better at finishing the to-do lists, then.

I raised an eyebrow. "I'm sorry, is that... snarkiness? Condescension? Should I be afraid?" I didn't know why I had such courage to say that. Probably because it was the middle of the day. I expected some sort of backlash for my brashness, but nothing happened.

The storage room was stocked to near bursting. The food had to be on shelves, while grouped items like tomatoes or clay bricks were on the ground. It would be nice to upgrade this unit, but no doubt it felt so full because I made a lot of soups.

"I *really* wanna try fishing." I checked the list one more time before creating more bricks. Once they were inside the tool, I climbed up the stairs to the second floor. The clutter was gone, though the room needed a good sweep.

Decluttering finished. Sewing machine activated.

Sweeping must not be necessary for this new tool to work.

"Okay, but what do you do?"

Killie perched near the door, her head cocked. A pattern book that hadn't been there before rested by the machine. I picked it up, seeing a page for every piece of clothing I owned, and then in the back it was all grayed out of the clothes I didn't have yet. I closed it and studied the cover. It glowed in my hands.

Upgrade book?

-1.00

"Sure. Go ahead."

My mind was telling me that was one stick's worth of dopamine points, and honestly, it was a fair enough trade. I was curious. I flipped through the pages again. The picture of the straw hat had writing underneath, and I brought it closer, squinting as I read.

Increases the probability of extra produce by 10%

The overalls said the same thing. If I upgraded both, that gave me a 20% chance of an extra tomato or potato. If I had all five clothes, that would give me a 50% chance of receiving extra produce. I flipped another page and found myself in the cleaning section.

Increases the probability of a stamina burst by 10%

Okay, I sensed a pattern here. The logging gave a 10% chance of dropping something. Either logs, boards, firewood, sticks, or matches. Cooking got a bonus for extra food. That had to be some strange level of law breaking physics. Fewer building materials for an item sounded excellent, and animal care meant Daisy would have a higher chance of giving an extra egg. I wasn't sure if Killie got anything. She was always pretty consistent in finding ghosts.

As a test, I tried it on my plaid shirt.

Warning!

This machine will take hours to complete

If you are upgrading an article of clothing, you cannot use it until the upgrade is complete

Did this mean that while it upgraded my logging shirt, then the trees would only drop five logs instead of six until it was done? I didn't want to chance it. Since I had finished farming for the day, I set my straw hat near the sewing machine. A sand timer appeared as the needle moved. No one sat on the chair. This timer was definitely longer than the fire and the fridge.

Killie jumped onto the table, mesmerized by the machine. Despite the hat shape, it had flattened so the needle could run across it.

"It's not the weirdest thing I've seen."

I walked down the stairs and almost went outside when I glanced around the kitchen again. Specifically, the calendar. I had upgraded it like I did the book. The upgrade had been toward the beginning of my time here, where dopamine points were scarce. I studied it with a slight frown.

Upgrade Calendar for -0.35?

Y/N

What more did it have to give me? I mentally chose yes and waited. Nothing happened to the calendar, but underneath my bars in my vision, a timer showed up. I assumed it was a timer until the lamppost turned on until I saw the picture next to it. It was a simply drawn wolf's head. Was it counting down until the wolf came? I thought the beast showed up when the lamplight flickered on. I had been so scared I always stayed inside right at sunset. But if I could know when it arrived, that would be fantastic! I could work until the last moment of the day. Every second counted. I tucked this away again as an experiment.

I walked back outside and made sure the brick tool was going. I double-checked my list, but I had to wait for that tool to upgrade, which meant I was at a bottleneck. The bricks would finish tomorrow afternoon, and I'd still have a full day and a half before *they* attacked. I hoped it wasn't a long list of resources the tool needed.

Alright. It was a matter of waiting, which meant that, for now, I had some free time to do what I wanted, and I felt like going fishing.

Chapter Twenty-Two
The River

Once I got enough dopamine points, I bought a fishing rod. I walked down to the river, my cooking clothes jumping onto me. I didn't know why I needed to wear a chef's cap and jacket to catch fish. If they had any sort of intelligence, they would suspect something was up. Maybe they weren't that smart, but if I were a fish, I'd be worried if someone arrived dressed to deep-fat fry me.

I studied the river, noticing dark shadows in the middle of it. Despite playing farming games, I didn't know much about the actual fishing people did in real life. Good thing this followed game logic, because I doubted the alien overlords would throw it out now. If I could drop ingredients into a pot and have them make soups, then I wouldn't be standing in a river for hours to catch one fish. I threw out my line and waited for it to jiggle. It triggered my muscle memory, waiting for the handheld device to vibrate before pressing a button. Would it be the same here?

Right before I wondered about trying a different tactic, the line pulled. I reeled the fish in. It worked for a few seconds, but then I watched as the rod bent dangerously. I stopped reeling for a bit to make sure it wouldn't break before another attempt. I did that two more times before the fish finally sailed out of the water. It was magically placed in a basket next to me.

"Alright, then." I already sensed recipes being unlocked on the clipboard back home. I also noticed a small bit of stamina vanish with that endeavor. It was a worthy sacrifice. Did fishing mean I was gaining experience in my cooking level? I hoped so. Of all the skills I had, that was the lowest. No doubt because I waited until I obtained at least an hour's worth of food to cook at the firepit before it died out.

I kept fishing, studying the scenery. Most of the trees around the fence were gone, which meant I should look for a new place to cut them down. It might be a smart idea to chop trees from the house to the riverbank to make a path somehow.

The moment I thought about it, a war of ideas started inside me. Logistically speaking, cutting all of those down would take *ages*. At least a full season. I couldn't possibly be here that long. The calendar showed two seasons, but that didn't mean I was staying here for both of them, right? I wanted to figure out a way to leave before the end of spring/summer. I had no time to start a project of making a path. But just in case I was wrong, and I would be here for a while...

My shoes did not make any crunching noises as I walked back with my basket of five fish. Once I returned to the house, I checked the bricks. They were almost done. By tomorrow afternoon, I would have all I needed and could move on to the next materials for upgrading.

I grabbed the clipboard, flipping through the recipes.

Fried fish
0/1 fish

Fish omelet: basic
0/1 fish
0/1 egg

A fish omelet didn't sound appetizing, but I needed to think more game-logically. That recipe had both high-level food sources. It might bring more stamina, especially with my longer bars. Words blinked at the top of a page. I brought it closer to my face to read it better.

Upgrade cooking fire to unlock a new category of recipes
Cannot upgrade fire until you reach cooking Level 10

Huh. With all the other instructions over buildings, I hadn't noticed one over the fire. Perhaps nothing came because my cooking skill was still below 10.

I flipped toward the back to see my progress.

Farming level 12

Cleaning level 14

Logging level 15

Cooking level 7

Building level 16

Animal Care level 11

In the clothing section, I studied my options. Cleaning was close to level 15. Logging and building's fourth article of clothing would unlock at level 25, which seemed so far away. I wouldn't be here that long, right?

"I *will* figure this out and leave before spring/summer." I tried to believe it.

My wolf timer continued to tick down as the forest blocked the sunlight. I hastily placed the newly cooked bricks into the tool. Ten more to go. I'd get them cooking in the early morning and have them in there by the afternoon. With the time remaining, I entered the carport and kept throwing clutter into a bag. I hadn't touched this place in a while, but the possibility of an upgrade made me curious. It was also the easiest room to declutter, with it being so close to the dumpster.

It got late enough that I turned on my flashlight as I worked. I glanced at the bare lightbulb on the carport ceiling, wondering when the electricity would work. I had long since ignored the logic of the whole thing. A single power pole next to the carport, not connected to anything else, would undoubtedly have enough electricity to power the carport and the entire home.

As I finished stuffing some junk into the dumpster, my timer started flashing red with one minute left. Though it was dark, the lamppost hadn't turned on yet. I didn't want to push it because I wanted to keep my sanity, so I quickly slipped inside the house. The timer dropped to zero. A few seconds later, the light flickered on.

I leaned against the door, which somehow made my panic spike. Night swallowed the sunlight, leaving me with a faint electric orange glow. Crushing feelings of solitude hit me as the walls shrank around me. I didn't understand why this sudden panic struck me. I was doing well. My to-do list was almost done. I had strengthened the fence. I could do other things while waiting for the bricks to finish tomorrow afternoon. Fish. Clean the carport. Protect my sanity from the wolf and the ghosts.

But I was still here. It was the conversation warring inside me ever since I thought about the project of cutting down the trees to the river. I was here. Those alien overlords had set this game up to make me feel like I would stay here for a long time, even though I didn't know what was going on in my old life. I had a family that missed me, no doubt. But I wasn't there. I was here. Here in a haunted house. Here with a monster prowling. Here where *they* attacked. As the only light source cast shadows blacker than the star-speckled sky, it was hard to ignore the wave of overwhelming isolation. Once again, I was swimming in the ocean and glanced around to see no island in sight to rest.

My lungs demanded another breath, so I let them. I had done it. My metaphorical moment of gasping for air in the middle of the sea. I had a choice to panic and sink or keep going.

Killie leapt off the couch, hissing at the doorway of the bedroom. I grabbed her, staying out of the kitchen to avoid losing a chunk of sanity from those bloody footprints. We jumped from room to room, ignoring whatever ghost Killie saw. Once the hour was up, I went to sleep, another day of swimming completed.

Chapter Twenty-Three
An Upgrade

My morning routine reminded me of the straw hat I had forgotten on the sewing machine yesterday. I replaced it with my logging plaid shirt, since I planned on gathering more resources today. I collected it before gardening, watering, feeding my animals, and collecting an egg.

Stones and clay took forever to drag to the house. Especially since I could only carry one at a time. It caused me deep frustration simply because of the monotony. I needed to figure out how to hold more resources. If I created a wheelbarrow, that would be a game changer, but I sensed I couldn't build anything unless it was part of the suggestions on the clipboard. Most of my building skills involved stuffing items where I was directed to. Either way, I figured it was a great thing to stockpile while I waited for the bricks to finish.

Strange as it was, I sensed that the more experience I gained with building, the ability of carrying two resources at a time would unlock. I didn't have it yet, but I wanted it. Two whole stones! I attempted to carry a couple once to experiment, and it wiped out half my stamina to walk to the house. I tried not to get frustrated. Instead, it fueled my desire to stockpile these resources. *They* were coming tomorrow night. Anytime a unit required anything from the river, it always stole hours of my day. So I used the time now while waiting for the bricks to finish.

I had a collection of five stones and clay stacked by the tool when I finally took out the bricks and finished the upgrade. I held my breath, hoping I wouldn't need more resources.

0/25 boards

Okay, that wasn't too bad. I pulled my leftover boards out of storage and into the tool before chopping down two more trees. After waiting so long for the next item, it was almost euphoric to have the second part of this done in less than an hour.

0/15 stones

That might take a little more time. At least I had the foresight to bring stone and clay in. Though if I *really* had insight, I would have just focused on stones and would already have ten of them in there. Instead, I put the five in the tool and turned toward the river.

"I'll be fine. The tool upgrade has to be close. There can't be much more. We can do this."

When I noticed the wolf timer had half an hour remaining, I only needed two more stones. I grabbed them and sacrificed a huge chunk of stamina to carry them both back to the house at the same time. I shoved both into the brickmaker and waited.

"This is it, right?" I asked the tool as if it could talk to me.

After a pause, words filtered above it.

0/5 firewood

My lips glued shut to keep the frustrated groan inside me, but it was fine. I still had some boards left over.

After eating soup to get more stamina, I made quick work of the boards and stuffed the firewood in there.

"How about now?" I asked.

Another pause.

0/5 sticks

"Yeah, okay." I quickly did what it requested.

0/1 match

After cutting down an entire board to reach one match, I stared at the tool, waiting. "This feels like the end. Is it? It'd be really nice if it were."

A larger brick and stone unit materialized. Information filled my mind as the sheen ran over the brickmaker. I frowned, sifting through the new knowledge.

"If you need to relay details, most games usually give a notification to read instead of downloading the data right into my brain. It's a little boost of dopamine, too. You make words pop into my head, anyway. This'll be nicer to visualize exactly what this improved brickmaker can do," I said to the sky.

After a moment, words floated into my mind.

Congratulations, you did what we expected of you.

It was so random it made me choke on my laughter. "Seriously, are you alien overlords snarky?"

The tool is now upgraded. You may enjoy the following benefits:

It can make the following resources during the day or night:

Glass

Required: 1 bag of sand

Maximum of five in a batch

Time: one day

Bricks

Required: baked clay

Maximum of fifteen in a batch

Time: half a day

Stone blocks

Required: broken stones

Maximum of ten in a batch

Time: half a day

Stone blocks were new. I wasn't sure how to break up stones without a pickaxe. Was it something to discover, or to buy?

A buzzing noise hit my ears as the lamp turned on, but it was still a good ten minutes before my wolf timer showed the beast entering the clearing. So, the wolf was inconsistent. Well, that was perfect. I needed every second.

I grabbed the leftover materials from the boards and firewood and walked toward the storage area. I headed down the stairs when an invisible wall stopped me.

Unit full. Would you like to discard some items?

Panic seized me. No. No, I did not want to do that. I glanced around. It didn't look full. The food shelving annoyed me. Each bowl needed a certain spot on the shelf, even though I wanted to shove them together.

"I could totally fit it all." I dragged the boards and firewood outside. After some consideration, I set them against the house. Nothing happened. They might be fine on the back porch.

My wolf timer blinked with a minute left. I peeked over to see the lamppost already on, giving a deceptively warm, yet not bright, glow. I slipped inside. Killie was curled on the couch in the entertainment room, asleep. I sighed as I settled into the recliner, staring at the bowl of pink candy before picking one up and sucking on it. I kept a careful eye on my stamina, but it looked like this food source didn't give any. Oh well.

I leaned back, thinking about what I had accomplished. With the tool upgraded, it gave me a full day to finish my list. I pulled it out to check what I still had left.

Repair all damages caused by them
~~Strengthen the wall around the house and greenhouses~~
~~Buy a chicken~~
~~Upgrade brick tool~~
Make glass
~~Declutter pink room on second floor~~

As soon as I figured out how to make glass, I'd be ready to repair the damage. According to the new information, even if I had sand, it would take a full day to make glass. *They* were coming tomorrow night. Despite everything, I still couldn't finish repairing all the damage. If I had found sand before I came in, it would have worked, but where would I find it? The obvious answer was at the river. From what I recalled, it was mostly stone and clay. I hadn't noticed any sand.

One of these days, I would complete my to-do list and go to bed early. As if on cue, the child giggled upstairs. I closed my eyes, my shoulders tightening, as a sliver of blue faded from my sanity bar. Killie remained asleep on the couch.

"Not that big of a deal. Killie's not reacting. The ghost is harmless. I should not be freaking out over this."

Saying it out loud didn't make me feel better. This was the night before *they* came. If I dropped below fifty percent, I wouldn't recover my full sanity. The encounter reminded me to dress in my nightgown as two females whispered upstairs.

"Fine. It's fine."

It was dark, but I noticed a reflection of someone standing behind me in the huge nineties-style TV. My heart stuttered as I flipped around and saw nothing. Why was I so surprised no one was there? I glanced back at the TV to see the figure moving toward the couch with some sort of wooden spoon over their head, aiming right at Killie.

"No!"

My shouting woke Killie up, who looked directly at the ghost and started yowling. I leapt out of my chair and grabbed my cat, running into the living room. I could have sworn I heard echoing shrieks as my sanity lost another sliver.

"Fine. I'm fine. Fine." I hesitated at the entryway to the kitchen. I did not want to see those footprints. But the echoes of the screams forced my hand. Instead, I ran into the bathroom with Killie and shut the door. There hadn't been any hauntings in here, right?

I had my back against the door. My cat was meowing, distressed. I turned on the flashlight so it wouldn't be pitch black. Killie stretched on the dirty tile. I heard nothing but my breathing.

"Did you sense her at all, girl?" I asked, petting her. "Is that the ghost you hiss at all the time? That shrieking grandma? She doesn't like cats, does she?"

Killie meowed, then kept circling around the small bathroom. I rested my head against the door, assessing the chunk of sanity taken from my bar. I was still a little over seventy-five percent. It was okay. I had less than an hour before—

My cat's back arched as she stared at the showerhead, making warning noises. I grabbed the flashlight, shining it toward the tub, even though I didn't expect to find anything. I was ready to sprint out of the bathroom when a force rammed into the outside wall, and I screamed. Ghosts couldn't do that. In answer to my screams, I detected the wolf's wet snarling. Killie shrieked, backing away from the door, pupils dilated. The wolf had never attacked the house. This time was different. It snarled and tore as panic seized me.

"No, not the brick tool. Leave it alone! I just updated it!" I shouted into the darkness. Did I really want to scream at that beast? It might break in.

I scrambled out of the bathroom and into the living room. Killie's body shook, no doubt from the encounter with the wolf creature. I triple-checked the locks on the front door, then the back door. I didn't like the kitchen at night, and I refused to go to the second floor.

The snarls and scratching could be heard from the living room. Killie remained stiff, claws out, staring wide-eyed at the wall. The snarling finished, and the wolf sprinted away. I sighed, dropping my head as I tried to control my fast, yet uneven heartbeat pounding in my chest.

Two ghosts spoke in muffled whispers again, male and female. I covered my ears, hoping that if I couldn't detect it, then it wouldn't hurt my sanity. Tonight was crazy, and it made me anxious. It was the night before *they* arrived. I was supposed to hop between rooms to keep my blue bar full. At least I had learned something; reflective surfaces helped me see spirits. The mirror, the TV reflection. I should stay away from those.

Once I felt the pull to go to bed, I abandoned the living room and moved to the bedroom. Something flickered in the mirror, but I refused to look. As soon as I climbed under the covers, I forced myself to sleep. This day needed to end.

Chapter Twenty-Four
A Loss

I didn't bother looking for anything poetic about that red dawn light. Instead, I threw the covers off and ran to check if my upgraded tool was fine. It was. But the boards, firewood, and clay that I'd left outside because the storage was too full had been torn to bits. I dropped to my knees, trying to mold it back together, but it was contaminated and refused to meld. The wolf had destroyed it.

Losing everything hurt, especially the clay. Even though *they* were coming tonight and I still needed to get stuff done, I spent a few moments on the ground staring at nothing. All that time gathering resources wasted. It did not bode well for my mood today. I climbed to my feet, numbly going through my morning routine, replacing another article of clothing at the sewing machine, farming, and egg collecting. Once those tasks were done, I left for the riverbank. The pain of the destroyed material tugged at my soul, but I needed to focus. It would take an entire day to make glass. The sooner I found sand, the better, and the only place I considered it to be was by water.

At the river, I focused on the task at hand. I crouched down, seeing the words above the clay and stone. Packed mud lay beneath them. I studied the riverbank before glancing over at the other side of the rushing water. I spied the lovely sandy hill I needed and groaned. At least I'd found the sand. It was just a matter of getting it.

Was I a swimmer? I started walking; the water touching my feet, yet I felt no coldness. This was a time of experimentation. Smoke formed at the corner of my sight as I stood calf-deep in the river. I glanced around to find a fire that would explain the smoke, but saw none. I pushed forward, and the further I got, the more the gray wisps covered my vision.

As my eyesight returned, I found myself dry, back on the banks of my side of the river. I folded my arms. Fine then. I couldn't swim, and this game had a weird way of showing that.

I chopped down a tree and grabbed one log. I tried to place it on the bank and angle it toward the other side, but this river was at least two logs wide. No doubt about it. I needed a bridge.

Perhaps this followed the same logic as the chicken coop. What if I could buy the bridge and then build it here? It was worth a shot. I ran back to the house, watching my stamina. A small chip of yellow left, but I wanted to make that glass. I flipped through the clipboard to the building section. Despite a few grayed-out buildings, I found it.

Bridge. 30.00 dopamine points.

"I'm starting to believe you guys don't want me finishing my to-do list." I glanced at my total. 22.32. Not bad.

I grabbed a board from the storage room and placed it in the dumpster, rushing past the scene of the crime with the other shredded boards. Once I had bought the bridge, I hurried back to the river. A ghostly outline glowed as I put on my building outfit and read the words above the water.

0/4 stone blocks

I leaned over, gripping my knees. Things felt too overwhelming, but then I closed my eyes and squared my shoulders.

"It's okay. Quinn, you'll be fine. The fence is strengthened. You wouldn't repair all the damage today, anyway. *They* cannot hurt you."

With that, I sacrificed more stamina to sprint to the house to check the clipboard. There, as an option to buy, was a pickaxe. After dropping more boards into the dumpster, I bought it. It was a rusty one, and if I had the 0/2 stones, I could have upgraded it, but I was out of that resource.

Back at the river, I tried breaking up stones. I watched my stamina. It took a large chunk with every swing of the pickaxe. The words above the resource changed from *stone* to *broken stone*. I flinched, realizing I should've taken the intact material to the house before whacking them. Lesson learned. The morning had turned into afternoon by the time I had carried, broken up, and gotten the stone blocks in the tool. Until they were finished being made, I had some time to kill. I looked around, figuring out what to do. The storage area needed an upgrade. That would take a ton of resources, with it needing 0/100 boards at the start. Since I couldn't store things outside, filling the upgrade became my new storage place for boards, just in a more permanent manner.

I studied the clipboard again. Cleaning was finally at level 15. I went to check out what clothes to buy, but they remained grayed out. At first, I thought it was because I didn't have enough points, but words were written over it.

Cannot purchase this until carport is upgraded

Huh. Odd. I had a lot of things to upgrade in my little paradise of horror. The firepit begged to be upgraded, too. I almost decided right then to go fishing and bring my skill level to ten, so I could upgrade the firepit when I hesitated. If I brought back another basket of fish, it wouldn't fit in the storage unit. I entered the unit and pulled out six boards and placed them in the wall outside. Could the wolf get these, too? No, it had never touched the brick tool while I was upgrading it. With more storage room now available, I did more fishing to level up. Cooking was my lowest section, and I needed more experience points.

In the late afternoon, the stone blocks finished. My wolf timer told me I still had a few hours. *They* would arrive at midnight, and it was important to get as much done as possible before then. After tonight, *they* would come in four days. Then, in another four days. Then in three. I had a bad feeling the last three days before fall/winter would be busy.

Me carrying one stone block was the equivalent of two stones for my stamina. I don't know how the math worked out, but I no longer applied actual logic to anything going on here. Eating helped clear out some space in my storage room. I downed a couple of soups before lifting the stone block and carrying it to the river. Sweat appeared on my forehead the longer I drained my stamina until I finally dropped the block in the ghost of a bridge.

1/4 stone blocks

Three more to go.

Tomorrow morning, I would do more cooking. I had used up a lot of soup in carrying the blocks. By the time I was carrying the final stone block, I was walking in the dark. I did not have the option of using the flashlight, since both my hands were busy. It made me uneasy, even though I kept looking at the timer and knew the wolf wouldn't be here for another hour. I dropped the last stone into the ghost bridge and watched it shift. Two solid foundations took shape at each end of the riverbank.

0/50 logs

Perhaps my project of cutting down trees from the river to the house would finish sooner than expected. I chopped down one tree and stuffed the six logs into the outline. I would have done more, but my stamina was dangerously low, and I wanted to keep something in reserve. The stress knots in my shoulders released as I shone my flashlight on the sandy banks.

"Soon." Hopefully before *they* came in the next four days.

Twigs cracked on the other side. My heart dropped to my stomach as I shone my light in the forest. *They* shouldn't be here yet. At least... I was pretty sure. I tried to see what made that noise, but the trees blocked my view.

That bush by the bank just moved. I trained my flashlight on it, waiting to catch it again or if it was a figment of my imagination. The night played tricks on me. No way a bush could—

It rose, then eight stick-like legs unfurled, scuttling around as its jaw opened, revealing razor-sharp teeth. No eyes appeared on the bush, but I was distracted by those teeth. My back was to the creature before I fully comprehended what I had witnessed. Whether an illusion or real, I would not stay to find out.

Halfway to the house, nausea slammed into me, and I collapsed in a fetal position, moaning. Stupid stamina. Why did I need it for running? I spared a moment, coughing on the ground. That was a monster. A small one, but still a monster. A horrifying thought hit me. I didn't know what was out there, and I was about to build a bridge. I hadn't stopped to think about the implications of this. If I made a link between the two sides, if darker creatures lived out there...

All the stress knots returned to my shoulder before I pushed myself up, already feeling tears on my cheeks. I walked as fast as my lack of stamina would allow; the house coming into view. Should I build a bridge? It was the thought that plagued me the entire walk. Did I have a choice? Maybe I could find a sandy bank on my side of the river, but that would require time to go exploring. Tomorrow would mark four short days before *they* attacked. I doubted I'd have a free day to explore more of this place. I held off on deciding about the bridge until I knew how many chores I needed to do. It might even be on my next list.

I did not want to be in a haunted building right now. That monster took a small chunk of my sanity, and I didn't know if I could be inside losing more. With fifteen minutes left until the wolf came, I gathered the last bits of clutter from the carport and dropped them in the dumpster. I watched the glowing words above the small roof change.

0/10 stone blocks

Since the brick tool was closer than the river, it shouldn't take as much stamina. I didn't have any stones, or I would have broken them up and placed them in the tool now. I wandered over to the front yard, studying the darkness beyond the orange glow of the lamplight. The front porch was still a dilapidated mess. The dead hanging plants were sad. Despite the haunting aspect of this house on the second level, I was growing to love this old home. It had a charm to it in the daytime, and the night would go better after a thorough exorcism. I wondered if I could do yardwork as part of this, too. Like planting flowers on the path leading up to the door.

My wolf timer turned red and blinked. I didn't dare waste any time as I slipped into the house to wait for *their* attack.

Chapter Twenty-Five
Singing in the Dark

Killie was on the couch, making warning noises at the empty corner. I grabbed her and ran straight to the bathroom as the nightgown materialized on me.

"Despite the wolf attacking last night, nothing else has happened here. But you warn me if my theory is wrong."

Was there something in this game to help me sleep through all the attacks and hauntings? I would willingly travel to the other side of the river for such an artifact.

Killie remained near, and I held my flashlight. It kept the impossibly dark bathroom lit. The noises had a muted boisterousness to them. I didn't want to know what they said. My cat was against my leg, trembling. I remained on the ground, my back against the door. There was a mirror here, but I ignored its existence.

A child started humming above me, and all other sounds reached a standstill. Despite being a ghost, the child skipped in a circle. The blue room was above the kitchen, and with all the baby stuff in there, it was probably that child's space. A boy? But this house also boasted a pink room, where most of the giggling came from.

The humming changed to singing.

"Ring around the Rosie,

"A pocket full of posies,

"Ashes, ashes,

"We all fall down."

The song was so familiar to me I was positive my mind was filling in the lyrics even as I couldn't make out the child's voice. The only noises were the child's singing and my own rattled gasps. I placed the flashlight on the ground because it trembled in my hand. I tried to talk myself into calming down. What was so terrifying about a ghost child reciting a rhyme about death?

"Ring around the Rosie,

"A pocket full of—"

My palms slammed over my ears, giving my brain a shake inside my skull as I did so. Killie pressed her back against me as I shut my eyes. My sanity took a dip. "Fine. I'm fine. Completely fine."

I hadn't received a memory orb in a long time. It was a strange place for my mind to go, but I was no doubt panicking so badly that I latched on to a thought that wasn't about ghost children. I usually got an orb before *they* attacked. I wonder why it hadn't happened.

The light from the flashlight flickered, and it threw me back to the present. My only source of light slowly dimmed. I grabbed it.

"No. No, no, no." It was like losing a flotation device in the middle of the ocean. "Please don't go."

My mind recalled all the times I had used this tool. Batteries didn't last forever, but I also assumed game logic would apply by always staying on as long as I needed them. But that was stupid. I'd found multiple rusty batteries in the carport, all of which the dumpster prompted me not to throw away.

The light flickered out. My heart pounded in my chest so loud I was sure someone heard it. It was pitch dark in the bathroom.

"The fence is strong."

My voice cracked, but I clung to the hope in my words as I repeated them. *They* couldn't hurt me tonight.

"Ring around the Rosie,

"A pocket full of posies,

"Ashes, ashes,

"We all fall down."

Palms returned to my ears. Tears dripped down my chin. Sanity took another hit as I sank onto the grimy bathroom floor, curling. The child's singing grew more muted before fading entirely. Despite my hands blocking the noise, I still heard the creaking of footsteps on the staircase.

What would my next memory orb be? I hoped it would be a happy one.

The stairs groaned with the weight as someone finished walking down them.

Maybe it would be of me and Theo going on a random trip somewhere.

Dull thuds sounded in the hallway.

Or some amusement park, like Disneyland. A place where we're joyful, and laughing. Theo would finally be talking. That would be great!

The footsteps padded into the kitchen, slow and careful. My body curled tighter into itself.

What was my favorite ride at Disneyland? I'm sure I went before. It was strange that I remembered these amusement parks so easily and yet not my mother's name.

The floor creaked next to the fridge.

It's a Small World? Constant singing, non-stop talking. It fit my personality as a child. Why did I remember what this obnoxious ride was like?

The footsteps moved toward the bathroom.

I quietly sang It's a Small World. What was I doing? Why was this noise leaving my mouth? A ghostly figure was roaming by my hiding spot, and I made noises, a sorry excuse for singing. The ghosts would find me.

How did I know this song? The verses, not just the chorus? Perhaps it really was my favorite ride. Despite all the fear, I had a small and trembling voice. The footsteps moved past the bathroom. I cowered on the ground, hugging my knees, trying not to imagine what the kitchen carpet looked like.

I kept the sobs inside me as I remained on the grimy floor. The longer I stayed in this game, the worse the hauntings became. So logically, I should not stay in this game much longer. I needed to discover the answers this place meant to give me. But how? Especially when I wasn't getting a memory orb? Was that up to the alien overlords?

I didn't know how long I was on the bathroom floor crying, but I did notice when every hair on my arms shot up. Killie moved next to me, cuddling close.

"The terror of the monsters comes mostly from ambiguity. Like Jaws. Or the aliens in Signs. Once you see a monster in daylight, it's never as scary. No more dread because of the unknown. I've seen *them*, therefore I'm not scared. *They* can't hurt my sanity."

What was I saying? Someone had told me this before.

A thud rumbled the ground. I didn't know if I could curl into a tighter ball, but my body took the challenge.

"*They're* just sludge. That's all."

Thud

"Full of teeth and hair."

Thud

"Nothing scary about that."

My soul tried to wriggle out of my body to escape *them*.

"Probably... a real-life... explanation..."

Thud

"Some... coma... medical reason..."

Crack.

I didn't realize my hands were over my ears until *they* bellowed. I stopped breathing, curling tighter. The complete darkness did not help. My sanity was below twenty-five percent. *They* had to be leaving soon; I couldn't take much more of this.

Another bellow plummeted my blue to a dangerous level before the thuds departed.

On the grimy tile, I took my hands from my ears as my body didn't stop shaking. I clung to my fragment of sanity. If I saw those bloody footprints on the ground, I would lose my mind. I gathered Killie and left the bathroom with my eyes closed. It was still dark, but I didn't want to risk anything.

My hip hit the cherry wood table, so I used that as a guide as I moved through the kitchen, then into the living room. I kept my cat in my arms. My entire being quivered as I realized this would happen every time *they* attacked. If I hadn't upgraded my stamina and sanity...

Killie remained calm, purring as I shuffled to the bedroom. My shoulder eased open the door, then I collapsed into bed. My cat snuggled up close, and I placed a hand on her. "Stay with me. Please. Don't leave me. I'm not okay."

She purred near my ear. I didn't order the game to put myself to sleep. I did it all by myself, listening to her purrs as I lost consciousness.

The night *they* attacked always left me shaking the morning after. I hated everything about *them*. Who were *they*? Why did *they* try to attack me? My sanity reached fifty percent, and I would need it. Because I only had four days to complete my to-do list, and I hated when the shadows inside the house scared me.

I stumbled into the kitchen. No bloody footprints covered the carpet as I checked the calendar. The rain cartoon was on the day *they* arrived. I could work with that.

The woman on the phone dove right into the chores, so I watched them get written out on the paper above me.

Repair all damages caused by them

Make glass

Strengthen the fence around the house and greenhouses

Upgrade carport

Purchase third article of cleaning clothing

Build a bridge to collect sand

There it was. The order to build the bridge. Whatever was on the other side of that river, the alien overlords wanted me to reach it. Would they tell me what that bush spider monster was? Would it hurt me?

A few steps outside, I saw blinking red words above the greenhouse.

Danger

Must be fixed or greenhouse will be destroyed in next attack

0/15 glass

It meant I had four days to make glass to repair the greenhouse or get it far enough along that *they* wouldn't make the glass break worse. If it broke completely, I would probably have to build it from the ground up. A time-consuming endeavor, no doubt. Considering I had not completed a to-do list yet since they'd become weekly things, I needed to get sand soon.

I did my morning routine, making sure to not forget to switch out the clothes on the sewing machine for upgrades. My farming outfit was buffed, and the sewing machine was now working on my animal care. I wore my logging and building outfits so much that I might have to start those upgrades towards the evening. The second floor at night made me nauseous, though. If I slipped up there fast, then came back down, it should be fine. Totally fine.

It was harder to grow things in a broken greenhouse. I needed to build that bridge soon and hope monsters wouldn't pour into my house to get me. No, thank you.

Since I had devoured so much soup yesterday, I spent an hour cooking more. I stayed near the fire as I chopped down trees to repair the damage to the fence. A reddish-black slime shimmered on the spikes. I averted my eyes, stuffing new boards into the fence, and the slime vanished. After a few more resources, I repaired the fence. The first resource it required to strengthen it was firewood. It was nice the repairs didn't require bricks or stones. I secretly cursed myself for having that thought as I placed the last firewood into it. The alien overlords were listening. I waited patiently for the next material.

0/15 stone blocks

"Seriously? You couldn't make it more obvious that you read my thoughts?"

After my initial annoyance, I let out a defeated groan. I might have to focus on the fence before the bridge. I could not get attacked by *them*, ever. Even *them* trying to attack had left me a complete mess.

Part of the day required the mind-numbing monotony of carrying stones from the riverbank to the house. I was close to lifting two at a time without losing stamina. I sensed it in my arms. Out of curiosity, I checked the progress chart and figured that level twenty in building was what I needed to hit.

Once I had fifteen stones, I broke them up. I stuffed ten broken stones into the upgraded tool and glanced at the hazy sky. It was barely afternoon. I could switch them out tonight and get another batch going before I went to sleep.

I collected the food by the fire when the words above the pit nabbed my attention.

0/10 bricks

I had finally reached level 10 in cooking. I added the firepit upgrade to the list of things that weren't technically my chores but made me curious.

The stone blocks were being created as I replenished my stamina, taking a moment to acknowledge that even after all that cooking, I was eating a lot of food. The greenhouse, broken as it was, wasn't growing vegetables fast enough to meet my demand. If I couldn't rely on my greenhouse, I'd have to lean on Daisy and my fishing.

As I made my way back to the river, I mulled over my plan. The next priority was glass. My veggies needed to return to producing fast. It took a day to make glass, which I also assumed meant the tool could run while I was sleeping, too.

As I approached the ghost of the bridge, I saw the words above it.

6/50 logs

My eyes traveled to the sandy bank, to where that monster lived. Maybe it only came out in the evening time like the wolf did. I pulled out my axe and started chopping. A bit of yellow dissolved with every thwack against the bark. As I chopped, I considered what the alien overlords were asking me to do. Building a bridge was on my list, so they had plans. But were these plans in my favor? They kept saying they were a neutral party. Would unbiased people ask someone to build a bridge next to the den of a bush spider? Besides, if they had to keep assuring me they were neutral, it probably meant they weren't. Or they were hiding something.

No, I refused to go down that road. I needed to finish my to-do list. It had not steered me wrong before. The only time the list failed me was when I didn't complete it. I could trust it. Right?

Chapter Twenty-Six

The Fear of Bridges

As the afternoon turned into early evening, I hesitated as I held a log over the bridge.

49/50 logs

Four logs remained on the ground from the last tree I cut down. Was I prepared to deal with the consequences of connecting to a monster land?

We will sell you the information about the other side for a price, if it helps ease your anxiety.

It always freaked me out when the alien overlords entered my mind whenever they wanted to. I hadn't heard from them in some time.

"How much?" I asked.

After a pause, numbers emerged.

-50.00

I hissed from what I was certain was physical pain. "Are you... open to negotiation, by any chance? Or... haggling?"

I love haggling

The words surprised me. I almost sensed excitement in the emotionless words.

"Negative fifty is more than I've ever spent on anything in the game. I'm willing to spend negative fifteen."

-45.00.

This information is rare

I chewed the inside of my cheek. "Negative twenty."

-40.00

This was because I had gotten ridiculously excited that one time when knowledge was cheap. I knew that would return to haunt me.

"Negative twenty-five."

-37.00

I mentally braced myself. "Negative thirty?"

-37.00

That was as low as they'd go, yet it was still so high. I didn't have that many points right now. I would have to take these logs back and cut two of them into boards to get that much, plus a little extra.

We'd let you dip into the hole for this.

If you choose to spend more than you have, you may purchase nothing until you return to a positive sum.

I pursed my lips. "Part of haggling is knowing the person you're negotiating with can't actually read your thoughts."

We cannot turn off our access to your mind.

Must monitor your constant ideas and movements.

I closed one eye and studied the canopy of trees. "That's really unsettling, you know."

Apologies

My sister will not let me lie to ease your discomfort.

The other eye snapped open at that, and I stared at the hazy sky, trying not to feel anything. I remembered why I didn't like it when the alien overlords chimed in. "You... can lie?"

I can. My sister cannot. Since we are working together, we keep each other neutral to—

Someone removed the words before I could finish reading them. As quickly as they vanished, new ones came.

Apologies. My brother spoke of things he should not. I had to stop him from tampering with the game. -35.00 is our final offer. I am incapable of going lower for the information you seek.

All the moisture in my mouth evaporated. A part of my soul screamed from the depths as I suppressed a shiver.

"Are there... only two of you?" I was probing for something I wasn't sure I wanted the answer to.

No other reply floated in my vision. I was too scared to think about the implications. A brother and sister, no doubt on a different plane of existence. Alien.

"And you're... a neutral party?" I asked again.

The letters moved around to create new words.

When we work together to keep each other in check, yes.

How much of that could I believe? They had to know I didn't trust them. I remembered the voices I had heard after *they* attacked me. There must be only two. Male and female. Brother and sister. My alien overlords. Beads of sweat appeared on my forehead. Would they erase my memory of this moment? They had that power. It was also distressing to me. Words materialized, and I braced myself for what they'd reveal.

-35.00

Y/N

The dryness in my mouth moved to my throat as I swallowed. I mentally chose yes because of my inability to speak. This knowledge might ease my fears.

Might.

They downloaded information into my brain, and a list of phrases began scrolling through my vision.

There are monsters of varying levels on the south side of the river

Traveling there is dangerous, as your weapons can only kill the most basic of creatures

The monsters might leave you alone; they might not

Depends on how far into the forest you go

The monsters will not move across the bridge and follow you home

They know it is wolf territory, and the smaller creatures fear the beast

The stronger monsters can kill the wolf if they wanted, but they don't, simply because they have no interest in doing so

Nothing on your side intrigues them enough

Besides, if those higher-level beings desired to cross the river, they wouldn't need a bridge

The information was done, and I was left on my knees, hugging myself tightly. I had a balance of -26.84 dopamine points, and I tried not to think about how that reflected on my state of mind. I didn't feel happiness right now. This world was about to get larger, and I rejected the idea of exploring any of it. Whatever my alien overlords had in store for me, I prepared to do it with only a sprinkling of trust. The bridge seemed legit, and I wanted it to be so. As long as I didn't wander too far into the other side of the river. Like they even needed to warn me about that. Monsters lived there. I had a hard enough time with a wolf. And *them*. And ghosts.

With all this information swirling in my mind, I stumbled to my feet and put the last log in for the bridge. Creatures wouldn't cross this in droves to eat me. That was all the knowledge I needed.

The log entered, and an unfinished crossway of mostly logs formed.

0/20 boards

Right. I'd had the impression I wouldn't need more materials, but the game thought differently.

It always felt dark in this area of the woods, no matter the time of day. Clearing a path from the river to the house sounded more enticing as the sun started to leave. I had enough energy to chop one log and stuck the boards into the bridge. Then, I carried a single mound of clay back home. No point in taking the journey without it meaning something.

Once the clay was in the storage room, I ate a fried egg, getting half my stamina back. With sunlight leaving the sky, I realized the wolf timer had a good two hours more than what I expected it to be. The beast wouldn't be here for a long while. That would be amazing to have more time, because I only had three more days left. If I had stayed outside instead of listening to the paranormal activity, then that, too, would be fantastic.

I placed the finished stone blocks into the main fence and put five more broken stones in the tool. Hopefully, that would be it, but the bridge proved I couldn't be certain. It was getting dark as I pulled out my flashlight.

Wait. My flashlight. It had died yesterday. Did I dare work in a thick forestry area without a working light? It might be okay if I didn't stay out long. I wouldn't cross the bridge without it, though. Not at night. Not with my imagination.

Inside the carport, I opened the drawer full of rusted batteries. After snatching a decayed cylinder, I pressed it and the flashlight together, but nothing happened.

"Come on. It works for building things."

Alright, time to not use game logic. I unscrewed the top, then flipped it over so the batteries tumbled into my palm. In the fading red sunset, I saw these were in the same corroded shape as the ones in the drawer. I guess the flashlight drained them until it looked like this.

"That's not... flashlights don't..."

Did I really want to have a conversation with those alien overlords about the logic of this place? I abandoned the carport and checked the clipboard. Maybe I could buy more. After a careful search through the pages, I found nothing. If all the batteries came from that drawer, perhaps upgrading the carport would give me answers.

I was losing daylight. Three logs were out there, and I had stamina to burn. The wolf wouldn't come for a while. I returned to the river in the swiftly fading sunlight, found the logs and broke them into boards. It didn't take too long. After placing everything in the bridge, I waited for something else to show up. The sheen racing across the bridge was easier to see than the structure itself. I blinked, staring at the dark sandy bank.

Yes, I'd said I wouldn't cross this at night. Yes, my imagination would undoubtedly get the better of me. Yes, I would regret this.

But if I could bring five bags of sand back?

No, there was no point. The stone blocks were already in the tool. If I couldn't place them in until tomorrow morning at the earliest, why bother? I had plenty of time to return during the day.

The sand was right there, though. At the foot of the bridge. I wouldn't have to go far. *They* weren't coming for three more days. If nothing happened, I would be at full sanity *tomorrow*.

Could I do it? Could I be brave? To prove something to myself? Have the courage to walk over to a land of monsters without a flashlight to get some sand?

I didn't answer, because my feet were already on the boards, crossing the river. Despite how much the information had cost, it helped me not feel as scared. I was still terrified out of my mind, but I wasn't a sobbing mess. Big difference.

The closer I got to the sand, the quicker I traveled across the bridge. The wolf wouldn't arrive for another hour and a half. I had loads of time.

As soon as I reached the bridge's edge, an invisible wall stopped me. My heart almost imploded when words emerged. They glowed because it was so dark.

Entering Monster Territory

Still wish to enter?

Y/N

The moment I said yes, my feet became unstuck, and I stumbled off the bridge. Then something changed in the corner of my vision. Instead of sanity, I had a health bar with a red heart next to it. The difference between the short health bar and my lengthy stamina made me nervous. I wouldn't survive here long. All the more reason to get working. I dropped to my knees, and a small sack emerged in my fist as I shoved sand into it. The hair on my arms stood straight up as I finished the first bag and filled another.

A screech echoed through the forest. It seemed far away, but it made my blood turn to ice. This side was way more active than mine. Monkeys chattered and screamed at each other. Bushes rustled, hiding monsters beneath. Nocturnal birds flew overhead. It was loud; it was terrifying. And if all the noises ever went completely still, I would drop everything and sacrifice all my stamina to run home.

The bridge was right there. If the sun were up, I'd be sitting in its shadow. I was safe. No beasts would follow me home, and the bigger creatures weren't interested in trying.

My eyes darted around in the darkness as I began my fourth bag of sand. I was fine. In fact, I was so fine, I said nothing out loud. Talking to myself, even quietly, meant I wasn't okay. Because I wasn't. Talking out loud, I mean. Therefore, I was alright because I remained silent. That would be stupid, come to think of it. Why would I talk to myself in a forest full of monsters? I've never done that before. Just in a house of ghosts.

Once the fifth bag was filled, I steadied myself as the trees echoed with noise. I lifted two bags, ready to spare the stamina drain it would take, when I realized that this was exactly what I could carry. I didn't question it. My feet moved to the bridge's edge, and I dropped the bags before retrieving the next two. Then the final one. I stayed on the bridge as I walked back and forth, carrying bags of sand to drop them at the edge. I was about to step off when everything froze.

Entering Wolf territory
Still wish to enter?
Y/N

Once I mentally chose yes, my health points vanished and my sanity bar returned. I dropped to the ground, with a good forty-five minutes until the wolf came. It was pitch dark. A giggle escaped me, and I tried to stifle my laughter. I did it! I had crossed this bridge with my sand and made it to the other side completely fine.

Sure, it was a sandy bank close to the structure, but considering how frightened I was and how much I thought I couldn't do this, I'd done it, anyway! I stopped stifling my laughter and let myself giggle. Euphoria filled me as I carried two bags back to my home.

It was dark. The house was already being haunted, and I didn't have to listen to it. Not only that, but I had also done something really hard, and I was proud of myself for it.

Once the five bags were safely tucked away in my storage unit, I glanced at the tool. It would keep cooking the stone blocks until halfway through the night. Which meant as soon as the morning hit, I could start glass. Finally.

This was a win today. After so long figuring out how to get sand, I'd gotten it. To celebrate, I pulled out my to-do list and saw it crossed off at the very bottom.

Repair all damages caused by them
Make glass
Strengthen the wall around the house and greenhouses

Upgrade carport

Purchase third article of cleaning clothing

Build a bridge to collect sand

Now all I had to do was make the glass and finally repair the damages. Those two items had been on my to-do list for a long time.

The wolf timer blinked red, and I smiled as I entered the front of the house. I slipped inside and locked the doors before entering the bedroom. My eyes didn't wander over to any reflective surfaces, nor did I focus on the muffled sounds from the second floor. I simply walked into my home and collapsed onto the bed.

It wasn't until I mentally chose sleep that I realized I had called this place mine.

Chapter Twenty-Seven
Shattered Glass

My morning routine was done with a healthy dose of adrenaline. The first thing I did, even before realizing I was still in my nightgown, was change the stone blocks with the five bags of sand. Once it started, I winced. Would I regret using up an entire day to make glass? I should have waited to see if the fence required any more resources.

The words above the greenhouse blinked red, being an obnoxious pull on my anxiety. Now that I was making glass, I was confident I'd have it partially fixed by the time *they* came so they wouldn't destroy it.

I placed the finished stone blocks into the fence, waiting for my new instructions.

0/5 shattered glass

My lips pursed in annoyance. True, it worked out great that the thing I needed was already in the tool. I assumed I had to break it with a pickaxe. It just also meant I would use all five panes and put off fixing the greenhouses *again*. I'd have to go across the bridge to get some more sand. It would be better to do that in the daylight. I was short on stones to upgrade the carport, and what with the chipped brick wall, I wouldn't be surprised if the carport asked for those, too. No harm in stockpiling some clay in my storage area. I fed Daisy and gathered an egg, then entered the blinking greenhouse to water the plants. Tomorrow, the tomatoes would finally be ready. I wasn't sure about the potatoes. I checked myself the moment I thought that, because honestly, they still grew in four days, despite the damage.

I switched out the last of my animal care clothes on the sewing machine and decided to upgrade the logging ones. I placed my hard hat and saw it flatten so the needle could go around it.

This was a day of monotonous gathering, and since the greenhouse wouldn't get fixed today, I wanted to save what food I had. Therefore, I watched my stamina and didn't push it. My first order of business was to gather sand.

The noises of monsters hit me again as soon as I mentally agreed to enter their territory. A smaller health bar replaced my sanity as soon as I crossed the bridge. Sure, it wasn't as scary in the daytime, but I was far more visible to these creatures, too.

"At least they don't have an anxiety meter. I'd destroy that every single day." The sunlight made me stupidly brave, so I just muttered that to myself on a side full of monsters. I gathered sand while constantly looking around. I was pushing my luck as the pile of bags grew. If I was serious about this, I needed enough to replace the fifteen panes of glass in the greenhouse, and then some extra, for good measure. The less I came over here, the better.

Once I had ten small sacks, I moved them to the wolf's side, then kept gathering more. Twenty would do it. The monster area was loud, but I still felt like the nighttime was louder. Some monsters must be nocturnal.

I grabbed the last two bags on the bank when something rustled in the deeper forest. My heart rate spiked, and I booked it onto the bridge, not minding that I was sacrificing stamina for this. I was making more noise than necessary, but I made it to the other side and hid. Another bush spider monster scuttled near the clearing. It didn't have eyes, so I wasn't sure if it saw me, but my fear kept me hiding.

It can't go over the bridge, I said in my mind, sweat forming on my hairline.

The creature returned to the forest, and I slumped against the logs in relief. I had twenty bags of sand. That would last me for... until I fixed the greenhouse.

For the rest of the day, I moved the sand into my storage unit, then gave a mini celebration when I realized I could carry two clumps of clay at a time without it hurting my stamina. It was a long afternoon of carrying resources, but a productive one. I got things done. It felt *good.*

I considered my next move. The brick tool worked at night now. Would I put in five more bags of sand, or ten broken stones? It was a tough choice. I disliked the idea of losing half a night when the stone blocks finished cooking. It all hung on whether shattered glass was the final piece in strengthening the fence.

When I had stored enough resources, I let out a sigh and admitted to myself I should experiment. I currently had -26.84 total points. Once I upgraded the carport, I'd need clothes. That meant I needed to pay off my debt.

I grabbed a clump of clay and dropped it in the dumpster, acquiring +5.00. Not bad, but considering how monotonous it was to get it, it was easier to farm dopamine from boards or firewood. I then lowered a stone into the dumpster. That too gave me +5.00 My debt was now -16.84.

Another experiment begged to be done. I broke a stone with my pickaxe before dumping it. +3.00 points. Alright, so an intact one was better. Sometime soon I'd have to discover what a stone block gave me. I was already planning on making clay to bake in the sun tomorrow with what I stored. I might relinquish a baked clay for research. And I *might* sacrifice a brick, too. But as of now, I needed those resources. With two more full days until *they* came, that experimentation would come after I completed my to-do list.

The hard hat was done, which made me think the sewing machine didn't run all day. I wanted to cut down some trees, anyway. I put the boards toward upgrading my storage unit. Extra room could only help, especially in my endeavor to stockpile resources and to fix the greenhouse to produce food faster.

The tool timer faded, and I immediately dropped my axe to run over there. I pulled the glass out, still cool to the touch, as I set it on the concrete. It took only one whack for it to change from *glass* to *shattered glass.*

If I'd spent most of the spring cleaning a musty old house and a dirty carport to get cut by broken glass now, I'd be angry. But something instinctual happened when my bare fingers reached toward the broken shards that forced me to be delicate. As I placed the last shard to strengthen the fence, I held my breath, waiting. The light danced over it. It was finished!

After taking a deep breath, I considered my next step. I had two days and two nights. It would be weird if bricks *weren't* required to upgrade the carport. In that case, it would be easier to make glass while I slept. I would need to spend the morning shaping clay mounds into bricks and baking them in the sun, and the tool could create more stone blocks while that happened.

I placed five more bags of sand to cook through the night and spent the remaining time cutting more trees down for a bigger storage unit.

Before going to bed, I checked my to-do list for an added dash of dopamine.

Repair all damages caused by them

~~Make glass~~

~~Strengthen the wall around the house and greenhouses~~
Upgrade carport
Purchase third article of cleaning clothing
~~Build a bridge to collect sand~~

Two more days of work, and I could actually finish my chores for the first time since they'd stopped being daily requirements. The excitement of crossing things off almost made it hard to sleep before I realized this was a game, and I happily asked to be forced to rest.

I was on such a roll. My stride had more confidence, and I wasn't as nervous. Then I put the five panes in the greenhouse and received five shattered glass in return.

It didn't completely break my spirits, but I hated that I had never considered this. It made sense using actual logic. After all, one would have to remove the broken shards to put in new ones. I hadn't thought about testing it out. There was nothing left to do but tuck this information away and keep going.

The words above the greenhouse didn't mark it as 5/15 like the other upgrades had done. Instead, it showed 0/10, and the red blinking finally stopped. I hoped that would prevent the greenhouse's destruction in the next attack. That at least was some good news. I was not ready to build this from scratch.

After stuffing ten broken stones in the tool to make blocks, I moved on to making twenty-five clay bricks to bake in the sun. Tomorrow it would rain, so this was the only day I could sunbake them. While I waited, I resumed cutting logs as I got closer to upgrading my storage.

The second the timer vanished, I shoved blocks into the carport.

0/5 logs

Okay, easy enough. That equaled one tree. I did as requested, watching my stamina.

0/10 boards

Also manageable. I chopped a few until the sunbaked clay finished. I stuffed the tool with fifteen pieces, the most it could hold. If the carport needed it, I would have it ready.

Once I filled the request for boards, the next resource was 0/15 firewood. I created quite a wide circle of cleared-out trees around the house.

Once the firewood was done, I got my moment of validation.

0/20 bricks

Semi-validation. The tool could only fit fifteen. It was fine. This was part of the game. I couldn't have everything go my way.

"The wolf dying would be nice, though," I said to the sky.

If I required five more bricks, it would be stupid not to make a full batch of fifteen. Working non-stop throughout the day made me realize something as the sun sank below the trees. I wouldn't finish this to-do list. Again. If repairing the greenhouse was the only thing left, then yes, but the carport needed upgrading, too.

I finished putting the bricks into the carport and placed five bags of sand in the tool.

"Maybe I'll complete the next list when I don't have to make so much glass."

This was the final week of spring/summer, and it didn't look like I would get a break. After tonight, I had four more days before *they* attacked again, and three days after that. Those last days all had rain cartoons on them, as well as one on tomorrow. That would be hard. I *really* needed my greenhouse to produce normally to cook as much soup as possible.

A part of me didn't expect another attack from *them* so soon. Even though *they* had only got me once, every time *they* tried to get me was a drain on my wellbeing.

"Why can't I forget when *they* attacked me? If you're so keen on erasing memories that distress me, why aren't you taking *that* one? You already mentioned it was a miscalculation, so why isn't it gone?"

No answer.

The day was over, but when the next day happened seconds after I hit the pillow, I didn't feel restful. I would rather wake up unrested if it meant no dreams.

In the pouring rain, I put five more panes into the greenhouse and received just two shattered glass in return. Some sections of the greenhouse had been missing, so I understood why I had less shattered glass. I was just annoyed when the game had realistic logic. Though it was a relief to wait only two days for tomatoes.

If I didn't need the additional stamina, I refused to waste my soup, so I suffered in the cold while doing my morning routine. I shook the entire time and lost small fragments of yellow as I gathered eggs and farmed, but I was reluctant to touch my stockpile of food. I placed thirteen baked clay items in the tool to cook. It wasn't a full fifteen, but I would still have extra.

And that was it. My chores now waited on the bricks. Once I finished the carport upgrade, I'd make another batch of glass. I was so close to crossing off everything on my to-do list. The glass would be complete when *they* arrived tonight, but I didn't want to be out here then. A part of me hoped that for the next list, I could finish it. I was confident the greenhouse would be ready in a day or two. That would be *such* a relief.

I decluttered everything on the house's first floor, wiped down the walls, and cleaned off the tables and cabinets. I would have to declutter the two other rooms on the second story, but I didn't know what to do with that locked room. Every time I thought about it, a dark feeling hit my heart. That place remained locked for a reason, and I wasn't curious enough to figure out why. Not when I'd seen that blood trickling out of the bottom of the door.

Since the pink room was done, I focused on decluttering the landing area and clearing out the hallway. I fell back into my pattern of stuffing everything on the front porch. Killie checked on me every once in a while, and I gave her all the love and attention she would let me give her. I seriously needed to make sure that cat never ran away from me. She was my lifeline.

It was almost time to check on the bricks. I used some stamina to finish decluttering the small room under the stairs before eating a bowl of soup to be warm enough to dump trash in the pouring rain.

As I dropped the stuff, I watched my dopamine points. It was a slow yet steady trickle.

-13.84

-13.80

-13.74

-13.68

I could, of course, drop two boards in the dumpster and be done with it, but I sort of liked the slow and steady climb back to the positive. Perhaps I was weird that way. This made me happy and calm, and that was an emotion I needed right now.

The last bag tumbled into the dumpster, and I checked on the bricks. They were almost done, but they'd probably finish a good twenty minutes after my heat timer ran out. I used the time to declutter the hallway from the kitchen to the bedroom. Hopefully, cleaning the second floor would give me another boost to my bars. I remembered the last time *they* had come. *They* hadn't broken the fence and hunted me, yet I'd remained curled on the ground, clinging to a fragment of sanity.

For the next little while, I stacked bags of collected junk onto the porch. Decluttering the green and blue rooms would undoubtedly take days of solid work, even if they were smaller than the pink room. I'll admit stuffing an entire mattress into a bag was a fun twist of physics.

Once I had a collection of sacks outside on the cement, I ate one of my last two potato soups and walked to the tool. I placed bricks in the carport, then waited. After it signaled its completion, my shoulders relaxed. Despite wanting to run inside right then to see what the upgrade did, I used my heat timer to put the rest of the sunbaked clay in the storage area, then started five more bags of sand. Another attack by *them* tonight would hurt the greenhouse, but I was confident I could get my veggies growing normally soon. I then dumped the remaining junk into the dumpster. My total hit -12.94, which was a boost of dopamine in itself.

I then ran into the carport, excited to see what the upgrade had given me.

Chapter Twenty-Eight
The Power of Lilac

Words covered my vision, and information filled my brain. It was a little overstimulating, so I tried instead to focus on one thing.

At the back of the carport was a large workbench, newly done up and varnished. I focused on the side with a charging station.

Battery charge

Can hold up to two batteries

Charges for 12 hours

Nice. Good. Great, even. I snatched a couple of rusted cylinders from the drawer and eased them into the black charger. A green light glowed, which was weird, but I wouldn't question it. I glanced at the other side of the workbench and read the instructions.

Paint making station

Room must first be decluttered, and the walls must be wiped off

Primer must be applied to room, will take half a day

Once primer is done, you may choose a color for the walls

Paint will take ten minutes to finish

I tried to hide my smile, but failed. Paint! I could paint rooms now!

"So, um, what about the paneling? Is that... magically leaving?"

Yes, once you choose a room

"And crown molding? You'll let me do that around the walls, right? Because this is a turn of the century home?"

A longer pause, and I waited, dancing on the balls of my feet.

We'll see

It was enough. No doubt the floors were something else, but getting rid of the paneling made me excited! I wanted to pick the paints now, but my entire body froze as I moved closer.

Must wear level three cleaning clothes to use this equipment.

"Oh, right."

In that case, this debt needed to go. With a sigh, I cut up some logs and shoved them in the dumpster until I had 14.94 total dopamine points. Paint was too exciting. The wolf timer still had a good hour left. It was hard to tell the time when it was raining.

I went to the clipboard, checking my progress.

Farming level 14

Cleaning level 16

Logging level 19

Cooking level 10

Building level 21

Animal Care level 13

I was building a lot. I supposed it made sense. Logging and building were still leveling up close together. I was close to buying a third level of clothing for farming. My morning routine tomorrow might push me over the edge to level 15.

Time to focus. I needed to see that paint! I mentally chose the gloves, apron, and recently purchased blue dress to figure out how to paint. Also on my body were my steel-toed boots and hard hat. Sometimes the combination of my clothes made me chuckle.

My heat timer was gone, but the run from the house to the carport was not that bad. The carport gave the same protection as the front porch, since a newly upgraded roof over my head protected me from the pounding rain. I approached the paint station, and more words filled my vision.

View model house?

Y/N

"Sure!" I was too curious and wanted to try out everything.

A three-dimensional image of the house popped up on the bench. My eyes widened as I studied it. Was this the level of technology I saw in movies? I tried touching it, smiling as the image followed my finger. I pinched it and watched as it zoomed in. It was a perfect replica. Even the books and the VHS tapes were all there. Every room on the bottom floor had a slight green glow, whereas the second story was red except for the locked room, which was grayed out.

Choose room

Prepare primer

Give half a day for the primer to dry

Once it is done, you may choose a color for the walls

My fingers tapped together in pure joy. I'd be clapping, but I didn't want to alert anything out there in the woods. An enormous smile crossed my face. This was one of those moments when I hated how I was in a time crunch. I wanted to spend *hours* choosing the color. I had woken up to the red dawn light on the weird green since I got here. Did this have a soft lilac? Ugh, I *loved* lilac in bedrooms. It was so nice and inviting and...

I glanced at my wolf timer. Ten minutes. Stupid time constraint. I had so many ideas as I touched the bedroom on the house replica. "I don't know if I'm a swearing girl, but god*damn,* I need to have lilac as an option."

Must paint primer first

Primer costs -7.00

Once primer is done, colors cost nothing

A quiet scream of frustration leaked out of me as I glanced at my dopamine points. I didn't have enough. I wanted to do this now. To change the rooms instead of cleaning them. And I *craved* that color in the beautiful, tall bedroom I slept in.

I needed to experiment anyway. I sprinted into the storage unit with eight minutes on my wolf timer, grabbed a brick, and dropped it in the dumpster.

+15.00

I squealed and returned to the carport.

"Bedroom, please! Primer on bedroom!"

The model of the house flickered into view again. A section of the bottom floor turned a solid blue color with that same sand timer I assumed was six hours long since it didn't show numbers. By tomorrow morning, I would see the catalog of colors. I tried to prime the kitchen, but got an error message instead.

Primer can only be applied to one room at a time

"Fine. Bedroom it is."

I could use the bedroom, though, right? My mood deflated. In all my excitement and giddiness, I forgot *they* were attacking tonight.

The wolf timer began blinking, and I winced. I rushed out of the carport and onto the front porch. I pulled out my list to see how close I was to finishing it.

Repair all damages caused by them
~~*Make glass*~~
~~*Strengthen the wall around the house and greenhouses*~~
~~*Upgrade carport*~~
~~*Purchase third article of cleaning clothing*~~
~~*Build a bridge to collect sand*~~

"I will finish my chores next time." I placed the paper in my pocket as I reflected on the next six hours.

"I'll be okay. Keep thinking happy thoughts. Like a lilac bedroom. It'll be gorgeous."

Nice lilac walls. The paneling would be gone. Then this place could reclaim some of its old charm. I had plenty of happy thoughts to ward off the ghosts in the house, who threatened my sanity. It would work. I would stay mentally strong.

Underneath the computer desk in the living room, I curled into the tightest ball possible, sobbing weakly as *they* left. *Their* echoing thud sent fear stabbing into my heart. I clutched my chest as if that could calm my erratic heartbeat.

I wanted to believe they might change with this attack, but it had been the same. Thoughts of that lilac bedroom made no difference. The ghosts, the giggling, the shrieking. *Them*, the thudding, the bellowing. I had a little more than a shard of sanity left, and I couldn't find the desire to climb to my feet and go to bed, even though sleep was everything I needed. I would experience this in another four days. A physical body could not handle this again so soon. Four more days, then three more after that. It exhausted me just thinking about it.

Once again, I did not get a memory orb. How did I stop the attacks? Despite how excited I was for the paint, I would give it all up to leave this horrible game for good. How could I figure out clues when my alien overlords weren't giving them to me anymore?

Would you like to be forced into sleep?

Y/N

Sometimes I forgot I didn't need to be in bed to sleep. A part of me rebelled against the idea of sleeping under this desk, but *they* had drained all the energy in my body without breaking the fence.

Killie climbed into my arms, purring. I didn't care if I saw a ghost. My entire frame shrank, and the thought of climbing to my feet made me nauseous. Why did *they* successfully drain me every time? Why did the ghosts terrify me? I was doing so well. I was close to completing that to-do list, and I had such excitement about the new abilities I earned. It was all gone now, and I had little energy to stand up and go to bed.

"If there's no lilac..." I whispered with all the strength I had left, "...I will hurt you..."

With that, I ordered the game to force me into a dreamless sleep as I curled under the desk.

When I opened my eyes and the red light of dawn filled the bedroom, I saw the white primer all over. I almost ran straight for the carport, but I stopped at the front porch.

"To-do list, Quinn." I walked inside and shut the door. "You will finish your chores for once, and it'll be this time."

As I passed the desk, I acknowledged feeling a lot better than last night. My sanity was at fifty percent, and I had all my stamina back. If the carport hadn't been so tempting, I might have stayed in bed a little longer, but I was ready for the day.

I grabbed the phone, pressed number one, and listened to the woman while I watched the list being written.

Repair all damages caused by them

Strengthen the fence

Prime and paint three rooms on first floor

Upgrade cooking fire

Purchase third article of clothing for farming

Plant lettuce and carrots

"Oh, some new produce!" I tore off the to-do list.

This got me excited. In fact, judging by my adrenaline this morning, I could have the entire first floor primed and painted. I had already finished the bedroom, after all. A job requesting me to upgrade the cooking fire made me happy, too. What would that give me? Would it help me create more complex recipes besides soup, cooked fish, and eggs? I hoped so.

I walked out the back door to see how much the greenhouse had been damaged in *their* attack.

0/7 glass

Not bad at all. Yes, *they* had left me shaking and scared last night, but I had four days to prepare for *them* again. And double plus, I wouldn't have to build the greenhouse from the ground up.

"I will finally finish my to-do list. When I complete it, I will go to sleep an hour earlier with Killie snuggled next to me!" I headed toward the carport. "But first I need to make sure lilac is an option."

It was. My alien overlords listened to me! I had never mentally chosen something so quickly. I paid the dopamine points to prime the entertainment room. Maybe a really nice forest green for that whole rectangle space. I tried not to think about what it would look like with the brown carpet, because I would tear that up as soon as the game allowed me to. I needed to see that beautiful hardwood floor! Until then, I had plans, and forest green would be so cozy. If only the horror movies and books would disappear.

While I was still in the carport, I checked on the charging batteries. When I'd put them in the charger last night, they were corroded. Now they looked like normal batteries. They should finish charging by later this morning, and I would have to remember to get them. If not, it might be an added feature of my morning routine.

I retrieved the finished glass and placed it into the greenhouse. Now it read 0/2 glass to fix, and my bags of sand were gone. The tomato plants grew faster, though. If anything, I would stockpile more food. With it raining every day for those last three days, I wouldn't be able to cook over the pit. I hoped I would have enough room to store it all.

My morning routine was finished by complimenting Daisy on a beautiful egg before placing it in the storage and checking my progress. As expected, farming hit level 15. After dropping firewood in the dumpster, I purchased my third article of clothing. I passed the tool on the way back to the clipboard. Every moment it wasn't making something made me anxious. So many times I would be at a standstill because I was waiting for bricks or stone blocks or glass. Having it empty felt wasteful.

I bought a red checkered button-up shirt for my new farming collection and smiled when I put on my farmer overalls and straw hat. I then paused when I heard the distinct click of a lock before it fell to the ground.

Congratulations! Second greenhouse now unlocked.

With so many decisions to be made, I froze. I could almost feel the deadline coming. The fence was always my priority, and bricks and stone blocks might be required. Yet another greenhouse just opened up! What decision should I make?!

Fence. I did not want to get hurt by *them*. Yes, I had new produce to plant, but if I had them planted and watered before going to bed, they would grow at the same rate as if I planted them right now.

With my axe, I took the twenty minutes to chop down some trees into logs and boards to set into the fence and await my next order. 0/15 stone blocks. I could do that. I already had enough stones in the storage unit; I'd just have to do them in batches. Once the tool had ten blocks, I pulled out my list to help me decide. Perhaps I should work on the fire. The firepit requested 0/10 bricks. I had only seven in storage, so I needed more. I also wanted to carry as much sand as I could for glass, because if I had to go to the monster side, I wanted it to be worth it.

As the tool worked its magic, I explored the new greenhouse, thinking about the produce that would be in here. Did lettuce grow from seeds? Despite how many farming games I played, I had no knowledge of how to grow it.

This second unit looked slightly bigger than the first. I pushed open the door and saw that this greenhouse, too, was disorganized, with six broken soil beds instead of three. It wouldn't take me long, but I couldn't plant the produce until I had this place cleared out, and the boxes fixed. I gathered items I knew were junk while saving two more bags of fertilizer.

It took a couple of hours to dump the clutter and rebuild the soil beds. Enough that I checked the carport to see the entertainment room had less than half of its timer. I purchased the seeds from the clipboard and planted them. It was strange being in an intact greenhouse as I watered them. The lettuce and carrots grew, with little green leaves already poking out of the ground. Would I have to keep buying seeds, kind of like how I had to cut up a new potato? I honestly didn't know. The carrots weren't *that* expensive at .50 dopamine points, but it could be pricey after a while. It would depend on the carrot recipes.

Once it was all done, I still had plenty of time before the tool finished the stone blocks and the entertainment room got rid of the paneling. I went back to my original plan to make this a re-source-gathering day. It always took a while, even with carrying two at a time. I was burning through my resources, since the fence and upgrades used up my stockpile fast.

Tomorrow would be a ridiculously hot day. I might hold off on cooking food to gather all that clay instead. If my theories were right and a hotter sun made the clay bake faster, I wanted to form a nice collection of sunbaked rectangles.

As I got closer to the bridge, I pulled out my to-do list, beaming.

Repair all damages caused by them
Strengthen the fence
Prime and paint three rooms on first floor
Upgrade cooking fire
~~Purchase third article of clothing for farming~~
~~Plant lettuce and carrots~~

A half a day and I already had two items crossed off. By tonight, the sand would be in the tool and I'd have glass out tomorrow morning to finally repair the first greenhouse. I'd have the painting station start in the living room once the primer was done. Tomorrow, two more things would be checked off, with three more days to finish strengthening the wall and upgrading the fire.

"This is going so well!" I said to myself.

When I reached the bridge, I tucked the list into my pocket and glanced over at the other side of the river. A spider monster waited there. It turned fast when it heard my approach. It opened its mouth full of jagged teeth and sneered. Everything inside me froze.

I spoke *way* too soon.

Chapter Twenty-Nine
Killie's Judgement

Okay, okay, so I didn't *need* the sand yet. I still wanted to get as much clay as my storage unit would hold, as well as fifteen or twenty bags of sand. Maybe ten. I could plausibly do ten bags. Technically, I only needed five for a whole batch. Or two. Two bags to repair the greenhouse. And it wasn't required until tonight. It was nice to let the tool run while I slept.

It was decided. Clay first. I gathered some, watching the monster remain on its side of the bridge as I walked back to the house, trying not to imagine it tearing me to shreds. It was as high as my mid-calf. I could take it, right?

As I returned to the river, I hoped it would get bored and scuttle off. This was a bush spider monster, though. The only reason it would leave was if a bigger creature chased it away.

As the sun reached its peak, I focused on clay mounds. I shaped ten bricks to start baking them. I would have done more, but ten was all I had. It was time away from the river, and hopefully the monster would lose interest. When the stone blocks were finished, I placed them in the fence before making ten more.

I don't know why I put so much hope in that monster feeling bored. Despite it having no eyes, it could clearly see me and wasn't going anywhere. I wanted that sand. It was always on my mind, even as I got enough points to prime the living room. The monster might not be there tomorrow, but I couldn't wait that long. I needed sand to start in the tool tonight. It was this stupid time crunch coming back to haunt me. If no horrors or haunts plagued me, I would absolutely love to go at my own pace to make this house beautiful. But no. There had to be giggling ghost children and shrieking grandmas, as well as wolf creatures that could run on their hind legs and *them* that drained my energy. And now, a bush spider monster blocked me from getting the one resource to complete my list. If I weren't careful, that creature might alert more friends. It was living on a side covered with monsters, after all.

It had to be done. I had to attack that monster to collect sand, and I couldn't avoid it forever.

"Stupid game," I muttered to myself as my hands balled into fists. "Stupid, stupid realistic game. Why am I not making cucumber sandwiches for a lovely tea party with a bunch of NPCs?" I headed toward the river, my voice raising enough to let this out. "Pastries and cupcakes. Passing little jars of jams and marmalade for scones in my beautifully done up forest green living room. Sip tea with merchants as we talk trade. Better yet, where are all those NPCs I can romance?" I glared at the sky. "Where's my rugged logger eye candy? Or even a bookish nerd in the library down the street? Why can't I have *someone* to prepare a special cake or create a complex statue to win his heart? Get married to him so he can help around the farm? Make it so we keep the house beautiful and become the jewel of the town in the middle of nowhere. But noooo*oooo*oo." I held out the syllable in case the alien overlords weren't listening. "Somehow I'm stuck here, isolated and alone, except for all these stupid monsters that want to attack me."

I kicked a tree for good measure. It didn't sting, but I was also on the side of sanity, so my health points were unaffected. "Whoever thought of horror should die!"

Perhaps I was being harsh, but I saw no appeal in this whatsoever. Though the horror genre was old enough that the person who founded it might be dead already. Which meant I wasn't only harsh, but insensitive, too.

Despite my need to vent to the sky some more, I approached the bridge, and it was smarter to stay quiet. I wanted to do this well before sunset, because if I really was facing a spider monster, I'd rather do that in the daylight.

My breath remained in my lungs as I pulled out my axe and crept forward. I hid behind a tree before glancing around and realizing the monster was gone. I found myself with a quintessential horror of spiders. Which was worse? Seeing it, or knowing it was there before and not seeing it now?

If I wanted to survive, I needed to treat this as a trap. I kept my axe in my hand, gripping it as tightly as on the nights *they* attacked. I was pretty sure I created grooves in this handle by holding it this hard.

I placed one foot in front of the other as I moved across the bridge. The river masked most of the noise I made, but I was still in broad daylight. As soon as my sanity turned into health points, I sprinted toward the sand. I refused to lower my axe, so I took my time filling the first two bags, my eyes darting everywhere. I snatched the bags, ready to return, when something scuttled right behind me. The sacks slipped from my palm as I screamed and swung. The blade caught the spider monster, and it tumbled to the ground. I ran up to it, hollering as I slammed the axe down again and again and again.

The thing was a bleeding green pulp of shredded leaves and broken sticks, and I was still screaming at it, slamming my axe like it was alive and kicking. I stopped only when it was an unrecognizable blob in the sand. I backed away, panting.

"Right." I moved some strands of hair from my face. "Well... that did it."

In my overzealousness, I didn't count how many hits it took to kill the thing. I never wanted to know what it felt like to get hurt, so I made sure the monster never had a chance to touch me. I cleared my throat and grabbed my sacks, rushing toward the bridge, my limbs shaking. The monster might have buddies.

"The more sand I have now, the less likely I'll need to cross here again."

It was a mantra I repeated in my head as I packed two more bags. I started on a third when the entire forest grew still. My heart rate spiked as I dropped the partially filled sack.

"Nope."

I grabbed those two bags and booked it over the bridge. A monster screeched behind me, and I couldn't tell if it was close or far. Big or little. It was angry; that's all I knew. Four bags were more than enough. I never felt more thrilled when my health points turned into a sanity bar.

According to the timer, the wolf wanted to stay in the forest for a long time tonight. Perfect. I required all the minutes it would give me. Once the second batch of stone blocks finished later, I would put in the four bags of sand so they'd be complete in the morning.

In the dying sunlight, I entered my little clearing and studied the firepit. It needed 0/10 bricks, which I hoped to have a healthy supply of by the end of tomorrow. What I wanted to focus on was upgrading my storage in order to fit all those bricks and the extra produce I'd gather with a second greenhouse. I worked on cutting down logs for boards, stopping to transfer stone blocks from the tool into the fence before storing the rest.

Blocks were the last thing the fence needed, which I was relieved about. I would be protected, even if I never felt safe. I placed my hard-earned four bags of sand in the tool before chopping down trees to upgrade my storage. Much like the carport, I was certain this would ask for bricks, which meant I was doubly glad I was planning on baking those clay pieces tomorrow.

The storage unit read 86/100 boards when I entered the back door and locked it. I pulled out my to-do list.

Repair all damages caused by them
Strengthen the fence
Prime and paint three rooms on first floor
Upgrade cooking fire
Purchase third article of clothing for farming
Plant lettuce and carrots

The living room had finished priming! I should have started a new room! I glanced at my timer, seeing I had a minute and twenty seconds left with a half-full bar of blue.

"Do it, Quinn. Be brave. You killed a monster today." I grabbed my last two bundles of firewood from the storage unit and sprinted out the front door. "For the kitchen!" came my quiet battle cry.

The carport and the dumpster were close. I dropped the fire-wood without staying to acknowledge my dopamine points, then dashed to the paint station.

"Kitchen, kitchen, kitchen." I slapped my palm against the workbench, waiting for it to respond, watching my timer. Something glitchy happened. The timer counted down as normal, but as soon as it hit the minute mark and started blinking, it jumped to fifty-five seconds, then to forty seconds, before it dropped to zero. My heart stopped as I stared at it.

"Oh. I didn't realize..."

The wolf snarled right next to the carport, and my eyes grew large. Despite all of this, I double-checked to see the kitchen on the replica had turned blue and had a six-hour timer.

"M'kay," was all I said before I booked it out of there.

Claws scraped against the fence as I sprinted away. With a leap that should not be possible, the wolf sailed over the fence, the spine-snapping sound echoing across the lawn. My legs pumped as the house got closer. My brain was frozen, unable to think, which was a miracle.

That beast sprinted *fast*. Those two hind legs moved up behind me at an inhuman rate as I stumbled up the stairs, then shoved myself through the front door. I slammed it, locking it tight, gasping as the monster snarled again. It threw its body against a rotten pole. I panted, leaning against the door as I heard the wolf retreating. My brain unfroze as a million thoughts stormed into my head. It was crazy I had even succeeded, and I also never wanted to leave this house again.

It was stupid, and a learning experience. Especially with how close that beast got.

Something moved inside the house, and in a panic, I turned on my flashlight and shone it toward the movement. It was Killie, lying in the middle of the floor, thumping her tail from side to side as she looked at me with deep judgement. I didn't see the point of defending myself against my cat, but I couldn't help it. I pointed at my chest with a shaking finger.

"But did I die?"

She blinked, then blinked again before heaving herself up and walking toward the bedroom. I sighed, then followed her. The entire endeavor had made a chunk of sanity vanish, so I needed to wear my nightgown to get that back tomorrow. It was terrifying what I did. I might have lost all my blue, but I didn't. Tomorrow I'd be at seventy-five percent. The kitchen would be ready to paint in the morning. I doubted I would do anything so reckless again, however... if I *really* needed to....

Killie shot me another look as though reading my thoughts. It seemed paint made me reckless. What would happen when floors became an unlocked ability? I ran a finger between her ears.

"You still love me."

She responded by rubbing her back across my legs as she always did before jumping onto my bed. Killie had her own place in the corner, but she took it as more of a suggestion. I collapsed on the covers as my cat snuggled up to me, and I forced the game to let me sleep.

Chapter Thirty
New Recipes

My body relaxed in bed, not sore at all from the stress of last night. I had three full days until *they* attacked, and my to-do list was well on its way to completion. Despite the glass needing to be moved to the greenhouse, I took a moment to admire the bedroom walls. With all my excitement at painting them, I was too busy yesterday and hadn't gotten to appreciate them. Now I could. Lilac was the best color for bedrooms. It was a hill I would die on. I wondered how to strongly encourage those alien overlords to give me crown molding. And a small, yet beautiful light fixture. And a coffered ceiling. It would be exquisite.

No, I wouldn't ever stop appreciating these walls, but I had work to do. I walked out into the entertainment room to see the gorgeous forest green. Alluring, as long as I kept my eyes on the color and didn't compare it with the crusty carpet. In the corner was a bundle of paneling. That must have been leftovers from the walls. A similar collection sat next to the door. I should dump them, considering it was clutter.

The artificial ceiling tiles were gone, and it was the same height as in the bedroom. The forest green was a lovely color, but I definitely wanted to work on the light fixtures. Also, I wanted to paint the ceiling to not be so stark white.

"Coffered ceilings, guys." I let out a sigh. "It'll give some lines and definition to a blank canvas. Something right out of the eighteen hundreds. Or my version of that time period."

This old house was beautiful. Charming, even with the wall of horror novels and VHSs. The living room wasn't painted yet, but I imagined it with the same forest green. I gathered the paneling and took it outside. Today was a hot day, and it reminded me of that fact as I stepped into the heat. Sweat formed on me as I sacrificed a little stamina to drop the clutter into the dumpster. When I saw a huge +9.43 boost, it made my sacrifice worth it. So much, in fact, that I grabbed the other paneling and dumped it. +7.57. Nice! Altogether, I had a comfortable 25.94 total dopamine points. That would last me a bit.

In three bites, I ate my chilled tomato soup to give me fifteen minutes to do my morning routine. Killie was unaffected by the heat, so she zipped between the chicken coop and the carport. I took the glass and put two in the greenhouse and the rest in storage. I then pulled out my list just to make sure.

~~Repair all damages caused by them~~

~~Strengthen the fence~~
~~Prime and paint three rooms on first floor~~
Upgrade cooking fire
~~Purchase third article of clothing for farming~~
~~Plant lettuce and carrots~~

One chore with three days to complete it? This was *so* getting done. I considered buying Daisy another chicken friend, but I didn't want to do that until I knew how much space the storage room gave me once I upgraded it. I got to work making clay into rectangles and shoving thirty on the patio to bake. It took two more tomato soups to do it. Then, I used the rest of my timer to chop down trees to keep upgrading the storage unit. By the time it read 100/100 boards, I had five uncut logs left.

0/50 stone blocks

That was a lot. I tried to stick the logs inside the storage room floor, but after the second one it stopped me, another phrase telling me the room was too full. This did not bode well for how many bricks I made today. I grabbed all the finished bricks I had and placed them into the firepit to store them there, in a way. I took out ten more stones to clear up space in the storage unit. With a thwack, I broke them up and placed them in the tool. I could do a batch of fifteen bricks after these blocks and put the remaining resources in the cooking fire before tonight. Yet I still had so much to do to fit all the bricks I had just assembled into the storage room.

I had one more chilled tomato soup left. I was ready to declutter the second floor when the baked clay gave a sheen. My experimentation paid off. The hot day made the bricks finish in three hours instead of six. A nagging feeling said I would *have* to juggle what was in my storage to fit this all.

With a slight change of plans, I ate my final chilled tomato soup before gathering all the baked clay and setting them inside the covered back porch. I placed the last four tomato soups into the fridge to chill. I needed to cook more food. The last days of the season had three rainy symbols. I'd need a lot of soup, but had no room for it.

"One game I used to play had an unlimited amount of storage space. You know why I remember that when there are so many memories I don't?" I grunted, trying to shove baked clay into the door. "Because of the overwhelming *relief* I felt, knowing I didn't have to worry about it. Not needing to rearrange everything all the time. Just stockpiling to my heart's delight." I let go of the baked clay as it clattered to the floor. On a whim, I tried to move it into the house. Logic told me that the wolf would only destroy resources if they were outside. Someone already used the second story as storage anyway, so imagining it as another warehouse wasn't a big stretch. I opened the back door, but the invisible wall kept me from entering with the resource. I grumbled, setting it on the ground and folding my arms.

The stone blocks would soon finish, and I could place fifteen baked clay to store them in the tool while they cooked. I sighed, feeling like this was taking too much time. I didn't want to worry about this until the wolf came tonight. Until then, yes, I would have more bricks to deal with. Since I had nothing else on my list except upgrading the fire, I would focus on upgrading the storage unit as my new priority.

I finished molding the rest of the clay into rectangles, even though they would never fit in the unit. I hoped to get some inspiration and figure out how to store them before tonight.

In the green room, I began decluttering. It was much smaller and had boxes of old books with blurred-out titles. I stuffed them all in sacks. The old wallpaper made me wonder. Did I have to paint every room? What if I had the option of a nice floral green wallpaper?

"Mmm, yes, please."

With so many options besides painting, my imagination ran wild as I moved bags of clutter to the front porch. Decluttering and imagining that beautiful wallpaper distracted me from the storage problem. I took a break to withdraw the stone blocks and place fifteen baked clay into the tool. I placed the blocks into the storage room for upgrading and returned upstairs. That at least got rid of ten stones. Instinct told me I needed to take the logs out. They occupied too much space and weren't as valuable as the other resources.

I kept working throughout the day, waiting for the bricks to finish. I wanted to know what else the firepit would need, because upgrading units was now a great place to store things. Despite the gigantic boxes stacked high, the green room wasn't that big. With a third of the room decluttered, I walked downstairs to eat chilled tomato soup, then check on the tool and dump the clutter on the front porch. The wolf timer still had six hours. It was a handy thing having a clock in my head.

The tool was done, and I got so excited I momentarily forgot about all the junk as I grabbed the fifteen bricks out. I set two in the firepit and waited eagerly. To my surprise, the pit finished. I would have loved to get rid of more storage room stuff, but I would take this. Words entered my vision.

New Recipe Section Unlocked: Comfort Foods
Comfort foods restore a small amount of sanity

A gasp escaped my lips. I remember thinking about it as a possibility. This was excellent! Did this mean I wouldn't be such a sobbing mess after *they* attacked? To restore sanity, not just by sleeping? This could build my confidence against monsters! Okay, so maybe this would only make me a little braver, but it was a step in the right direction.

In my excitement, I almost forgot about the junk on the front porch and the fact that I had a good ten minutes left on my chilled tomato timer. I practiced a level of self-restraint I didn't think was possible and cleared off the cement. Once that was done, I remembered I hadn't painted the kitchen. Mint green might be nice, though I wasn't sure how I'd feel about it until I walked inside. The bathroom also needed a decision. Should I use a much darker color in a windowless bathroom? I couldn't deny that dark blue or red would be gorgeous.

I had enough points to prime the bathroom, since the paneling gave me so much, but it still floored me to see 47.03 total points. It only took a moment to remember that I had finished my to-do list, and must have received an enormous bonus for completing it. Yes, it felt amazing. It also pained me that I missed out on the bonus throughout the season because the greenhouse got so damaged.

I raced to the clipboard before my chill timer ran out to check what recipes had unlocked under comfort foods. I saw only two.

Basic fries and ketchup
0/3 potatoes
0/2 tomatoes

Fish and chips
0/2 fish
0/1 egg
0/3 potatoes

Many other sections were grayed out. I was curious to try the recipes out to see how much sanity they gave me. No doubt more recipes would unlock as I explored. With two whole greenhouses still locked, how could it not? I would have to cook some tomorrow. I had a bunch of potatoes just waiting to be used up. As long as I had the room.

My gaze traveled to the stuffed storeroom. I had put this off for too long. It was late enough that I needed to plan how to fit a small stack of twenty bricks and baked clay from my experiment into the storage area. The first thing to do was to extract the logs. Those were easily available resources. With those logs gone, I stored half the waiting pile of bricks inside. It made sense that bigger things took up more space, but sometimes game logic applied. It still annoyed me I couldn't stack bricks in a heap. They, like cooked food, demanded their place.

In order to stuff the rest of the bricks in the storage room, I became more selective of what I needed to toss. Since I needed stones for the blocks, I kept those. I broke the logs into boards, then carried them all outside. By the time the excess resources were in the dumpster, I had 187.03 points! Despite the pain of losing them, at least they gave me something.

As I walked back in the house, I pulled out my paper for that last burst of dopamine.

~~Repair all damages caused by them~~
~~Strengthen the wall around the house and greenhouses~~
~~Prime and paint three rooms on first floor~~
~~Upgrade cooking fire~~

~~*Purchase third article of clothing for farming*~~
~~*Plant lettuce and carrots*~~

To-do list finished, reward of +20.00.

I tucked the paper away and opened the front door, seeing the beautiful forest green in the living and entertainment room. Killie meowed as she ran to me. I picked her up, holding her close.

"How about we go to bed early tonight, huh?"

She said nothing, just rubbed her head under my chin as we headed into the stunning lilac bedroom. I stared at the ceiling, sighing.

"Also, I don't think you understand how gorgeous a light fixture would look in here with those little plaster floral decorations at the base. Is that an option?"

The alien overlords didn't respond, and for the first time, the game put me to sleep well before the hauntings started.

Despite the low stress, it remained weird to wake up with no genuine sense of rest. Just the end of one day, and the start of another with full stamina and sanity. I walked outside to the tool, putting the finished stone blocks toward upgrading and adding ten more broken stones in their place. If everything went smoothly, I would finish filling this requirement by tomorrow morning. The storage would definitely require more materials, but I was fine with that. I hoped it would take bricks next so I could free up more space. I should keep some in case the fence requested them on the next to-do list. The game might not let me bake clay while it rained.

It was anyone's guess about what that final list of the season would need.

But I also wanted to cook more food. I had one potato soup, four chilled tomato soups, two cooked eggs, a basic fish omelet, and four fried fish. I had a basket of three caught fish and a bunch of vegetables. After doing my morning routine, I added more tomatoes and carrots, as well as another egg. I needed seeds to plant carrots, but so far, no new recipes have unlocked for them. I wouldn't buy more unless I had a reason to grow them.

I sat down at the newly upgraded firepit and set firewood, sticks, and a match in there. I placed potatoes and tomatoes in the pot. Comfort foods took longer than soup to cook, but I technically didn't have any chores to do.

Fries and a small bowl of ketchup emerged, and I put them aside with a smile to stick two fish, an egg, and three more potatoes into the fire.

My mind wandered as I studied this place that turned cozy in the morning light. Killie explored the tall grass. Despite all the work I had done inside, the outside looked dilapidated. Some of the brick was crumbling. Even the updated carport was nicer than the house. There must be something to unlock for outdoor labor.

Fish and chips took longer, but once they finished, I made soup. The three upcoming days of rain pressed on my mind, and I lacked food to prepare for it. I planned on fishing later today to make a few more comfort foods. *They* were attacking tomorrow night. Maybe *their* arrival wasn't the best time to experiment with how much sanity these gave. A test run shouldn't be on the day of the race. I didn't have to go to bed tonight. I could stay up and get spooked. Then I'd have an entire morning again to cook and strategize. I knew what I had to do, but I didn't feel excited about it at *all*. Technically, my blue bar could drop to fifty percent, and it'd still be fine. I sighed, then glanced at the trees. I had another source to fill up my sanity. It would be stupid not to try this. But it also seemed stupid *to* try it. I—

My brows furrowed as my eyes lingered on the treetops before darting over to other trees. The breeze playing over the grass wasn't hot, nor cold, yet I sensed a shift. I had not noticed it until I saw the trees; the hazy sky remained, but the leaves were touched with color.

A breath escaped me as I finished up the last of my cooking. When the final tomato soup started, I walked over to the carport and chose a dark blue for the bathroom. If the alien overlords didn't count the hallway, I had the entire first floor primed and painted. It only took a few moments of satisfaction before my thoughts again drifted to the ceiling. Or even some wallpaper. I waited for my bar of sanity and stamina to grow, but it remained the same. Either I didn't get a reward for finishing this, or I needed to wipe down more walls.

With that, I spent the rest of the morning fishing. I expected it to be quicker, but as soon as I got to the bridge, another spider monster tumbled out of the forest and growled. I had been thinking I might gather some sand while I was at it, but that would prove difficult with the creature. At least it didn't chase away the fish, but it still took longer than I'd like to catch two. I wanted more, but the tool was almost done. I needed to make sure that was constantly going with new stone blocks to upgrade the storage.

When I returned, I marched right to the tool. I reached in to grab a stone block. A memory orb came out attached to the stone. I raised my eyebrows in surprise.

"Oh, it's been a while!"

That was all I said before the sphere smacked my chest and everything went dark.

Chapter Thirty-One

Them in Broad Daylight

A montage of events came in quick succession, showing Quinn and Theo growing up.

The six-year-old kids were sledding down a hill, Quinn screaming in excitement as Theo had the biggest smile on his face. They flew over a bump on the ground, causing both of them to tumble out of the sled. She shrieked with laughter, and he could not stop giggling.

Brenda, Doug, Quinn, Theo, and two more adult children attended Derrin's high school graduation.

More foster kids came in and out, but Theo and Quinn remained. Quinn always helped give instructions to the newcomers, whether they were six months old or sixteen. She was a chatterbox. Theo was quiet, but respectful.

Theo and Doug stayed up late on the weekends, watching scary movies, eating popcorn as they watched either at home or at the movie theater. The ten-year-old boy hounded the increasingly gray-haired man for higher-rated shows.

"Miss Nichole even suggested I should watch harder stuff! It's good for me!" Theo said.

"No, she and I both agree. Nothing R until you're sixteen."

The boy groaned before the memory shifted to the next scene. It was Quinn's eleventh birthday, and she unwrapped one of her presents. She frowned, studying the case. "Harvest Moon," she read out loud.

Theo snorted. "Isn't that a game for babies?"

"I've been asking other people," Brenda said, patting Theo's shoulder to quiet him. "You haven't loved the games we got as a family, and Anna said you should give this one a go."

"I don't know." Quinn turned the case around. "I'm not a fan of shooting creatures or killing bugs."

"Oh, no, this has none of that. It's a relaxing game. Repair a farm and get it thriving." Brenda checked with Doug, who nodded.

"So... no murdering anything?" Quinn asked.

Brenda shook her head. "Nope."

Theo's breath hitched. "No defending your camp from space aliens?"

"I hate that game." Quinn crinkled her nose.

"I think you'll enjoy this." Doug tapped the case. "Give it a go. And if you don't like it, then that's fine, too."

Quinn shrugged. "I mean, it's worth a shot."

The scenes went through rapid succession, Quinn playing game after game, her small bookshelf filling with cases of farming games.

Thirteen-year-old Quinn and Theo were near a Christmas tree, unwrapping a box with papers inside. Brenda and Doug hadn't had a new child come to the house in months.

"We've ended our time fostering," Doug said when Theo gave him a questioning look, holding the pages.

Brenda squeezed her husband's hand. "End it, so we can start something else."

Quinn gasped, eyes widening with excitement. "Adoption!"

Brenda couldn't stop her beaming smile. "Adoption."

Doug grunted. "As soon as the judge makes it official."

"We both agreed they simply can't split you two up, and the best way to keep you together is to let you stay here."

Quinn squealed and hugged Brenda. She hugged her back, tears in her eyes.

"So, um..." Theo trailed off.

After a sip of Brenda's famous Christmas morning hot cocoa, Doug shot a knowing glance at the boy. "You can still call us Brenda and Doug if you want."

Relief flooded his face. "I would... rather do that, yes."

Doug's knowing look turned into an encouraging smile. "That's fine." Doug opened his arms. Theo welcomed the bear hug from Doug.

The scene shifted to the courthouse. They each put an arm around each other as they smiled for the camera. Derrin and his siblings were there, too. The family was growing, with one of Brenda and Doug's adult children already with a baby on her hip.

They went out for ice cream later, just Brenda, Doug, Theo, and Quinn.

"You two needed each other, you know." Brenda licked the twist cone she had gotten. "You're like yin and yang. I've never seen kids with completely different likes and dislikes come together the way you have."

"We're not that different," Quinn said, glancing at Theo. "Are we?"

Doug chuckled, moving his spoon around the banana split he shared with Theo. "Says the person who doesn't go to every horror movie that hits the big screen."

Quinn's shoulders quivered before it traveled down the rest of her body. "Ugh, those are gross."

Theo got himself some banana split. "Speak for yourself."

"I am speaking for myself. They're gross. Why do you watch those?" Quinn asked.

Theo shrugged. "Because they're cool."

"Isn't there enough evil in the world?" Her lips pursed after the question, waiting for the answer.

Doug patted Quinn's arm. "Monster movies aren't that bad once you figure out the secret."

"Secret?" Quinn asked.

"The terror of the monsters comes from the viewer's ambiguity. Like Jaws, or those aliens in Signs. It taps into a universal dread of the unknown. Once the movie lets you see the creature in broad daylight, it's never as terrifying as the uncertainty of what you thought it was, and the group of heroes usually kill it soon after."

Quinn nodded thoughtfully.

"Or the heroes all end up dying from the attempt," Theo added.

Quinn gave his shoulder a shove. "Seriously?"

He snickered before taking a bite from his spoon.

The scene shifted, and fourteen-year-old Quinn came home from school, shrugging off her backpack and coat. "Theo!"

"What?"

She followed the sound of his voice. "Did you really punch Anthony in the face?"

"Sorta."

She pushed open Theo's bedroom door to see him sitting on the bed with an ice pack against his cheek. "What do you mean, sorta?"

"I mean, he sorta asked for it. He punched me back, so no, I don't feel bad."

Quinn was about to say something else when she paused, then folded her arms. "What'd he do?"

"Oh, come on. You've heard the rumors. I was trying to stop it once and for all, because it's disgusting."

She furrowed her brow. "You mean about us being adopted? Everyone knows that."

"Not just that." He got up. "About how people figured out we're not biologically brother and sister. Anthony's a nauseating kid who assumed we were secretly dating."

Quinn paused, then leaned over, gripped her knees, and made a gagging noise.

"I thought so, too." Theo continued holding the ice pack on his cheek.

"What kind of gross lies are those?!" She still gripped her knees. "Why is this kid your friend?"

"You haven't heard the rumors?" He blinked a few times. "Aren't you more popular than me?"

"Well, I mean... maybe talk to more people and you can make better friends than Anthony. The sick child." Quinn straightened. "I just assumed that he... you know..."

Theo raised an eyebrow. "That he what?"

She paused, then her gaze shot to the ground as she shuffled her feet.

"That he what? Seriously? What could be worse than rumors of us secretly dating?"

"I thought Brady finally squealed and told Anthony your last name. From... before."

Despite it almost being ten years ago, the haunted look returned to his face in full force. "I am not Theo Wolfe," he whispered before moving past her to the kitchen.

Another scene sprung up, this one far more relaxed as it lingered on Brenda reading a book on the couch, sipping coffee before placing the mug on a coaster. Seven-year-old Quinn walked into the room, arms folded, confused.

"Brenda." Quinn's brows furrowed. "Theo's... being weird."

The woman glanced up. "Oh? What's he doing?"

"He's... in bed. Under his covers. Every time I think he's sleeping, but then I leaned over today, and his eyes aren't closed. I try to talk to him, but he ignores me. Can he sleep with his eyes open? Ashley says some people do that."

A small, sad smile flickered across Brenda's face. "It's good of you to be concerned about Theo. That's a lovely quality you have."

"But what's wrong with him?"

"Nothing is wrong." She closed her book and put it next to her coffee mug. "It... he has..." She let out a sigh, organizing her thoughts. "Theo has depression."

A deep frown tugged at Quinn's lips. "What's that?"

Brenda patted her hand. "Something I hope you never experience, but it's still important to show compassion to those who have it."

"But what is it?"

Brenda closed one eye, thinking. As she did so, the scene shifted. It was of seven-year-old Theo, curled in his blankets, staring at nothing.

"It's hard to explain because depression is different for everyone." Brenda's voice came, despite the scene staying on the little boy. "Some people might love doing a hobby, then for weeks or even months, not find enjoyment in it anymore. Some get angry at the drop of a hat."

"Theo does that sometimes," Quinn's voice said.

Theo closed his eyes.

"Yes, he does. It's because his energy is low, and he has to do so many things, and the poor kid is so tired. He will often lie in bed."

"So why doesn't he sleep?" Quinn asked.

"Because he's too exhausted."

"Too exhausted to sleep? How is that possible?"

"Even though it looks like he's asleep, his mind plays images of the past while depression fills him with ideas that don't leave him alone. Thoughts that make it difficult for him to feel relaxed enough to sleep."

Theo didn't move, burrowing deeper into the covers until his face was covered in shadow.

The scene returned to Quinn and Brenda talking in the other room.

"How did depression happen?" Quinn asked.

"We're not sure, because it's different for so many people. Some people are born with it. Some only have it during the wintertime. For Theo, Ms. Nichole believes most of it comes from the bad thing that happened in his past."

"Is that why you never want me to ask questions about his family?" Quinn asked.

"Yes. And you continue to respect his privacy that way. When he's ready, he'll tell you himself, but you do not pressure him." She touched the little girl's nose. "He is working it out with Miss Nichole, and Doug and I are here, too. You help by being his friend."

Quinn folded her arms. "But how can I when he never responds? He doesn't want to play with the toys I give him."

"No, he wouldn't have the energy to do that." Brenda said.

"I don't get it." Quinn stared at her, trying to understand.

Brenda tapped her book in thought. "You know all those movies Theo watches?"

The little girl screwed up her face in disgust. "Yeah. Those are creepy."

"In a way, he is fighting his own monster."

Quinn raised an eyebrow. "Depression is a monster?"

"For many people, yes."

"A scary one?"

Brenda nodded. "It can be."

The little girl lifted her palms, curling them like claws. "With teeth and hair?"

"Possibly. Though maybe it's better to imagine it as... as a big black blob of slime." Brenda said.

Quinn dropped her hands, her eyes wide in fear. "But he's not actually getting attacked, is he?"

"In a way, yes. But this sludge monster doesn't tear him apart limb from limb like in the movies. It covers him, then sucks all the energy out before leaving him with thoughts of hopelessness. He has a hard time picking himself up after each attack."

"Can he kill it forever?" Quinn asked.

"I don't know." Brenda shrugged as tears pooled in her eyes. "Some people can. Other people..."

The scene changed again, even as Brenda's quiet sigh was still heard. It was Theo's bedroom, but the boy grew older, playing with toys in his room. Sometimes he was fine and happy, being with friends or drawing some pictures.

"...for other people, it'll be a constant in their life," Brenda's voice said as the scene shifted. It showed a growing Theo doing homework, then times where he would trudge over to his bed, the weight of the world on his shoulders as he collapsed into it. Barely able to do anything else but grab the covers and stare blankly at the wall.

"And it might be a constant for Theo."

Theo kept growing. Kept smiling. Kept laughing. Kept collapsing. Kept curling into a ball. Kept staring at nothing. Kept closing his eyes as if he was asleep, but the furrow on his brow deepened as thoughts did not give him peace. The weight of life pressed deeper into him as his face grew devoid of emotion.

"But it's not fair," Quinn's seven-year-old voice said.

"No. No, it's not. But until we figure out a way to kill depression everywhere, Theo will have times when he's being attacked by a monster none of us can see. Miss Nichole, Doug, and I are doing our best to help him fight back. I want you to worry about giving him all the love and compassion I know is in that heart of yours, to give him time to recover from each attack."

Theo remained in bed, hardly moving.

Quinn sighed. "Yeah. Yeah, alright."

Theo stared at nothing. His face changed and morphed over the years that passed. Child to tween, tween to teenager.

"But why does he watch those scary movies with monsters if he fights a monster himself?" Quinn's voice asked.

"Sometimes it's nice to know they can be defeated."

"But... but in so many of those stories, they never succeed. Theo talks about it a lot. The monster can't be killed, and the hero... the hero dies."

"I... don't know why he's so drawn to them. But Theo... he has something the heroes don't have."

"What?"

"You. You and your big, loving heart."

The voices vanished. Seventeen-year-old Theo remained in bed, staring at the wall. Time passed as he didn't move a muscle, looking asleep except for the furrow in his brow.

The door opened, and Quinn walked in.

"Hey, Theo, did you say you had your AP English te—" She stopped at the sight of her brother barely doing enough to breathe. Quinn hesitated, then slipped out of the room. The only thing that made anyone believe he was still alive was his eyes focused on a point on the wall instead of being sightless.

The door opened again, and Theo stayed motionless. Quinn walked in with two handheld gaming consoles. She placed one by him with no expectation that he'd take it before she herself sat down on the ground by his bed, her back to him. It was similar to their first night together at Brenda and Doug's house, yet this time Quinn stayed quiet. Instead, she turned on her game, remembering where she was and started mining for ores to upgrade her tools.

She said nothing, because she didn't have to. She was busy, lost in the rhythm, gathering resources and farming crops. Whatever monster he fought, it was invisible to her, so she sat there, unafraid. The peaceful music rising from her console was the only sound. After a while, Theo sucked in a deep breath as though coming to himself and glanced down at the device near him. He picked it up with trembling hands and turned it on. He loaded his favorite first-person shooter game, remaining on the bed as he played. Gunshots and splattered brain matter punctuated the soothing nature sounds. They remained that way for an hour, ignoring homework and other responsibilities.

"Kids!" Brenda called from the kitchen. "Dinner."

"Coming!" they shouted back.

Quinn stood up before offering a hand to Theo. He took it and forced himself out of bed.

"I hope she made tater tot casserole. I'm starving," Quinn said.

Theo didn't look at her as he tried to straighten his posture. "Do you think we'll ever convince Brenda to make french fries as a side instead of green beans?"

"Doubtful. Besides, tater tots are the fried version of potatoes. It's in the casserole itself! I love that stuff."

He folded his arms, with no smile on his face, but Quinn didn't expect to see one so soon after an attack. She turned around to grab the gaming consoles before the two of them left his room.

Chapter Thirty-Two
Paranormal Detective

I gasped, stumbling back, clutching the stone block as I reoriented myself. I didn't want to drop it on my foot, but my hand trembled. My knees sank to the ground, resting the block on the cement as I stared at the base of the tool. Was this entire game some super strange analogy to help me know how Theo experienced depression? But... why? Why would the alien overlords be involved in something like this? To study human nature and figure out how to replicate depression? Because that was undoubtedly what *they* were. It was too uncanny to listen to my younger self and Brenda talking about a monster I saw in this world. The fur, the teeth, the slime, there was no other way to describe it.

And the wolf creature? The game had shown me a memory of Theo's haunted eyes when he revealed his last name. Theo Wolfe. I remembered his drawing of the same monster prowling this house at night. Somehow, the memories, the experiences, were tied to him. Was this his house, too? A childhood home and life I could never ask about? Part of me was waiting for this clue to confirm what I had been guessing at for a while. This house belonged to Theo.

As always, the memory orbs left me with so many questions, and the one constant was why. Why was I here? Who were the alien overlords? What was happening? I learned a lot, but I didn't know the most important thing. How could I get out?

After a moment of recuperation, I lifted the stone block and placed it in the storage unit before returning for the others. My mind reeled from the memories. Those last ones were very depression-heavy, and I got scared. I had been here for almost thirty-five days, an entire summer, according to the calendar. I felt sad and alone, but I'd never reached the level I saw Theo experience. Not unless one counted the times after *they* attacked. But that was the point, right? To know what it was like to be hit with depression. By *them*.

The pickaxe broke ten more stones, and I placed them in the tool. By tonight, I'd get a batch going. Tomorrow morning, I'd get another list of resources above the storage room.

As I walked to catch more fish, I rubbed my chin as my mind swirled. I was certain this was Theo's childhood home. Doug and Brenda had forbidden me from asking questions, and therefore I had no recollection of it.

My thoughts plagued me as I threw my fishing line into the river. I was slowly but surely getting memories back. I thought I had been learning more about myself, but Theo seemed to dominate these flashbacks.

Them being depression made me uncomfortable in a way I had trouble placing. Brenda's descriptions were too close for it not to be an obvious reveal, but... why? Why would alien overlords create this world and place me in it to let me experience the horrors of a wolf and *them*? All the while cleaning a house and farming in my greenhouses?

It also didn't explain the monsters. I glanced up, seeing another bush spider monster on the other side of the river. What were those things supposed to be?

I reeled in a fish, turning around to look at the trees keeping the white brick home hidden. The wolf and *them* had some connection. So, what about the hauntings? Were they part of this?

Theo's fit of giggles on the sled came back to me, the very first memory I'd seen today. With a sinking heart, I realized why that giggle sounded so familiar.

"Oh... my god."

He was the giggling child upstairs. The one chanting nursery rhymes. This was undoubtedly his house. Perhaps the ghosts were nothing more than clues to what had happened in Theo's past. I remembered the blood leaking out of the bottom of the locked door, and my throat tightened. I'd been so horrified I made a vow never to go up to the second floor at night. But now, to put clues together, I would have to do some experimentation tonight with the phantoms haunting this place. With unlocking the comfort food part of the cooking fire, I had a way to replenish my sanity without sleep. Everything hinted that I needed to stay up and do research.

My soul shriveled, but I held on to one important understanding. I was confident the child was Theo. That knowledge alone helped ease my fears. Perhaps it would even give me the strength not to lose any blue whenever he giggled. Killie was never afraid, so I didn't need to be either.

From what I remembered, the shrieking grandma ghost traveled and hated cats. I had also heard two adults talking, but they were in the locked room. There might have been a male voice among them. I had never gotten close enough to listen, and I hadn't *wanted* to. But now I had a purpose. A terrifying one. I would figure out what happened here at Theo's childhood home. I already assumed some things with the clues I had.

"So..." I started speaking out loud. "All those times I thought I was a rat in a maze. Is this the actual reason I'm here?" No reply came as I felt the fishing line jiggle. I gently reeled in a fish. "It's not a maze, I am just... figuring out what happened to Theo?"

Again, nothing. I placed the fish in the basket. Two more and I'd have enough to make five fish and chips. Hopefully, it would give enough sanity for this to be worth it. Any percentage would be wonderful, so I wouldn't complain.

"But why do you care?" I asked the sky. "I get that you're a neutral party and whatnot, but... but why did you create this world for me to experience? Steal me from Earth? Why did you choose to bring me here to figure out Theo's past? To erase my memory and force me through these hoops. Isn't there an easier way? Like, I don't know, me asking him while on my planet? He is my adopted brother, after all." I threw my line back in, sighing. "Can I leave once I find out what happened?"

Words came, and I braced for the interaction.

You will get your answers. Just play the game.

A lock of my hair danced in the burst of air I let out from my mouth. I'd thought I was patient until I traveled to a game with wolf monsters, *them,* and a haunted house in need of cleaning.

Once I had my fish, I returned to drop them off in the storage. I brought out ten more stones to fit in the basket. I'd be breaking it up for blocks to put in the tool soon anyway.

I spent the rest of the afternoon and evening decluttering the hallway. I forced myself to get used to the darkening place. Yes, a few windows were here, but not enough light from the covered back porch would trickle through. I turned on the flashlight and started scrubbing the walls. I wanted a brighter color in here. Maybe some light, happy wallpaper.

My heart pounded in my chest. Every instinct told me I shouldn't be here. Not when it was this dark. My natural response was to flee. The pure terror of remembering the creaking floorboards and seeing those bloody footprints made my palms sweat. I never wanted to see those again, but they were a clue.

"This sucks." I did not want to do this. I hated the idea of figuring out what the hauntings meant, but the more mysteries I solved, the better my sanity would hold up. At least, I hoped it would. "It'd be nice if I weren't such a scaredy-cat."

Killie's head emerged through the door, staring at me like I had called her. I sighed, then wiped down the wall. "I stand corrected. You are braver."

Once the stone blocks finished cooking, I stuck them in the storage unit, then put the last ten broken stones in the tool to free up space. I crossed my fingers that bricks would be next.

My wolf timer wasn't blinking yet, but it was close. I stared at the back door of the house, took a deep breath, and prepared to do some late-night paranormal detective work.

I gripped my flashlight and a plate of fish and chips as I walked into the kitchen. A container of regular fries and ketchup fit snugly in my pocket, since I needed my light. The mint green paint really clashed with the faded red carpet, and I wasn't sure if I could last until I tore it up. Perhaps brown for the walls would look better, but I didn't *want* to put that color in here. I wanted a mint green and nice floors. These hardwood floors would be gorgeous, and I...

...was one hundred percent distracting myself from what I had to do.

It did not help that I walked into the living room, admiring the forest green and ignoring the brown shag carpet. That color looked so much better than the paneling. The green also brought out the beautiful built-in bookshelf, even if the contents inside were things I'd rather not focus on. The thing I *needed* to focus on was clearly not on my mind.

Killie sauntered through the house. I stood in the middle of the living room gripping my fish and chips, trying hard not to feel like an idiot, shining the flashlight around.

"I know you're here."

True, I never sought them out. They usually found me. It was dark, the wolf prowling outside. I swallowed, holding my plate, waiting. Time ticked on, and in the quiet, I was sweating.

"Seriously?" I asked.

Where was the shrieking grandma? The giggling child? The conversations?

Killie meowed, getting my attention. I glanced down, seeing the cat swipe her paw at the beams of light. The realization hit me, and I whimpered.

"I hate this." I then took a deep breath and switched off the flashlight.

Chapter Thirty-Three

Another Nursery Rhyme

The house was completely dark. I listened to every creak and groan, waiting for something to happen.

Killie kept rubbing her back against the wall, meowing, trying to communicate.

"What is it, girl?" I asked. If I had a high enough animal care level, would I understand her better?

She stayed near the forest-green walls. I glanced around, then my brows furrowed. I had wondered whether painting and priming the entire first floor would give me a reward. Perhaps the grandma ghost Killie hissed at so much wouldn't haunt here. After all, it was becoming unrecognizable, which meant the hauntings weren't as prevalent.

Which... fantastic! That's not a bad trade-off. Except I needed to find out more about these ghosts.

The giggling sounded from above the entertainment room, and I took a deep breath.

"It's just Theo." I watched my sanity, preparing myself. I wanted to start with the shrieking grandma, but eventually I'd have to go to the second story. Truth be told, I was simply a wimp and terrified of walking up that staircase at night. I spent half an hour waiting for something supernatural to happen on the first floor when I already knew that up the stairs was a magnet for ghosts.

I sighed, once again holding my plate, and headed through the bedroom.

"Just Theo." I closed my eyes. "It's just Theo."

My sanity remained full. Once I heard the giggling, my mind was certain. The problem was that finding out more required me to go up the creaky staircase.

"How is this my life right now?"

Little ghost Theo giggled again, and my heart pounded. Despite knowing who it was, it was still a mystery. Yet he sounded so cheerful and happy.

The wood groaned as I walked up the staircase, clutching my plate like a lifeline as I closed my eyes. My lips moved in the motion of saying "Just Theo," but no sound escaped. I didn't dare talk as I approached the second floor.

I turned, followed the last few steps, and arrived on the landing. My breathing was the only noise. My soul desperately required the flashlight, but I needed answers more.

The giggling happened again, this time in the blue room, the one I hadn't started cleaning yet. I swallowed, and my legs moved as if they were under water. With a courage I did not possess, I pushed the door open. I didn't get in far with all the clutter, but I held my breath, my eyes lingering on the shadows.

"All around the mulberry bush,"

It took all the strength I had to keep my hands on the plate so it wouldn't slip from my fingers.

"The monkey chased the weasel."

He sang somewhere in here, yet I couldn't see him. How could he be anywhere in here with all this junk?

"The monkey thought, 'twas all in good fun.'

"Pop! Goes the weasel!"

My sanity lost a chunk of blue. "Just Theo." No sound escaped my lips. I pulled out my flashlight and turned it on, trying to locate the ghost child. I imagined him as he was in the memories, but without that haunted look on his face. The cheerful, giggling boy I saw later.

"All around the mulberry bush,"

The beam of light jumped all over, trying to pinpoint where the singing came from.

"The monkey chased the weasel."

The voice echoed throughout the room. My palms shook as the words reverberated off the walls.

"The monkey thought, 'twas all in good fun,'

"Pop! Goes the weasel!"

My sanity dropped, and I did my best to stay brave. "You can't scare me. I have fish and chips." Sound came out of me for the first time since stepping foot on the second floor.

"A penny for a spool of thread,

"A penny for a needle,

"That's the way the money goes!"

He held out the last word for as long as he could, his voice trembling as he lost air. Perhaps it would have been cute, but the echo quality didn't help. He took the biggest breath.

"Pop! Goes the weasel!" the boy shouted with everything he had before giggling up a storm.

I covered my ear. It was nothing more than an adorable child singing a nursery rhyme. That couldn't be scary, right? My sanity told a different story. It spasmed before losing a few chunks. Once I'd been in the room long enough, the voice seemed to come from all over, echoing off the walls. It wasn't exactly a calming voice, either.

"This is what I need. My blue to drop. To find out how much fish and chips will recover. It's okay to be scared. I'm not—"

"THEO!"

The plate clattered to the ground. It should have made the contents spill all over, but the food remained glued, holding true to game logic. My lungs sucked most of the air in the room. My flashlight shot in every direction to find the woman who shouted, whether ghostly or otherwise. She was nowhere. The voice vanished, and I became aware that I had placed myself in a darkened, cluttered space. I sensed the lack of spirits. Both the female and the boy had left.

Whispers traveled from the locked room. I picked up the plate of food and moved onto the landing. I hated getting so close to this place. My flashlight lingered on the floor. If anything resembling liquid trickled out, I was sprinting out of here.

The hushed tones remained the same. I expected them to get louder as I got closer, but that wasn't the case. It was the same volume of muffled noises I'd heard from downstairs in the living room. I approached the locked door, trying the knob again to be certain. It didn't alert the people inside as they kept talking. I placed my ear against the door, my head bowed to stare at the base.

One was male. I could differentiate that much. From the tone of his voice, he sounded more laid-back than the female. Despite the two whispering, the woman did the most to keep her words nearly silent to make sure nobody overheard them. Perhaps I'd hear them better if I were in that room, but the thought of stepping inside filled me with nausea. All the hardship, all the evil, all the haunting, stemmed from this place. My bias started from that blood trickling from the base of this door, but I felt justified in that prejudice. That was a pretty freaky thing to happen. Later in the game I might find the key, but it would not be tonight.

My sanity dropped more than a quarter as I backed away. I had gained enough information this evening. I made a final trip to the pink room to switch out the clothes on the sewing machine, to pretend I wasn't trembling the entire time. The bright orange building overalls should finish by tomorrow morning. I had buffed everything in my logging now. Building clothes would be harder to buff because I used them so much, but coming up here at night to swap them out would make it easier.

I moved down the stairs, diving into my fish and chips as I watched my sanity fill up about fifteen percent. I pulled out the container of fries and dropped them into my mouth. They gave about five percent back. It wasn't a lot, but then again, this was better than nothing. No doubt higher levels of comfort food would give more sanity back.

My inner gamer felt hurt that I wasted the food on something I would gain when sleeping anyway, but it was for experimentation. Now I knew if I had six fish and chips on hand, I could go from next to no blue to well past ninety percent. Considering *they* would attack tomorrow night, this was vital information to have.

As I relaxed in bed, I took a moment to process. My sanity had taken a few hits tonight, but I was almost back to normal. I wasn't sure what those two ghosts were talking about in the locked room, but it made me uneasy. Despite knowing for certain Theo was giggling and singing, it still hurt my sanity. It was this house. It was absolutely charming in the morning and afternoon, yet something shifted in the evening.

There was a purpose to all of this, and food to help me regain the blue I had lost. That alone helped me to not be so terrified. Well, still a bit terrified. But now I would figure out what happened to little Theo. With those thoughts, I closed my eyes and asked the game to force me to sleep.

The red light of dawn found me rushing out of bed and doing my morning routine. Part of that momentum was to the sewing machine to collect the bright orange pants. I wore all my building clothes before pulling out the stone blocks and placing them into the storage. I waited patiently, staring at the small unit, as the words shifted and changed.

0/75 bricks

A smile came to me. "Perfect." I grabbed the thirty bricks I had ready to go and dropped them one by one into the foundation. About halfway through, I contemplated what I was doing. It would rain for three days straight. If the fence required bricks, then I would need enough baked clay to strengthen it.

A chill raced down my spine, staring at what I had left. I got too excited. It would be stupid not to have something prepared, or even start cooking more bricks to make sure the tool didn't get clogged up. Three days wasn't a long time.

I stopped adding to the upgrade and counted the remains. Ten baked clay and fourteen bricks. If I saved all of them, that would give me twenty-four in total. Despite how much I wanted to update the storage unit for more space, I had to stock up. Clay needed sunlight, and I wouldn't get that for three days.

Today's morning routine involved cooking more fish and chips. I had enough for five plates, and I would have the room to store it. Could I cook in the rain? I hadn't actually thought about it. Since *they* were attacking tonight, I would eat most, if not all the comfort food to help my sanity. I planned on staying above fifty percent. As I started the fire and put the ingredients in the pot, I wondered what would happen if I ran out of food during the next three rainy days. I wasn't sure if I could make anything.

Despite my ache to get the storage room upgraded, I waited. Tomorrow, I'd have my new to-do list and would find out if I would need those bricks. If I didn't, then great. I would dump them all into upgrading. I could spend one more day waiting.

In the greenhouses, I collected my veggies. The lettuce was ready to be picked. This would be the first time harvesting it, and I wanted to figure out exactly what this would give me. As I broke off the leaves, a recipe unlocked on the clipboard. Once I finished gathering the lettuce, I watered the stubs before grabbing my baskets of food and returning. I dropped the produce in the storage unit before flipping through the pages of recipes. The one new recipe covered an entire page.

Salad Bar

Every salad must have a base of these three ingredients:

0/5 lettuce

0/2 carrots

0/2 tomatoes

The more complex the ingredient, the higher the percentage of stamina you get back. The optional ingredients to put on the salad are:

Basic: Add a small percentage to overall stamina when consumed with salad

0/1 onions

???

???

???

Complex: Add a larger percentage to overall stamina when consumed with salad

0/1 cooked egg

0/1 meat of choice

???

???

???

Requires a chopping station in the kitchen to create this

This made my eyebrows raise. A salad that provided different amounts of stamina, depending on what was in it? I would have to test the base to see how much it gave. A lot of the add-ons were still locked. What hit me like a ton of bricks was that final sentence. Chopping station. I could make food independent of fire! I turned the pages again, searching through the kitchen section. A grayed-out area caught my attention.

Must reach cooking level 15 to unlock this

In excitement, I flipped to the back to view my progress.

Farming level 19

Cleaning level 21

Logging level 23

Cooking level 14

Building level 24

Animal Care level 16

Level 15 was close. Considering I was making food now, I might get it. Also, I was slacking on the animal care clothes. I needed to check this more often. I checked all the other sections to see if anything was available, but they were all either bought already or locked away. My logging and building levels, too, were near level 25.

For not having a to-do list, I had certainly created a lengthy one for myself today. I made another plate of comfort food, hoping a few more of these would help me reach level 15. Between a fireless cooking place and collecting more clay to bake, I would be busy.

I finished the last few things in my morning routine before lingering by the fire, staring at the trees. No doubt about it now. The golds, reds, and oranges spread. Summer was ending. To sit felt wrong when I had so much to do, but I couldn't purchase that chopping thing for the kitchen without raising my cooking levels more. It required me to stay here and cook. Once I had the final food in the pot, I glanced at my progress. Still not enough. With that, I began my trip to the river. Once there, I caught a fish, gathered some clay, and returned. I did that one more time before finally reaching level 15. I tried to buy the cutting station, but it told me to get the outfit first.

"So picky." I chose a pair of black slacks, which left me with a nice 177.03 total dopamine points. Another ten points went toward the chopping station, which I gladly gave up for the opportunity to have a place to cook inside. As usual, this came with some assembly required, but honestly, two boards seemed almost insulting compared to all the other things I'd had to make recently. Cutting down an entire tree, however, felt wasteful. I wouldn't have enough room to store all those logs.

This didn't seem to take nearly as much to build. Now that fishing counted as part of gaining experience, cooking was finally catching up with the other skills. I placed two boards on the table. At the end, a huge cutting board with a sharp knife sprang into existence.

Animal care was the next lowest at level 16. I'd have to experiment to bring both animal care and cooking up. With dopamine points burning a hole in my pocket, I spent ten more to get scratch-resistant gloves. I had barely bought the item when the entire clipboard glowed. Out of instinct, I dropped it, backing away, eyes wide.

All levels at 15

All level 15 clothes purchased

Upgrading...

My heart pounded. "This is good, right? Because this is scaring me, but it's supposed to be good. Right? Right!?"

A breeze picked up my hair, blowing it around as I lifted off the ground an inch. I glanced down, surprised to see my body glowing as well. Before I had time to fully freak out about the whole thing, I dropped to the floor again and the light faded. I stood there, panting. I patted my clothes. It was the oddest sensation, but for whatever reason, I felt a pocket dimension in the small of my back. I reached in, frowning.

Upgrade complete

Inventory granted

Can have TEN *inventory slots*

I stared at the words as they faded away, then excitement bubbled up inside me.

"This will make getting clay. So. Much. Easier."

Chapter Thirty-Four
To Forage

It was still mid-morning by the time I pulled my second ten mounds of clay out of my inventory. It was the oddest experience, reaching into the small of my back into a pocket dimension there. I didn't notice any added weight when I put the resources inside. I expected a fanny pack, but it was just something behind me I could tap into. Either way, before the sun was high in the sky, I molded and prepared to sunbake another thirty on the ground while fifteen more baked clay got placed in the tool.

With this new inventory upgrade, it cut my time down significantly. It didn't take all day to gather resources anymore. By the end of the day, I would have sixty total bricks, more than enough for the fence. Then I could dump the leftovers into upgrading the storage. My job was making sure I had adequate room to store them all.

Once that was done, I changed into my cooking outfit. This lesson taught me that it was ideal to keep all levels matched. I needed to be certain my lower skills weren't too far behind. I headed toward the river, prepared to do more fishing when I slowed my walk, information entering my mind.

Level 3 clothing, new ability unlocked: skilled forager

I blinked at it. Foraging? I had to wait until level 15 to forage? Out of curiosity, I changed into animal handling and waited.

Level 3 clothing, new ability unlocked: cows

That shouldn't have surprised me, but I still raised an eyebrow. My cooking clothes returned. At least that meant replenishing my nonexistent milk supply, right? That'd be nice. I'd probably have to build a barn before I could buy a cow, much like how I had to construct a chicken coop before getting Daisy.

I turned toward the sky. "Again, I don't want to critique your game, but foraging is one of the first things people do. There's always berries or mushrooms in the wild that a person can collect right from the get-go. It's a level 0 ability, honestly." I glanced around. In my black slacks, chef's jacket, and cap, I looked like an idiot, but I waited to see the words over bushes that revealed resources I could get. It didn't take long before I realized I hadn't explored my side of the river that much.

"This one might be on me." I walked deeper into the forest near the carport. "Granted, if these woods didn't look so terrifying and creepy, I might've done more exploring earlier. Like, come on, what is this?" A few strides into the area, and it plunged into darkness, the thick trees blocking out the sun. "I would've taken two steps in here and noped the hell out."

It started to make sense that this was a level 15 skill. I took out a flashlight and turned it on. In my cooking clothes, I sensed the direction of my home.

"At least I'll never get lost. Correct?" I plunged forward. "Okay, this is why you waited before giving me this skill. I know where the house is, and I also have an inventory now."

That's right. My inventory. Did it work while I slept? Did I gain ten more spots of storage? Maybe I could place a bowl of soup on my person and a plate of fish and chips to prepare for anything.

Some green words glowed in the distance. I headed toward them when an invisible wall stopped me.

Entering enemy territory. Do you wish to continue?

Y/N

I stared ahead, wishing I hadn't rambled to the sky so loudly on the way here. Enemy territory? As in... the wolf creature? The beast that came closer to my house every night? Who could stand up on its hind legs and sprint at an inhumanly fast rate? This shouldn't surprise me. I left on the carport side of the forest. I let out a soft groan. Perhaps this was why foraging was a later-game feature. There must be something to help me, and I knew where the house was. I mentally chose yes, and the wall vanished. I walked toward a bush with the words above it, the beam of light wobbling.

My vision shifted. Ten spots of inventory appeared at the bottom. The wolf icon moved from underneath my sanity and stamina to the other corner. Instead of a timer, it had three question marks around it, which did not help me feel better. I tried to pretend bravery into my system as I approached the strawberry bush with *forage food* above it. I knelt down, picking them and placing them in my pocket dimension. A picture of a strawberry popped up in the first slot, with a number next to it every time I put one in. Since they were so small, they didn't take up all the rows. I finished gathering all the strawberries, and the green glow disappeared from on top. More words glowed deeper in the forest, and I took a deep breath, steadying myself as I allowed my feet to carry me farther into enemy territory.

I knelt, harvesting nuts and mushrooms. Despite being all the way out here, I sensed recipes getting unlocked on the clipboard. I didn't want to stay out here too long because the thick trees made it difficult to determine what time of day it was. Also, since my wolf timer gave me no clues, I would have to judge for myself. I knew the direction to the house, so I wouldn't worry about that, but the three question marks caused a knot to form in my stomach.

Through experimentation, I figured out I could collect fifteen bunches of each foraged item in a single inventory slot. If it filled past that, it got placed in another slot. I refused to stay here too long, since I was filling up those slots fast. Every second I remained here made me worried about the wolf.

My flashlight spotted an apple tree near me. As I approached, I froze when I noticed the claw marks on the bark. I gave myself a moment before creeping forward, touching the trunk. Words filled my vision, and I blinked, alarmed. They went too fast to read before new phrases came.

Information download. Wolf was here an hour ago. No sign of him now.

These sentences shrunk and replaced the question marks. I froze, blinking. This must be part of foraging. I mentally chose the wolf icon again, and the words returned to full vision. Whatever skill I had let me track it.

The apple tree wasn't large. A stepladder would've been nice, but I didn't own one. Instead, I set the flashlight on the ground and grabbed a branch, climbing up and picking fruit. I stored seven before it jumped onto the next slot. I remained in the branches until I had two slots of apples, then hopped down and snatched my flashlight. The natural pull toward my house helped me find the right direction. I stopped to pick more nuts on the way to keep filling my inventory, but I refused to relax until I moved out of enemy territory.

Once I selected to leave, my view shifted again. My inventory shrank, but it was kind of nice to notice how many spots remained. The wolf icon returned underneath the stamina and sanity bar, showing I had a good five and a half hours left before it came. I stretched, heading for the covered back porch. It was time to see what recipes my foraging had unlocked.

After snatching the clipboard, I checked the progress bar first. Foraging helped my cooking levels grow, which meant I had another thing to help gain experience. I then noticed a note underneath, written in the same perfect handwriting as the to-do list.

Foraging: level 2

The information came to me without words in my vision. Every time I foraged, I gained more tracking skills to deduce where the wolf was to protect me from stumbling into that creature. This was clearly its own kind of skill in cooking. Though why I had to wear a chef's hat and jacket was beyond me. Who even forages for food in clothes meant for a fancy kitchen?

I flipped through the many pages of unlocked recipes. Peanut butter and berry jam stood out to me. I might unlock the ability to make bread soon. On the salad bar recipe, one of the question marks was replaced with 0/10 foraged items to give it a more complex stamina addition.

With the cooking section behind me, I moved on to the buildings and found a barn unlocked. It would cost 50.00 dopamine points, but I had that. Having something to build was another way to store logs or boards instead of filling up the storage unit. I purchased it and heard it settling in the backyard. This would take a while, but that was okay. Maybe my building levels would reach twenty-five when I finished. The base was nearer to the final greenhouse and had words glowing above it.

0/200 logs

For that many logs, it wouldn't be hard to clear out this area of the forest to make more of a clearing for the barn. Despite how tempting it was to start swinging my axe, I instead walked to the tool to switch the bricks out, putting them into storage. I gathered up the thirty baked clay from the ground and placed them on the shelves. With that finished, I started storing my foraged food. A basket appeared, and I was relieved to see that all the strawberries fit. A new one materialized for the nuts, then I tried to do the same with the mushrooms, but it stopped me. It had reached capacity again. Thirty baked clay were inside, with fifteen bricks currently being created in the tool. I supposed it might protect them while I slept. I had already planned on keeping some things in my inventory for the night. While thinking about it, I grabbed a tomato soup and all the fish and chips I made. *They* were attacking tonight, and I would need them all.

It got darker. Not dark like when I was in the woods, but the sun dipped below the tree line, and it was getting harder to see. I pulled out my axe as I walked toward the fence, crossed over it, and started swinging at the nearest trunk. A barn could hold a cow, which meant milk, and a few more complex recipes asked for that. I worked for the next hour, clearing out a section of trees around the barn base. Two hundred was a lot, but I felt elated when seven logs dropped instead of six because of the buff, creating its own kind of dopamine. I also tried out a salad for the first time when my yellow sank to the lower end. The lettuce had some nuts and mushrooms on it and gave me the same amount of stamina as a bowl of soup. In true fashion, I ate it in three bites.

All this chopping burned through my energy as I cleared out trees. I would no doubt get strong enough in building to reach level twenty-five soon, especially if this barn needed two hundred logs. I kept going until I had a small percentage of stamina left. The last log almost fell off my shoulder when I hesitated, and curiosity struck me. I moved the large resource to my lower back. I waited, feeling the pocket dimension do the rest, sucking the entire thing into whatever was now on my back.

"Alright, well, should have tried *that* from the beginning." I pulled it out again and dropped it into the barn. This could work for so many things, like if I put bags of trash in my inventory to declutter.

49/200 logs

Not bad. It would be a lot harder in the pouring rain, and of course I'd have another to-do list tomorrow, but if I spent a solid day chopping down trees, I could fill all the requirements for logs.

The wolf timer still had forty-five minutes, so now was as good a time as ever to test how my inventory helped with decluttering upstairs. I didn't want to use up my sliver of stamina on trees, and I wanted to save my soups for the next three days. I crossed the fence and was about to head around the storage unit when some strange shadows caught my eye. The flashlight beam hit it, and my heart skidded to a stop. I expected creepy things inside the house, not outside. The beam landed on a pile of trash. I had rarely been on the side of the house near my bedroom window and the entertainment room. It had some lovely, yet overgrown, lilac bushes. Honestly, if I cut a walkway through the large lilacs and placed a bench between them, it would be the coziest reading spot in the spring/summer.

I had a bad habit of jumping to decor ideas when I got scared out of my mind.

The light remained on the pile of trash. I approached it cautiously, crouching down to inspect the garbage in the dead grass. Beer cans and cigarette butts. I could have sworn this wasn't here before. I would have noticed this when I first circled around the property. Which meant this had been collecting for some time.

My mouth went dry. I tried to keep my wits about me as I counted them. Fourteen cans, and plenty of cigarette butts to go with them. Someone had been here, smoking and drinking, and I hadn't even noticed. If I threw all this trash away and returned tomorrow morning, I'd be able to figure out when this person came. Did I want to know that? The idea of running into them made my stomach drop. I was on my knees, a sizeable amount of blue drained from my bar. I thought I'd been taking things well, but I didn't expect this. Something had been happening here for at least a week or two.

I stood up, brushed myself off, then tried to look past the bushes and into the window. I cupped my hands around my eyes and leaned over to see my bedroom. Yes, I knew it was the right window, but I needed to make sure. From where the pile of beer cans sat, they had a perfect view of me sleeping. What did this mean? Part of me refused to go down the obvious road, even as it was halfway there before I mentally screamed for that line of thought to come back. I couldn't deny the chunk of sanity that vanished, the way my breathing hitched, the fear that gripped me. Something besides the wolf lived in these woods. Possibly human. Someone who watched me while I slept.

Another slice of blue evaporated from my bar. I backed away from my bedroom window as my mind shut down.

Chapter Thirty-Five

The Second Floor at Night

I gave myself ten seconds to freak out about this discovery. Five seconds as my sanity twitched and dropped, then five more to confirm it wouldn't drop anymore. I sucked in a deep breath, then let it all out. Then I gathered the trash in a bag and headed toward the dumpster. It was important, in order not to panic, to treat this all like an experiment.

"This is great," I said, returning to my bedroom window. "This way... this way I can start... checking. Checking when this person comes here. See... see how much they drink. At night. While looking... while looking..."

All speech ability left me as I stared at the crystal clear shot of my bed through the yellowed curtains. I backed away, forcing myself to think of other things. It didn't help that *they* would attack tonight. It always put me on edge, even if I had fish and chips.

My breathing would not remain steady if I stayed, so I turned and walked through the back door and up to the second floor. I had two empty inventory slots, and I wanted to see how this would assist me in decluttering. The wolf wouldn't be here for half an hour, and I needed to stay up here to get clues during the haunting. I chose the blue room, since little Theo was here last night.

Each slot held two bags of clutter, which was a lot more than I expected. It was so much easier to walk down the stairs, and strangely satisfying to stand at the dumpster and pull out the sacks of trash from my pocket dimension. I had to watch what I dropped, though, because I wasn't interested in dumping my fish and chips. The dumpster might warn me first, but I didn't want to chance it.

This made decluttering a room easy. It was like having a wheelbarrow strapped to my back that weighed nothing when it got full. I did one more trip to get a good section cleared and was in the house before the wolf timer was even blinking. I leaned against the door to give myself a moment. *They* were attacking. If tonight followed the pattern of other *them* nights, the hauntings would be worse. Tonight was an excellent opportunity to study more about Theo's childhood. It still didn't cure my terror. A *powerful* part of me wanted to hide in the bathroom again, curled in a ball, devouring my comfort food whenever the need arose as I waited for *them* to attack. I had already lost sanity at the discovery of the beer cans. Another incident, and I'd start eating my fish and chips.

Killie started hissing. It was how I knew she was in the entertainment room. I went over to see her snarling at something in the corner. I scooped up my cat. Instead of running, I attempted diplomacy to the empty corner.

"We... we mean you no harm. Please. I'm... just figuring out what happened here."

Silence. Then, a wall-shattering shriek rattled the windows. I sprinted to the bathroom, Killie in my arms. The lesson learned from this was that I was neither brave nor diplomatic. Nobody found this surprising. I slammed the door shut, trying not to sob.

"That grandma is crazy."

Maybe she had a method to her madness, but right now, when my sanity had taken another blow, I didn't have the most charitable outlook. I sank to the grimy floor, pulling out a plate of fish and chips from my inventory and ate it in three bites. I learned an important lesson as I watched more blue fill the bar. Eating comfort foods did not make me braver. If anything, my sanity rose, but my physical exhaustion remained. It was simply giving the ghosts, the wolf, and *them* more opportunities to frighten me.

Something inside me deflated. I'd put too much hope in food, but I wanted to waltz out of the room and demand what that grandma meant when she shrieked at me. Or march up the stairs to study what happened. Instead, I remained a trembling mess on the grimy bathroom floor as I gathered what little of my shattered courage I could.

Killie hopped into my lap, and I placed a hand on her back. She seemed to understand I was struggling.

"I admire you. Your first response is to hiss and fight. I just run. Must be some instinct of mine handed down from my ancestors. See the supernatural, sprint the other way. It's kept me alive for this long. How are you so brave?" I rested my head against the door, my eyes shut as Killie remained on my lap. "If I became unkillable, I'd be braver, too."

"Ring around the Rosie,

"A pocket full of posies!"

I flinched, even though I knew it was Theo.

"Ashes! Ashes!

"We all fall down!"

"Just Theo."

"Ring around the Rosie!

"A pocket full of posies!"

"He's switched from Pop, Goes the Weasel to Ring Around the Rosie," I told Killie.

"Ashes! Ashes!

"We all fall down!"

If I wanted answers, I would have to go to the second floor to check this out. My inventory was loaded with fish and chips, and I could do this. But my body froze in the bathroom. I was terrified. *They* were coming tonight. Shouldn't I save my sanity?

I forced myself to stand. My blue bar was almost full, and I had food to keep it that way. I could do this. My feet teetered as I opened the door. Killie remained by my side as we walked through the kitchen and into the hallway. It was at the foot of the stairs when my cat froze in her tracks. Little Theo still sang to himself, and Killie stared up at me as though I were crazy. This did not bode well.

The singing stopped, and the real unsettling nature of it all hit me. I didn't know what to expect, but silence made everything worse. I took a step, then used about three minutes to prepare to take the next one. My sanity flickered, but my feet couldn't move faster. The trek to the next floor lasted an eternity. I heard every creak of the wood as my soul screamed the whole time. I repeated in my head that I was here for information as I approached the landing. Theo hadn't sung in a while. I wasn't sure what I expected when I reached the second floor, but my mind certainly created plenty of terrifying things. The stairs felt coated in molasses. Killie remained at the bottom, her fur standing up. I kept my gaze forward, because I didn't want the reminder that my brave kitty refused to walk upstairs.

My flashlight materialized in my hand. The beam wobbled. It was supposed to be a comfort, but with how much it shook, it messed with my head. I did not want to be up here, but my gamer self said I had plenty of sanity to lose, so I should take this opportunity to learn.

Whispers drifted from the locked door. I tried to approach, but it took a mental strength I did not possess to walk up the stairs. I would listen from here. Perhaps it followed the same logic as last night. They were quiet enough that I couldn't understand them, even with my ear against the wood. It was a perfectly good excuse to remain where I was.

The whispers continued, and I kept my eyes wide open. It sounded like two females. Both in hushed voices, the kind where they understood a child was sleeping and didn't want to wake them. Then all at once, the murmurs cut off. I waited at the stairs in case I needed to make a hasty getaway. More silence filled the space, and I checked my sanity. A little over seventy-five percent. That had to be good. It would—

Liquid trickled out from under the door. I knew this would happen, especially tonight, with the higher frequency of haunts. It still did not prepare me for how rapidly my body recoiled.

"Information. Here for information."

It was my mind trying to calm my heart down, but I couldn't do it. I threw myself down the stairs, tears in my eyes as a mass of blue faded from my bar. A murder scene was behind that locked door. Perhaps those two women. Perhaps someone else. I didn't know the logic of how these hauntings worked. Theo had mentioned his mom had died. Was this how? On a quiet night?

I stumbled into the kitchen before collapsing to my knees. The sob I held back came through in force. I refused to see the murder scene that was behind that padlock. I lacked the strength to find out tonight.

As I stayed on the faded red and gold carpet, I ate two more fish and chips to fill my sanity. I wasn't sure how long I was on the ground when I heard the creak of an entity at the top of the stairs. Whatever blue I had gained disappeared in a second. It was those bloody footprints. Things clicked into place for me in the worst possible way. Someone was still here, and it was most likely the murderer.

One of these nights, I would be brave enough to remain in the kitchen to study the footprints and gain information from them, like if the murderer tried to attack me. Tonight, I was too exhausted. I scrambled into the bathroom, shutting the door once Killie leapt inside. I heard myself breathing, so I placed a hand over my mouth to keep quiet. The staircase creaked as the mysterious person walked down it. I must have been a ridiculous sight, curled on the floor, pulling out a plate of fish and chips, listening to the groaning wood.

The being moved into the kitchen at a careful, slow pace. I held my breath, tears streaming down my cheeks. Despite my sanity hovering over fifty percent, I was exhausted. The person entered the entertainment room, and I remained in the bathroom. I couldn't go out there again. I had done enough exploring. My comfort food test had taught me something. It was more exhausting to have it than not. I never got braver; instead, I gave the phantoms more opportunity to scare me, and it was so draining. However, I didn't want to know what would happen if I ran out of sanity.

I waited in the silence until the air shifted. My neck hair stood on end as pressure forced into my lungs, squeezing everything out. *They* were here.

Chapter Thirty-Six
Exhaustion

"Just depression." I tried to do the same thing with *them* as I did with Theo. Pinpointing what it was made it less terrifying, right?

Sure. Take a concept like depression and stuff it in monster form, and somehow that didn't make it as harrowing. I almost heard the sarcasm leaking out of my mind.

Thuds rattled the mirror as *they* approached the fence. Tears continued to flow down my cheeks. My sanity dropped, and I could do nothing about it. Everything about *them* unsettled me. A crack sounded, then *they* bellowed. I let out my sob while they made their noise to hide mine. I was exhausted and couldn't keep doing this. But I didn't have a choice.

They tried breaking the fence again. The fear that came over me was so primal, so instinctual. It was like falling into the ocean, dropping deeper and deeper into the dark. The farther I went, the more twisted the creatures became.

I couldn't breathe. Not unless I focused on the mechanics of breathing and reminded myself to do it. The pressure of *them* pushed me on every side.

Another crack, another bellow. I pulled out some fish and chips and ate it in three bites.

Consumed too many comfort foods. Penalty applied.

I didn't have the energy to ask what that meant. The tip of my stamina bar grayed out. Until that gray mark was gone, it couldn't be full. I wanted to scream. To shout. To fight. But I had no strength. It was gone.

They gave a final bellow, and my sanity dropped so fast that I pulled out another plate without thinking about it and finished it in three bites.

I had a lump of sanity left, with a larger portion of stamina grayed out. *They* retreated as I climbed to my hands and knees. I thought having more sanity would make me less susceptible, but I was more drained than before. I crawled to the bedroom as I considered what had happened tonight. Thoughts were the only things churning through my mind as I lifted one foot in front of the other.

Theo, Ring around the Rosie, whispers, posies, dead, ashes, blood, murdered, footsteps, fish and chips, stamina, lost, grayed out, *them*, exhausted.

Exhausted...

...exhausted...

My body dropped onto the dusty covers. I was aware of the window, of what I discovered at sunset. Someone might be out there. But the energy and mental fortitude it would take to get out of bed and check was too much. I ran out of strength to care.

"Tomorrow." I would worry about everything tomorrow. I forced myself to sleep.

And woke up in a dark room. I stared at the wall, took a deep breath, then let it out. I hated this feature. *Their* attack always felt like such a huge thing, and I wanted to be restful. Instead, I sat up, staring at the ground for a few moments to reorient myself to what had happened.

They attacked, and *they* will return in three days. It would rain the whole time, and I wasn't sure how to remove the cap from my stamina. I had assumed sleeping would do it, but the grayed-out area remained. I would get that back, right? The mental question was for the alien overlords, as I still tried to wake up. My sanity was at seventy-five percent. My yellow only filled to halfway, and about twenty percent had been capped. It must be another penalty. I couldn't chow down on comfort foods without any consequences.

"I hate this." The words plopped out of my mouth like mud.

It took most of my mental fortitude to force my body out of bed and walk into the entertainment room. The steady rhythm of the rain was almost melodic, but it instilled a sense of dread, too. I needed to start my to-do list. I rubbed the sleep from my eyes, hoping it gave me energy, but what I wanted was a good, long, relaxing nap. Something I hadn't had since I entered this strange place.

I grabbed the phone, pressed the number one, and waited to hear the familiar female voice.

"In three days, they will come. In three days, they will destroy. This is the last attack of the season. They will have grown stronger than at any other time they've attacked so far."

That alone sapped the strength out of my knees, causing them to quake.

"There are two things you must do if you hope to survive. Strengthen the fence and find the furnace. It will rain for three straight days. On the second day, your house will grow cold, similar to outside. If you do not locate the furnace, you must eat food even inside to warm you up.

"Further instructions will follow..."

My mind sputtered with horror as I stared at the kitchen island. Only two things on my to-do list. Those jobs were daunting. I grabbed the paper and tore it off, reading it.

Strengthen the fence

Find, fix, and feed the furnace

The window was blurry as rain pelted against it. I let out a sigh, trying not to panic. I hadn't seen a heater the entire time I was here. Did I need one? Where were furnaces, anyway? This seemed unnecessary. How could a furnace run with no electricity?

The fridge started whirring, and I blinked. It was almost as though the alien overlords sent their own message without putting any snarky speech into my vision.

"Fine. I'll find the furnace." The words forced themselves through my pursed lips.

My priority, as always, was the fence. I walked outside, quivering in the rain as I checked the tool. I had been so distracted with the process of waking up that I'd forgotten my experiment. The finished bricks remained inside untouched, and the food left in my inventory was there, too. I had a feeling the tool would be in a constant state of making resources, though, so I wouldn't use it as a storage space.

I remembered the other thing I needed to do. Even thinking about it made my energy leave again.

"Quick look." I moved near the barn. "A fast one. Just to check. Need information."

My head eased over the stucco exterior of the storage unit, staring at the ground. It was hard to see with so much rain. I approached the window and saw it. Another beer can. The second my sanity wobbled, I ran from the trash. I didn't want to think about it. Someone was here. That was... good information to have. I'd study it more. Later.

I quickly did my morning routine, refusing to touch my soup until my stamina got low. I picked tomatoes in the greenhouse, my mind wandering.

"The thing about rain in farming games is that... it's nice to not water the crops that day." I finished picking the veggies and grabbed the watering can. "Like a free shift from these responsibilities, because the rain already waters them. It gives me something to look forward to and more time to do other things." I walked out of the first greenhouse and into the second. "Food for thought." I snickered. "Food. That was funny."

No reply as I watered the lettuce. Now that I knew carrots were a core ingredient in salads, it wouldn't hurt to plant some more. I needed more options of food to cook inside and not over a fire for the next three days.

"To be clear, I'm talking to you, alien overlords. We haven't talked in a while. Just thought you wanted my opinion."

Silence again. I sighed, moving to buy some carrot seeds. "A shorter morning routine would give me more time to find a furnace, anyway. Where is the furnace? I do not know."

My mind focused on that as I finished planting seeds and moved on to the chicken coop. I complimented Daisy on her beautiful egg. Once everything was done and I had eaten a bowl of soup, I walked to the fence and stared at the words above it.

0/150 logs

The more I stared, the more nauseous I became. That was a lot. That was more than they've ever required. *They* would be stronger, the female said. If I didn't strengthen the fence, if they broke through...

If they asked for bricks...

The sixty in storage that had felt like a plethora the other day didn't seem enough now. That thought caused all the warmth from the soup to leave. I had to know how many bricks it would need, which meant I had to chop trees. No more time to waste. I only had three days.

I stuffed logs into my pocket dimension. I focused on this, and didn't dare let my mind wander. *They* would be stronger than at any other time, but *they* would meet with a fortified fence, because I would finish this.

Chapter Thirty-Seven
Cold

Despite juggling to get more space over the past few days, I devoured so much food that the storage unit shelves were turning quite bare. I needed to eat not just for warmth, but for stamina, too. Another thing I didn't want to focus on. This was an enormous order of logs.

Tears stung my eyes as the rain continued to pound. Hopelessness tugged at my soul as I studied the white brick house, torn between two demands. The fence was always my priority, but this home was where I stayed warm. Tomorrow, nowhere would be safe. I had eaten a third of my soups already, and it was barely the afternoon. If I didn't spend some time searching for a furnace, I was in danger.

With the fifteen-minute heat timer out, I made my decision. I stuffed all the logs from my inventory into the fence before running inside. It was warm, but I sensed the temperature dropping. I wiped the already evaporating rain from my face, glancing around the kitchen. Where would a heater be? There must be a utility closet somewhere, but I had been here all spring/summer and had never found one.

The clouds made it darker, so I pulled out my flashlight to check every nook and cranny. It felt like a colossal waste of time. The longer I searched, the more anxious I became. I checked behind closets, cabinets, and drawers. Nothing. I remember seeing a chimney, so there should be a fireplace or a furnace of some kind, but I'd never put two and two together. Not until I had to look for one. It wasn't on the first floor, so I inspected everywhere twice.

I got more frustrated as I reached the second floor. It grew darker as the sun set. Hauntings would distract me from finding this. I should've started with the upper level, but I didn't think it would *be* here. Perhaps there was an attic entrance I hadn't noticed. That too seemed wrong. The shape of the ceilings in these rooms proved to me this was the shape of the roof, and therefore the "attic" area.

So... basement? No, this was a two-story house, and *only* two-stories. I would not expect to find a basement on the first floor. To test my theory, I ate soup to warm up and walked outside in the pouring rain. My flashlight beam was speckled with rain as I studied the foundation of the home. The overall structure did not hint at another level below. It made sense, because I would have seen stairs by now.

I used the rest of the fifteen minutes to chop more trees, refusing to panic. It was late. It always seemed later than it actually was when it rained. My mind wandered as I did my menial task of dropping a tree and filling up my inventory with logs. I tried to still my brain to keep myself from hysterics. It was easier to focus on a problem to solve. Forget not finding the furnace yet, forget darkness gathering around me, forget the rain turning cold. I glanced at the wolf timer and saw multiple hours left. I did the math in my head, noticing a pattern to the wolf's activities. The wolf did this a lot. Once in a while, the beast was gone longer than usual. What was the reason?

The log rested on my shoulders, then it all clicked in my mind. The monster always did this the day after *they* attacked. *They* must also frighten the wolf. Perfect. I wanted to spend more time outside tonight and stay up to find the furnace.

I devoured almost half my soups to finish the logs. Once I had placed the last log, I waited, fiddling with my hands.

0/100 firewood

With a determination that stemmed from frustration, I grabbed my axe and chopped down more trees. I pushed through, eating more food. I could make the fence strong enough. It would protect me from *them* at their strongest. When the final firewood dropped, I had a small chunk of stamina left. I waited for my next instructions.

0/65 bricks

My mind was a constant whirl of panic until I forced it to shut down. I stared at the words long and hard. I was five bricks away from my goal. All those logs, that firewood, it was pointless. Clouds blocked the sun and wouldn't come back until after *they* attacked.

Two options were before me. One, to give up and dump all the bricks into upgrading the storage unit and hope for the best in three days. Or two, ponder this for a while and figure out how to make what I needed without the sun.

Despite my panicking mind, I demanded experimentation. I refused to be five bricks away from this and not try. After scrambling to the river, I grabbed a mound of clay. I formed it into a brick shape as I returned to the house, then tried to stuff it in the tool. An invisible wall stopped me. No, there had to be a way. This was a purposeful trial from my alien overlords. I pulled out the list in the pouring rain. Even though water fell from the sky, the paper remained dry as I read over it.

Furnace.

Would clay near a hot heater be enough in a pinch? Is that the link the alien overlords tried to help me see? I checked the foundation of the house once more, crouched down on my hands and knees, combing in the mud next to the home. I let myself stay out until my timer was gone. No sign of a basement. I examined the front porch, but it was all cement. The back porch, too.

It still didn't stop me from walking inside, trying to tear up the living room carpet. Each time, my fingers couldn't grasp it. After the fifth attempt, words popped into my vision.

Cannot pull up the carpet. Flooring isn't unlocked yet.

"I need a hint! Please!"

I got no response, my frustration growing.

The wolf timer blinked, and I realized just how many hours I'd wasted trying to locate the stupid furnace. I tried not to panic. I ran through the house, attempting to break the backs of closets or find some hidden trapdoor in the flooring. The hauntings grew worse as the night darkened, but I was more afraid of falling asleep. I did not want to wake up cold.

"Please." It was the millionth time tonight I said that to the ceiling. "A hint."

Approaching midnight. Force sleep will happen.

A new timer blinked, making it difficult to see. My tears made it harder, and my dangerously low sanity did not help. Shadows wobbled, and whispers were everywhere, getting louder.

They were attacking soon, and I wouldn't have a full bar. The grayed-out cap on my stamina remained from *their* last attack. I was in danger if any more blue vanished, but that hidden furnace! That stupid, stupid furnace! Where was it?!

My body shot up in bed, unaware that the forced sleep had already happened. The chill turned my breath into wisps. The locked portion of my energy was still there. I hadn't slept in my nightgown. So many things backfired. *They* were attacking tomorrow night. I had fifty percent of my sanity and stamina. I was not prepared. But I also wasn't sure if I'd survive the rest of the day.

I ate my last soup while doing my morning routine as the rain beat down on me. This enormous weight pressed on my shoulders, as heavy as a furnace. I didn't have any other food to keep me warm. Fifteen minutes, which had seemed like such a huge amount at the beginning of this strange season, were now seconds to me. I stared at the house, willing some secret place on the second floor to pop into existence.

Was the heater in the locked room somehow? Did I have to unlock the door to find it? So many questions plagued me. So did terror and fear. I had no intention of stepping into that evil space. It couldn't be there. Entering that room would have its own main quest when the game was ready.

I collapsed to the ground, nauseated. I had spent so much time worrying that I forgot to eat something. My shaking ate up my stamina. "Damn." I could not stop shaking. The nausea was intense. Usually, when I ran out of yellow, I stopped running, and the queasiness went away. I'd never been caught outside on a super hot or rainy day before. With how my stomach rolled and heaved, I never wanted to again. But what could I do? It was just as cold inside now.

Warning! Must get somewhere warm!

A blinking timer started counting down from one minute.

I tried to crawl toward the house. Maybe I could climb into bed. That was warm, right? With how much my gut protested, I doubted I could make it to my bedroom. I had a hard time climbing to my feet, pushing past the nausea to move faster. I barely made it onto the back patio before the timer finished counting down. All energy drained out of me, my vision darkening. The last thing I saw was the concrete rushing up to meet me as my body braced for impact.

Chapter Thirty-Eight
A Hint

It was the most comfortable bed I'd ever been in. Like sleeping among clouds. Similar to when *they* attacked me. This time, however, I opened my eyes. I was in a strange white world. It should have been too bright for me to comprehend, but somehow I did.

"Hello!" I called out.

"Hello, Quinn."

I gasped and spun, arms raised to brace for an attack. A black-haired man stood there in a small cape and... tuxedo? I was so confused. I lowered my hands, eyes wide. He looked human, yet not. Like someone who had studied mankind and tried to replicate it. He shuffled a deck of cards, looking like a street performer doing magic tricks.

It was his eyes that drew my attention. They were windows of the soul, and try as he might, this entity could not pretend to be human. The more I stared, the more nauseous I became as I watched his iris and pupil shifting and churning, changing and falling.

"My sister didn't let you see us for your own sanity." The smile the man wore made me uncomfortable. "I am not her. She forces, I allow you to choose." What did he mean by that? "Therefore, the choice is yours. Keep my gaze, you lose your mind. Drop your gaze, and you'll keep whatever wits you have left."

The words hit me like a truck. It was an effort to tear my eyes from his, but as soon as I focused on the white ground below, I realized how badly my body trembled. I was on my knees, swallowing the bile that crept up my throat.

"As you wish." The man took a few steps around the room.

"Where... where..." I couldn't get the phrase out. Vomit threatened to leave my mouth.

"Where is my sister? Not here," he said.

I closed my eyes, willing a semblance of normalcy back into me. I tried not to be afraid, but I also had never seen my alien overlords. His voice was instantly recognizable. I had imagined what might happen if I were in their presence again, but I never considered how simply looking at this man would make me a twitching mess. What could I possibly do? I couldn't trust him. He'd admitted he could lie, and the only thing keeping him from lying all the time was his sister.

"Oh, not all the time." He continued to pace around the white room. "Then that would make me predictable, and that's something I never want. I usually tell the truth, unless I find it too delightful to add a little chaos to the world."

My gaze remained on the ground, but the trembling in my body did not stop.

"What... what..."

"You have questions for me." He shuffled his deck of cards. "But you know the answer to all of them already."

Play the game. It wasn't what I wanted, though.

"The answer is rarely what we want." The man picked up a card and made it disappear with a flick of his wrist. One by one, the deck got smaller. "I have only one question for you." I didn't dare turn my head to see him. "Do you give up?"

That was not what I thought he'd say. "Huh?" My arms and knees teetered, and I was scared I'd collapse and curl into a ball.

"Do you give up?" The request for him to repeat himself did not bother him. He focused on the cards, making them cease to exist. I had a feeling the flick of the wrist wasn't just a sleight-of-hand trick. His gaze was on me, but I did not return it.

"I... don't understand..." A billion questions were inside my head, and I only had the strength to ask a few.

"These are the rules of the game we set up."

"You... and your sister?" I asked.

"Me," a card vanished, "my sister," another one was gone, "and you." The deck disappeared.

Once again, I was confused. I breathed deeply, staring at his black dress shoes. "Me?"

"Funny thing about losing your memory. You wouldn't remember it, would you?"

He lies. He admits it.

"I... I don't know... you. Or your sister. Are you... God?"

The man shook his head. "We're older than God. Or at least the Gods that rule your planet and a few other planets. We have been here longer than the creation of everything. We *are* the reason creation began in the first place."

Did I have anything with mushrooms in it lately? I'd picked some recently, but I didn't eat any. Besides, I got those in the weird world where I was by myself, farming and cleaning a haunted house. Could I trust what I ate?

The man cackled. "See? This is why it's so delightful to admit I can lie. I *adore* how much you can't rely on yourself right now. I *crave* that kind of chaos." He cackled again, pulling a top hat out of a different dimension, and placing it on his head. "You have five minutes to answer the question, or my sister will demand one."

"Who... who..."

"Ah, ah, ah." The man pulled out a handkerchief from his pocket. A colorful one with multiple handkerchiefs attached to it. "I'm done with the philosophical discussion of my existence. Do you give up? Would you like this experience with cleaning and the haunted house to become a dream? Nothing but..." he chuckled at his own thought. "But wondering about the mushrooms you might've eaten when you wake up?"

My head pounded with a headache I couldn't be positive was real. This was more than unsettling. This man, this being, was casually talking about my life like he'd done this before. Taken people on trips into the mind and played some sort of sick game. Maybe not to me, but to others.

He sat down, crossed his legs, and picked something out of his teeth. "Only when I get bored. And I will admit I feel bored way easier than my sister."

Another chill raced through me.

"Does it comfort you to know that I'm not evil?"

"No." The word rattled out of me as I used the excuse to suck in some air. "You lie."

"My sister would promise we are nothing but a neutral party."

The only energy I had left was used to shake my head from side to side. "Leave me alone."

He leaned back with a smile. "So... do you give up?"

My breathing steadied. So many things didn't make sense. It was like I was trying to put a puzzle together, and this entity came over and dumped another huge package of pieces on the table before swearing they were all part of the same image.

I mulled over his question, but knew I couldn't give up. A quiet stubbornness said if this man wanted me to, then I should do the opposite.

"Hint."

Despite knowing the thoughts in my head, this caused him to pause, his head cocked to one side in excitement. "Hint?"

"Where... the furnace... where..."

He hesitated, then the smile turned into a smirk. With a twist of his hand, the cards fanned out in his palm. "Pick a card."

None of this made sense, but it was consistent with the entire conversation. My fingers pinched a card. I flipped it over to see a perfect replica of the covered back porch. I frowned, studying it to make sure.

The man clapped his hands, then lifted them up. A deck of cards flew out of his sleeves, and I flinched, scared I'd get sliced by them. The cards didn't follow any sort of rules of physics, nor did they fly around in a pattern.

"Pick another," he said.

This seemed like a perfect opportunity to cut me to pieces, yet I was drawn toward one. I reached out for it, and it flew into my palm. I turned it over, seeing a picture of a broom. One I was certain I saw on the back porch.

"Do you know what to do?" the man asked.

I frowned. "Sweep... the porch?"

He smiled, then winked at me. "Don't tell my sister I told you." He snorted. "Who am I kidding? She already knows." Then he began to fade from existence. "Remember, Quinn. We are not your enemies."

Things got blurry and dark in this impossibly white room. The shadow of a man kept his terrifying grin. "But... we're not your friends, either."

This made as much sense to me as everything else he said. With that strange, cryptic meaning, my vision went black.

I sat up with a gasp, glancing around. Rain pattered against the bedroom window. I scrambled out of bed. It was morning again. I entered the kitchen, turning toward the calendar, tracing my finger over the many X's. Today was the last day of spring/summer. Tonight, *they* would attack. I'd lost an entire day from my already short timeline.

All I did was let out a breath before sprinting to the covered back porch. I ignored my morning routine. Ignored checking if that creepy beer can was in front of my window. Ignored everything else but a hint I partially trusted.

The rain pattered on the roof as I searched through the tools shrouded in cobwebs. I snatched the broom and pulled it from the others.

"Okay, I'm sweeping!" I watched the yellow bar. It was still only half full, as was my sanity. I stuffed thoughts of doom into a corner of my brain. It didn't matter that *they* were attacking tonight. Or my inability to make comfort food with no fire. I needed to focus on this. And this was... a messy place. Old leaves that nobody had swept in years, no doubt building up after countless autumns. I'd never considered cleaning it, because I'd been rewarded for decluttering the first level without touching this porch. But why was I using a broom? This had a rug. I studied closer and realized that no one had nailed this down like the carpet in the other rooms. I already checked the foundation. Nothing was underneath it but dirt. It would be stupid, though, to go through all that and not check. It was so cold that I was losing stamina.

With a jerk, the rug came free. Then I saw it. My heart practically leapt out of my chest. I used the broom to brush more of the dust and leaves away. It was a rectangular piece of plywood on the floor. I didn't stop to examine it. I dropped to my knees and picked up the wood. Underneath were cement stairs leading to the foundation. The entrance to the basement wasn't outside the back porch, but *within* it. My teeth chattered as I moved the board aside. I climbed down the stairs, and did not expect to experience this much relief at entering a dark hole in a haunted house.

Chapter Thirty-Nine
Warm

I turned on my flashlight as I straightened, studying the maze of wood and torn insulation. This basement looked like a large crawl space. The floor was nothing more than a slab of concrete with some cardboard placed on the ground. The ceiling was barely six feet high, which was perfect for me. I maneuvered my way over the broken-down boxes, hearing a promising whirring sound. I followed it until I reached a strange contraption. It was a pipe leading out of the house. This wasn't the furnace. Perhaps part of the dumpster? A clipboard hung next to it.

The following points can be exchanged for items:

0.50–matches

1.00–sticks

5.00–firewood

10.00–boards

10.00–coal

15.00–metal shard

With every shake, my stamina dropped, but I remained studying the pipe. This was excellent to know. I would study the contraption more when I got the heat up and running. The cardboard path led me to the central part of the house and, to my delight, a rusted old cylinder furnace. I jumped into my building outfit as I approached.

0/3 metal shards

0/4 coal

The clipboard had mentioned that kind of stuff. I had dropped so much clutter in the dumpster that I'd have points enough for all of it. The relief that slammed into me brought tears to my eyes. I made the purchases, draining most of my dopamine points. It was cold. I had about thirty percent of my stamina, and I did not want another conversation with that male again.

I shoved metal and coal into the furnace, then let my shoulders slump in pure relief when it clicked and roared to life. I collapsed to my knees, a dead rat a few feet away.

"Thank you," I said to the man who was neither my friend nor my enemy.

The change was instantaneous. I stopped shivering. Even though I was in this big crawlspace, warmth washed over me, and my stamina no longer dropped. I let out another breath, letting myself revel in this victory before moving on to the next pressing issue on my list. Could I cook baked clay near the furnace?

With no soup left, I spent some time in my warm home making applesauce with my cutting station. Five bricks. That's all I had to make. I needed to reach the river to collect the clay. It would be so much easier now with my inventory. With nothing to beat the chill, I had to keep my energy maxed out. It was one trip to the riverbank. I could even run if I wanted to.

It took two apples for every applesauce. It gave about fifteen percent of stamina. A regular apple provided a fragment of yellow. It was far more valuable to grind them. I ate until I got a full bar. My sanity was halfway, and I had no more comfort foods, but I tried not to panic about that. I would build this fence. The furnace would work as a substitute for the sun.

Once every slot in my inventory had a basic food item, I walked into the cold. I jogged to the river and gathered five mounds of clay.

"This'll work. I got information about how to make bricks. It makes sense. Slide the clay close to the furnace. It'll act like a sun. Right?"

I didn't bother looking at the sky. Once the last mound was in my inventory, I headed for the house, watching my stamina. It was dropping, but I was fine. I had enough to get home. At home, it would be dry and warm.

In the covered back porch, I folded up the carpet and placed it to one side. I walked through the hole in the floor, molding the clay into a brick shape as I approached the furnace. I knelt on the ground again, sliding them near. For two seconds, I felt like an idiot. How could a furnace possibly replace the sun? But I was too stubborn to give up. The gamer part of me knew this might be an option.

"Is there a sign if this worked?"

No reply. I chewed the inside of my cheek as I stared at the clay. Despite my fear of that male, I combed through memories of our conversation to find a hint. I couldn't trust anything the man said. How could I? He could lie.

No, wait. I trusted *some* things. He got me here after all. He didn't deceive all the time. It made him too predictable. That, for whatever reason, rang true to me. Maybe because...

Because his sister *was* predictable. They were siblings, but opposites.

"You're like yin and yang. I've never seen kids with completely different likes and dislikes come together the way you have."

That phrase from my memories came back too fast for it not to be a clue of some sort. Brenda had said that about Theo and me, but what if it also hinted at my alien overlords?

Yin and yang. Opposites, yet in balance. The male lied; the female was incapable of it. Predictability and unpredictable. Together, they formed a neutral party.

I opened my mouth, but paused. What exactly should I say? It wasn't like I needed to. My thoughts were open to them.

"Is it true that I agreed to this whole situation?"

Enough time passed that I wondered if they would answer.

Yes

I swallowed, closing my eyes. This was the closest I had ever come to solid answers, yet I couldn't trust those words. This might be the male.

My brother may not lead you astray as long as I am here

More air left my lungs. Perhaps the female spoke, but I could see the male pretending to be her to trick me. I needed to do a few more tests. "So... you are incapable of lying?"

Lying is too simple a concept to describe what I do.

I am a higher being, beyond your comprehension.

Me using these words to communicate to you is, in a way, lying.

If I tried to use my pure language and reveal myself in my true form, you would dissolve at the sight of my existence, for your mortality cannot comprehend it.

Therefore, I lie because I keep myself hidden to preserve your existence.

But I do not purposefully lead you astray to do actions you should not.

I simply withhold the things that cause you harm.

I kept staring at the words until they slipped away. This was more existential dread than I wanted to feel today. Despite all this, I knew this was the sister. She went above and beyond to assure me I wouldn't get deceived.

"I, um..." I gave my head a little shake. "I was... hoping to convince you to... make a timer on the bricks? To see if the furnace is baking them."

It felt silly asking that after the existential conversation from before. I wanted to be more sneaky about it all, to pit one sibling against the other, but sometimes I forgot those entities are higher than gods.

It makes sense for that to happen. An upgrade of some sort.

Not just for bricks, but all tools that rely on a timer.

Even your stamina and sanity should have a number representation of what they are.

I like this.

I shall discuss this with my brother.

With nothing more for me to do, I waited. A small part of me beamed with pride. I knew how to talk to these two beings, and could request things. Another part said I would never try this again.

Once all levels reach 20, you will receive this upgrade.

I hesitated before climbing to my feet. I meandered through the insulation and cardboard, then walked up the stairs to the covered back porch. The clipboard was in my hand, and I got to the last page with my progress.

Farming level 21

Cleaning level 22

Logging level 26

Cooking level 16

Building level 27

Animal Care level 18

Once I brought cooking and animal care up, I'd get this upgrade. After that relief, a different thought hit me.

"Okay, well… I actually hoped to use it to figure out if the furnace bakes the clay." I glanced out the window, certain it was still light enough to be morning. "If it can make them, then by the time they're bricks, I'll…" Need to sneak them into the fence while the wolf prowled outside.

That realization made my heart want to escape my ribcage, but it was the only way. Even if the baking worked without the sun, I'd set the finished resources in the fence an hour before *they* attacked. That would cut it close, but the only other plan was to not have a fortified fence. That didn't feel like an option to me. Which meant I had to sneak around the wolf creature. Tonight. With no comfort food and the two fried fish I had left. I stared at my fifty percent remaining sanity, willing it to grow before looking away. I tried not to focus on the negative. This would still work.

"So, um…." I glanced at the ceiling. "Is the furnace turning it all into baked clay?"

No answer. I hesitated, then walked into the basement, to the rectangular-shaped clay. I cleared my throat. "Is it working?" It showed a sand timer on the patio. Wouldn't I get one here? I waited for something.

Information for -25.00?

Y/N

I winced, glancing at my total. 42.21. I had drained so much of it to buy the furnace materials. Yes, I had enough, but after the nice cushion of over a hundred, I didn't enjoy the thought of getting closer to zero.

"Can I barter again?"

The question wasn't long from my lips before I saw numbers.

-23.00

To focus, I closed my eyes. I had reached level 25 in both building and logging, which meant I could get the fourth set of clothing for 20.00 dopamine points each. Did I want information? Or clothes to help me out?

More than information, I corrected myself. This was peace of mind. How much would I spend to begin mentally preparing to sneak through the yard with a wolf nearby?

"Negative fifteen?"

After another pause, numbers materialized.

-20.00

Honestly? That was fair. The price of clothes. The moment I considered it, I knew they wouldn't go any lower. It wasn't as expensive as the other piece of information. And when I thought of it in terms of currency, it was as much as I earned from a log cut into boards.

"Okay. Tell me."

Yes, the furnace works, and the bricks are in place to be baked
They will take half a day
There can only be five clay at a time
The words vanished, and I sighed with relief. I was right and had so much stuff to do now.

Chapter Forty
To Deliver Bricks

I gathered all the bricks from my storage unit and dropped them in the fence, taking the blow to my stamina. Once they were in, I ran inside to dry off. I took a moment to appreciate how warm it was in here. I wanted to do some more cleaning, but I didn't want to go outside if it wasn't necessary.

Instead, I walked through the first floor, admiring the colors and how much this house had changed. Yes, the brown carpet still bugged me. Yes, the furniture belonged to a grandmother. Yes, I craved wallpaper, coffered ceilings, and crown molding, but it was beautiful regardless. The junk was gone. The walls were a lovely painted color. It was clean. It hadn't smelled of mildew in ages.

Killie walked over to me, purring as she rubbed her back against my leg.

"Hey, girl." I leaned down to pick her up. "I need to up my animal care levels and cooking, but it's raining. Playing with you helps gain experience. Wanna play?"

She glanced at me with those cat eyes, and I could hear the sass in her meow. My smile turned chagrined.

"Obviously, I would play with you even if it *doesn't* raise my levels. I've been so busy with all these chores and having an existential crisis. Or three. While waiting for the clay to finish, maybe we could have some fun?"

She let out a soft trill, jumped down, then faced me. She waited for me to pick the entertainment.

"Right." I glanced around. I didn't have a toy. She usually played with my feet. In my decluttering of the place, I hadn't seen cat accessories anywhere. But that was what an imagination was for. I had enough charged batteries that I let her play with my light for a bit. Killie chased it before getting bored. The biggest hit was the crumpled-up chore list. It was almost therapeutic to crumple that up and toss it to her. She batted at it, meowing as she pursued it. I smiled, following her, stealing it from her occasionally. She enjoyed it far more than the flashlight.

The hours passed. A part of me was screaming at me for playing with Killie while I had a to-do list to complete. The other part tried to calm down and remind myself I *was* working on it. I was at a bottleneck with those bricks.

My animal care levels rose, and I was delighted to see the time I spent with my cat let me reach level nineteen. I wasn't about to tell Killie that, though, in case she was offended I only played with her to gain more experience in animal care. I also bought sturdy jeans, which would increase my logging reward to seven whole logs for each tree. When the first extra log hit the ground, I'd chop it into boards to buy the building clothes. It was tempting to get building instead of logging, but I almost didn't want to know what that ability unlocked. Not until tomorrow.

It was time to gather the baked clay and stick it into the tool. I sacrificed some stamina to do that in the pouring rain. I imagined the seven temperate days I would have at the start of the fall/winter season. Seven whole days to replenish my food and upgrade the storage unit. It would practically be a vacation! As long as I survived tonight.

But... I would. I tried not to be overly optimistic, but I had learned things during my conversation with the brother. These farming games rarely ever ended. If anything, I usually had gotten bored and put it away for a few months or a year. Sure, they 'ended' with the storyline, but they kind of lasted forever. Forever cleaning, forever organizing, forever watering and picking veggies.

I had received a penalty for staying out in the rain with no stamina. I had lost a day. That hurt, especially losing sanity so close to *their* attack. But I had a feeling my alien overlords wouldn't force me out. This was a contract among the three of us. I needed to last long enough to figure out why.

As soon as the hauntings started upstairs, I scooped up Killie and barricaded myself in the bathroom. I had no comfort food, so I had to protect my sanity. I closed my eyes, ignoring the sounds and giving explanations for why the ghosts acted like this. It kept my blue bar steady for most of the evening until the staircase creaked. Try as I might, my only logical reasoning was that the murderer remained in the house. Despite all my talk about how this game would only end if I got bored, that was when I was playing with my cat, not huddled in the dark, waiting for a dangerous ghost to pass by. I was proud that I only lost ten percent of my sanity. With the footsteps fading, I shuffled to my feet, wiping sweat from my forehead.

"Alright." I gave Killie a pat. "Wait in here. I need to finish the fence."

She stared at me as I left the bathroom. Against my better judgment, I grabbed the latch and unlocked the back door. I didn't allow myself to think too hard about it. The rest of my food was stuffed in five inventory slots, and the rest were for the bricks. I was eager for it to be tomorrow, not just because *they* were attacking in a few hours. I knew what one season presented, so I would start mentally preparing for the next. Part of that preparation was to upgrade my storage.

My mind wandered, almost dissociating. How could I be thinking about tomorrow when I needed to focus now? I slipped the last brick into my inventory.

My feet tiptoed up the stairs, and I opened the screen door. The rain masked my steps, but it also hid the wolf's snorts and quiet snarls. I froze when I spotted the beast *inside* the fence sniffing around the dumpster.

I backed toward the covered porch again, not daring to breathe. I could use this to my advantage. The creature was there, so I should go on the other side of the house where... where I was ignoring the beer cans by my window. The ones left by someone I had deduced came at night. Like the current time it was now. Which one did I want to run into? The wolf? Or the creep?

Information. I could check to see... if a figure stood outside my bedroom. That would be a brilliant discovery, because... because... I had a slight chance I'd see the creep. A guarantee of running into the wolf. Simple logic ruled me.

I crawled past the storage room. I waited at the edge, then popped my head over the side. No one was there. Perfect. I used the opportunity to sprint to the fence, unloading the bricks into it. I let out a breath, checking my stamina to make sure I was alright.

The words shifted. My eyes snapped to them. Then, to my growing horror, new words glowed in the dark.

0/20 shattered glass

I stared at it long and hard until a part of my soul screamed that I needed to get back inside because my stamina had dropped low. *They* were coming, and I had to save every bit of my bars.

Because *they* would break through the fence tonight.

A snarl echoed across the ground way too close. I spun and saw the wolf staring right at me. The creature had been sniffing the storage unit when it spotted me. Adrenaline shot through my legs, and I bolted toward the front yard. It yelped, then broke into a run. The rain might have masked its feet, but it could not mask that sharp crunching sound as the spine broke.

I let out a terrified shout as I ran around the house. I leapt over the dead flowerbeds. It growled, its hot breath hitting my neck. I dropped to the ground out of instinct, and the wolf on its two legs tripped over me. I wasted no time scrambling to my feet and sprinting through the front door. My momentum didn't stop until I rammed into the living room wall. I gasped for air, trying to hold back a sob, my mind scattered. The only thing that brought me out of it was when I heard Killie hissing.

The door was wide open. The creature stood there, right at the edge of the cement stairs.

Chapter Forty-One
They Hunt Again

I covered my mouth to smother a scream, but my terrified curiosity kept me staring. It was such a horrifying sight I couldn't help it. Those hind legs shouldn't be able to hold that beast up. It was well over six and a half feet tall; the fur was matted yet soaking wet. In an act of bravery, I turned on my flashlight and pointed it at its face. It had beady black eyes, and the only emotion in them was rage and murder. It didn't bother looking at Killie, even though she was the easier target. She hissed at it, but the wolf ignored her.

The creature remained on the front porch, unable to go any further. That alone made me brave enough to keep a light on its face. To see those murderous eyes. The number of sharp teeth in its jaw seemed impossible. Its mouth held hundreds of serrated fangs, leaving little room for a tongue. Blood tinged the saliva dripping from its muzzle. It snarled at me again, batting at the air with its elongated claws. As the beast found itself incapable of getting me, it filled its lungs and roared. I cowered at the noise as a huge chunk of my sanity faded. I scrambled over and slammed the door shut. My hand went to my chest, trying to breathe, forcing myself to think about a different monster.

They were attacking, and the fence wasn't done. Twenty shattered glass! Even if I ran out to get sand, I wouldn't have enough. It took an entire day to make five panes in the tool. How many times would I fall for this? Thinking I was finished with the task I was working on? I softly banged my head against the door. I could have put all those bricks in the storage unit and had it completed by now. Or I could have saved all those points and spent them on another article of clothing for building.

My thoughts returned to the alien overlords, and I tried not to be bitter. They knew shattered glass was the next task. Perhaps it was my fault for not asking more questions, but I'd been so focused on the clay. I was so close.

Too close.

I thought about how lucky it was that I had sixty bricks already done. Fortunate that the furnace could bake five. The exact number I needed. It all came together a little too perfectly. Like my alien overlords dangled a carrot over my nose to get me to do this. Maybe they weren't setting me up to fail, but it was certainly suspicious how it worked out.

Until it didn't.

The familiar feeling of being a rat in a maze returned. My actions were under constant surveillance, and they injected tests I hadn't agreed to. So, why? Why did I subject myself to this? Was I tricked into this contract? That seemed like something the male would do.

Killie walked over to me, checking if I was okay. I patted her on the back, staring at my sanity. I had perhaps thirty percent to face *them*. No way would I survive the night.

Her fur brushed my skin, and I glanced down. I touched my reflective vest and saw a large tear. When did this happen? I remembered dropping to the ground to trip the wolf. The image of those enormous claws on all its paws returned to me.

Warning! Clothing damaged. Will not work until sewing machine has repaired it. Will take six hours.

I groaned, resting my head in my hands. It was better to know this now rather than later. I needed my building clothes, as I was pretty sure the game required all three levels to upgrade buildings. I got up and crept to the second floor, taking off the vest and setting it on the sewing machine. It started working fast, and I slinked down the stairs again, my heart hammering in my chest.

Before my panic took over completely, I tried to soothe my thoughts. I would experience what would happen after an attack and see if I talked to the male again after *they* sucked all my sanity and stamina from me. Could I spin this to my advantage? Get more information?

My foot hit the final step into the hallway, and I shuddered as pressure pinned me on all sides. *They* were coming. I could do this.

It was a talk with the brother. That's what would happen at the end of all this.

I picked up my axe, tears streaming down my face as I clung to my thirty percent sanity. I ate the last of my fried fish to fill my stamina up to about seventy percent to be safe. The grayed-out cap was still there, so I couldn't fill it all the way even if I tried. I was out of food.

Thud

I closed my eyes, shaking my head. Not a monster. More a blob thing. I could do this.

Thud

So what if they broke through?

Thud

I'd have a conversation with the alien overlords. I wouldn't give up.

Thud

I would figure out why I was here. I would.

Silence.

My palms were sweaty, but I refused to feel terrified.

An explosion rocked the house, and I fell to my knees, recoiling from the sound. I kept a grip on my axe, trying not to sob. My sanity took a hit. This would be a quick night.

Reddish blackness pooled at the base of the door before I heard a steady drip. I let out a gasp, backing away. Killie ran into the bedroom. I wanted to follow her. To go to bed. To ignore all this.

I backed into the kitchen. Despite knowing I wouldn't survive the night, my self-preservation kicked in. *They* hunted me, a sludge of teeth and fur. I didn't know how to kill *them*. My feet shuffled away as the slime followed, gaining speed. If I stayed in the house, I would be trapped. I whimpered.

To last as long as possible, I threw open the back door and stumbled onto the porch. Reddish-black pillars lifted, their bodies filled with jagged teeth. I staggered outside and slammed the screen door right as *they* attacked. The slime hit it, but specks of *them* landed on me. I shouted, shaking *them* off as the rain pummeled me. *They* attacked everything, breaking down the fence, the greenhouses, entering the house and the storage unit. I gasped, trying to hold my axe.

"Get out! OUT!"

Another reddish-black pillar reared up before slamming into me. I swiped at *them*, but it didn't work. It was like cutting a wave, hoping it wouldn't soak me. *They* hit my chest as tiny molars and canines tunneled into me, leaving no blood but filling me with *them*. I tried to scream, but my energy drained out of me. The rest of my sanity vanished, and I waited for the blackness to come. Instead, *they* started eating my stamina, too. I collapsed to my knees, more of the sludge rolling around the corner of the house to find me. I grabbed the slime from my torso, but when I pulled a bit out, the teeth transferred to what remained on me. More came every second, piling on me, pinning me to the ground. My fingers reached for my weapon. I struggled to breathe as *they* gathered into my mouth and lungs. My energy dipped below fifty percent as my vision turned wobbly. Why wasn't this over already?

They were strong. I no longer listened to the primal instinct to fight. I simply closed my eyes, ready for the darkness. For that white room. To see if my alien overlords would punish me for failing.

In the distance, a noise echoed across the lawn. If I had to put a word to it, it sounded like a chainsaw, of all things. *They* pulled away from me. From the house. From everything. *They* had found a new target, and I was too busy figuring out if I had really heard what I thought I did.

I leaned against the storage unit, hearing that noise as it cut into *them*. I suppose it was a chainsaw. *They* produced no shrieking, no crying. Just the wet slap falling to the ground before reforming again. My lungs flooded with air as I tried to focus. The chainsaw got closer, and I needed to leave. Meeting up with a crazed murderer was not something I wanted to experience right now.

The noise died down. I had spent so much time focusing on getting the energy to enter the house that I didn't realize how close this person was. A beam of light hit my face. I lifted a hand to block it, worried I wouldn't die from *them*, but from a murderer.

"Quinn?"

That voice. I recognized it in an instant. It was the one constant in all my memories. I dropped my palm as he raised his headlamp. The rain stopped pounding so hard as I breathed deeply. I saw him standing before me. The shaggy brown hair, the surprised brown eyes, the young man now my age. He wore rugged tactical gear, and the chainsaw was still in his grip.

"Theo?"

My brother stared at me, brows furrowed. He glanced at the house, his face falling as he staggered back. "What... what the hell..."

He was in this world, too. But... how? Why? No doubt he had a million questions himself.

Theo's head jerked to the side before he lifted his chainsaw and started it up again.

"Theo, wait!"

He didn't stay. He sprinted away, holding his weapon to destroy more of *them*. I wanted to follow, but darkness flitted around me. Fear took me as I glanced at my stamina, but I wasn't nauseous. I had a fragment of yellow left.

Attack is finished. Force sleep beginning.

"No!"

I stumbled forward as darkness consumed my vision. Theo was here, in this world. I needed answers, because I had a million more questions.

They were all put to rest as the game forced me to sleep.

End of Volume One

This story will conclude with

An Ill-Fated Cure

Acknowledgements

My first thanks will always go to my family. Thank you to my husband and kids for understanding how much I love writing. Thanks for letting me slip away for a few hours every weekend to do so. Thanks for your support, and for your excitement when I publish another book. Your cheers mean so much to me.

To my Royal Road fans, thanks for reading it first. Thank you for being touched by this story, and giving me suggestions and grammar corrections. I'm pretty sure I got them all! If not, that is entirely on me, not you. Thank you for being so invested in my characters.

If reading my story gave you a sudden itch to play cozy horror games, please check out We Harvest Shadows, Pumpkin Panic, and Kingdom Two Crowns. These three games inspired me to write this novel.

Many thanks must go to Emily Jensen for her expert editing. Thank you, thank you, thank you. If it weren't for Emily, you'd all get tired of the word sliver. Also thank you, JV Arts, for the delightfully spooky cover!

Last of all goes to the person and/or people who played a huge part in getting this story out there. I will remember who you are by name one random day when I'm vacuuming the floor and be so disappointed in myself for forgetting you in these acknowledgements. Just know that I appreciate what you did.

Also by Ellen Taylor

I Suck at Titles

I Still Suck at Titles

[Error] Title Not Found

The Altered Manuscript

About the author

Ellen Taylor enjoys living with her husband and three children, and also enjoys living in her head. She writes in her spare time, because sometimes she needs to be in control of chaos. Follow her on Facebook or Instagram for updates on future books at Ellen Taylor Books.

www.ingramcontent.com/pod-product-compliance
Lightning Source LLC
Chambersburg PA
CBHW020350010826
48973CB00005B/1344